TOO TEMPTING TO TOUCH

"Intelligently crafted, steamy . . . pure erotic romance with a dash of the gothic, never missing a beat. Her three-dimensional characters play out their roles while the sizzling love scenes flow and the suspense builds. This is what historical romance readers relish, perfectly balanced passion and plot."

—*Romantic Times BOOKreviews*

TOO HOT TO HANDLE

"Holt showcases what she knows, writing a luscious erotic romance as a coy innocent collides with an alpha male in steamy love scenes and hot sessions of temptation . . . settle in for a delectable night of reading pleasure."

—*Romantic Times BOOKclub Magazine* (starred review)

"Holt's erotic romances touch the hearts of readers with an even pacing of compelling emotions interlaced with seduction and intrigue."

—*Rendezvous*

"*Too Hot to Handle* is on fire! Reminiscent of the magic of *Complete Abandon*, this may very well be Holt's best erotic yet. The characters are lively, the erotic sweet, and the love between Michael and Emily so turbulent and emotional it has all the makings of a five-star romance . . . when you read Cheryl Holt, you enter a world of stunning passion, intrigue, and tender love."

—*Historical Romance Club*

"A book lush in historical detail that will transport readers back to a different time and place . . . love scenes are intense and sultrier than a hot summer day. Bestselling author Cheryl Holt proves once again why she is at the top of the list."

—*Romance Junkies*

COMPLETE ABANDON

"You can fall for this hero and know you'll be caught in strong arms. The ultimate, sexy, bad-bad boy, John Clayton, finds that lessons in passion can become lessons in love . . . fantastic. A keeper."   —*Romantic Times BOOKreviews* (5 stars)

"I fell in love with this story and hated for it to end. Emma and John are magnificent characters, and I loved watching them change and grow as love winds its tentacles around their hearts . . . This is a masterpiece of storytelling. A sensual delight scattered with rose petals that are divinely arousing. Oh my, yes indeedy!"   —*Reader to Reader Reviews*

"An enticing, sizzling combination of erotic passion, strong characterization, and a finely tuned plot. Readers will see themselves and their secret longings on each page and shiver with delicious delight."   —*Kathe Robin*

FURTHER THAN PASSION

"Fantastic . . . a keeper . . . Holt has finely tuned the art of delving into secret fantasies and drawing out what women want. In this deliciously sensual story, she keeps readers glued to the pages by infusing every one with plenty of sizzle. Very sensual."   —*Romantic Times BOOKreviews* (starred review)

"Holt pens a compelling, erotic tale . . . a sensual feast of love, betrayal, and sensual pleasure, *Further Than Passion* takes the reader beyond the typical consequences of desire for happily-ever-after . . . [a] powerful story that readers will find impossible to put down . . . each character springs vibrantly alive, living in the reader's imagination long after the last page is turned."   —*Midwest Book Review*

"A deeply passionate book . . . very seldom does a historical novel find its way to my shelf, but this is one author for whom I will always make an exception. Fans won't be surprised to find this book on their keeper shelf."   —*A Romance Review*

Forbidden
FANTASY

CHERYL
HOLT

St. Martin's Paperbacks

This is a work of fiction. All of the characters, organizations, and events portrayed in this novel are either products of the author's imagination or are used fictitiously.

FORBIDDEN FANTASY

Copyright © 2007 by Cheryl Holt.

Cover photo © Shirley Green

ISBN: 0-312-94255-9
EAN: 978-0-312-94255-7

Printed in the United States of America

St. Martin's Paperbacks edition / September 2007

St. Martin's Paperbacks are published by St. Martin's Press, 175 Fifth Avenue, New York, NY 10010.

10 9 8 7 6 5 4 3 2 1

This book is dedicated to the thousands of people who wrote to me over the years to tell me how much they enjoyed my novel *Complete Abandon,* and to everyone who waited so (im)patiently for me to finally tell Ian Clayton's story. Hope you love it!

Forbidden
FANTASY

Chapter ONE

London, Winter, 1814 . . .

I wish to speak with Mr. Ian Clayton."

Lady Caroline Foster stared at the butler who'd answered the door. She tried to appear imposing, but intimidation was difficult. It had taken weeks to learn where Ian was living, and now that she'd arrived, she was terrified over what she'd set in motion.

"And you are . . . ?" the butler inquired.

The question flummoxed her.

In her rush to confer with Ian, she hadn't stopped to consider that an employee's initial order of business would be to ascertain her identity. She needed to be ruined—and in a hurry—when she wasn't even sure what the deed entailed. Ian was the only person she knew who might assist her, but their meeting had to be a secret, and she couldn't risk discovery.

She'd traveled in a rented carriage, had worn a hooded cloak to shield her striking blond hair, her big blue eyes, her perfect and easily recognized face. Servants were the worst gossips in the world. If she stated her name, within minutes the information would be bandied about in every house in London that mattered.

She pulled herself up to her full height of five foot six and repeated, "I wish to speak with Mr. Clayton. Is he available or isn't he?"

A man approached from down the hall and entered the dim foyer, but she couldn't see him clearly.

"Who is it, Riley?" he queried.

The butler gazed over his shoulder. "It's a visitor for Master Ian, sir."

"I'll handle this," the man said. "You may be about your duties."

He urged the butler aside and insolently leaned against the door frame.

At first glance, with his golden hair and too blue eyes, his tall stature and slim physique, he so resembled her prior fiancé, John Clayton, Viscount Wakefield, that she nearly fainted. Luckily, he wasn't John, but someone much younger who had the misfortune of looking very much like him.

In the six mortifying months since John had ended their lifelong betrothal and had humiliated her by swiftly wedding a pregnant commoner instead, Caroline had avoided him like the plague. If she'd run into him now, she'd have located a pistol and shot him right through the center of his black heart.

"Who are you?" she demanded in her most authoritative tone.

"Who are you?" he quipped like an annoying juvenile, even though he had to be every bit of twenty years.

"I've come to see Ian Clayton," she advised. "Either have the good manners to notify him that I am here, or be courteous enough to apprise me that he is out, and I shall return later."

With her father being the Earl of Derby, she'd been raised to be haughty and proud, to peer down her aristocratic nose at those she deemed inferior, and it was a hard habit to break. Typically, she hated to seem pompous, but with how her knees were shaking, she was glad for her ability to condescend.

By venturing to Ian's as she had, she was completely out of her element, so it was comforting to revert to form.

"Ian's here," he admitted with a casual shrug.

When he made no move to go fetch him, she said, "Well . . . ?"

"He's in bed."

"But it's two in the afternoon."

"It certainly is."

She scowled. Ian was still abed? In the middle of the day?

As Ian was John's bastard half brother, she'd known him for over a decade, and throughout that period, he'd been excessively conscientious. What could have happened to alter him into a sloth?

"Is he ill?"

"Definitely not."

"Rouse him for me," she commanded.

"I imagine he's already *roused*," her mysterious host announced. "*Up*, too."

He was babbling in riddles that she was in no mood to decipher, and she pushed past him, barging in as if she owned the place. She proceeded to the stairs, acting as if she would brazenly climb them and find Ian.

She'd never previously visited a bachelor's abode, and couldn't quite articulate what had driven her to this one, so the prospect that she might was thrilling and ludicrous.

A hand on the banister, she whipped around. "Will you get him or shall I?"

"I'll get him," he offered after a lengthy pause. He evaluated her in an intense and unnerving way. "You must be Caroline Foster."

"Don't be ridiculous. I know Lady Caroline. She'd never behave so imprudently."

"Wouldn't she?"

"No. She's an absolute paragon of appropriate conduct. Ask anyone; they'll tell you what she's like."

He scoffed. "You don't have to pretend. It's evident who you are."

"I'm not Caroline Foster!" she tried to insist.

"Ian was extremely precise in describing what a rich snob you are. You couldn't possibly be anybody else. I wondered if you'd come sniffing around."

He'd leveled so many insults that she couldn't decide where to begin in chastising him. How dare he castigate her! How dare he criticize! He didn't even know her.

"What is your name?" she seethed.

"Jack Romsey. Jack *Clayton* Romsey."

"You're a Clayton brother?"

"Another illegitimate one, Lady Caroline."

He tossed out the word *illegitimate* as if it might cause her to swoon. "With your inflated attitude, I might have guessed."

"We're slithering out of the woodwork like mice on a cold winter's night. I'll get Ian for you."

"You do that."

"It might be a while before he receives you. Make yourself at home."

He sauntered off, leaving her to her own devices, and at suffering his disregard she was furious.

She'd been abandoned by him. No maid appeared; the butler had vanished. Of course, Ian was a bachelor, his wealth of dubious origins and not commensurate with her family's by any means, but still, she'd expected simple courtesy.

There was a parlor off to her right, and she strolled in, determined to do just as Mr. Romsey had suggested: She'd make herself at home. She and Ian had been acquainted forever, so it wasn't as if she'd invaded a stranger's residence, though he could scarcely be referred to as a friend, either.

They'd interacted merely because Ian had lived with John, but Ian being a poor relative, who'd emerged from nowhere and latched onto wealthy John like a leech on a thigh, she'd always considered his alliance with John to be suspect. On one despicable occasion, she'd stupidly voiced her opinion on the subject, so they'd never gotten on.

He went out of his way to bully her, and she detested him—as she did every man she knew—for his arrogance and patronizing. She'd spent all twenty-five years of her life letting men order her about, and she was sick to death of their superior posturing and asinine advice.

She dawdled, studying the furniture, the drapes, the paintings on the wall. She'd viewed Ian through his association with John, but for some reason, he and John had quarreled and were no longer close. Ian was away and on his own, and she was more intrigued than she should have been by how he was carrying on in his new situation.

There was liquor on a sideboard, and she boldly walked over and reached for a decanter of the whiskey that Ian's uncles brewed in Scotland. She filled a glass to the rim, and she sipped it, mesmerized by the sharp flavor.

She couldn't remember drinking liquor before—no male would have allowed it—so as a petty form of protest, she downed the entire amount. As the contents hit bottom, she felt much better. The imbibing of hard spirits was so sinful, and so out of character, that she resolved to make it a habit.

Fifteen minutes passed, then thirty. She poured another whiskey, the second one going down much easier than the first. She was overheated, the fur on her cloak stifling, but she didn't remove it. Her cheeks were flushed, her lips tingling, her body parts loose and limp.

The alcohol was awfully potent, reducing her inhibitions and circumspection. Her temper spiked. Why was Ian ignoring her? And what of Mr. Romsey? Had the infantile scapegrace even notified Ian that she'd arrived? He was probably sitting on the landing, snickering and watching to see how long she'd tarry.

Well, she'd show him! In the crush of recent weeks, any reticence or reserve she'd once possessed had fled. When she was about to be married off against her will, like a prized cow at auction, she wouldn't be coddled or sent away like an obedient schoolgirl.

She gulped a third serving of whiskey, deeming it the most delicious thing she'd ever tasted; then she started for the stairs. If Ian wouldn't come to her, she'd go to him.

She tromped up, listening and climbing, until she was rewarded with murmurs emanating from a room at the end of the hall. She presumed it to be the master suite, and she marched toward it, eager to strut in and demand Ian's attention, but as she neared, her confidence flagged.

She had no idea why she'd risk detection in such a precarious spot. If she'd been caught in his front parlor, she could have devised a suitable explanation, but she couldn't justify loitering outside his bedchamber.

The liquor had imbued her with courage, though not enough for shameless conduct, so shortly she was tiptoeing to the door. It was open a crack, and she peeked in, flustered to note that she was gazing directly at his bed.

He was awake and resting on the pillows, and while she knew she should sneak off, she couldn't pull herself away. He'd always fascinated her, and she hated to admit that neither time nor distance had quelled his allure.

With his black hair and blue eyes, his fabulous anatomy and assertive manner, he was just so blasted handsome. There was no denying it, and she was irked by how his looks tantalized her. Why couldn't she control herself around him? What was wrong with her that he had such an effect?

His hair had grown out, and it was held back in a rakish ponytail. He hadn't shaved, and his cheeks were shadowed with stubble, which gave him a dangerous air and exacerbated the rugged Scottish heritage he'd constantly striven to hide.

His untidy condition astonished her, yet she enjoyed this rumpled version much more than she had the polished, suave gentleman he'd been prior.

He wasn't wearing a shirt, and she couldn't quit staring at his bare chest. It was covered with a matting of hair, as dark as the hair on his head, and she suffered from the strangest urge to rush over and run her fingers through it. The quantity was thick across the top; then it thinned to a line in the center and disappeared beneath the blankets to destinations unknown.

His shoulders were broad, his waist narrow, and as he stretched and yawned, she could observe the hair under his arms, the round pebbles of his nipples. She was agog, and her heart raced at the sight.

"What time is it?" he asked, and Caroline was shocked to hear a female voice answer.

"Almost three."

He was with a woman! Had he a lover? Was she his mistress?

Since his fight with John, and his subsequently removing himself from John's town house, there'd been so little news. If he'd taken a paramour, Caroline would have had no method of gleaning the information, yet amazingly, she was angered by the notion. As she rippled with what could only be jealousy, she wanted to laugh aloud.

Jealous? Over Ian? She didn't even *like* him. Why would she care if he was consorting with a strumpet?

Still, his dalliance put a damper on her bravado. She'd planned to storm in and request his assistance with her dilemma, but with a trollop lying next to him, she never could.

She'd decided to turn away when Ian spoke to his companion, and Caroline was frozen in place.

"You have to be home soon," he mentioned, his soothing baritone wafting across the room and tickling Caroline's innards.

"Yes, so I suppose we should make the most of the minutes we have remaining."

"I suppose we should."

The woman shifted so that she was draped across his torso. The upper half of her body was naked, the bottom half concealed by quilts, but Caroline suspected she was naked down below, as well.

As a sheltered spinster, who'd waited through her prime for John to proceed with their wedding, she had few clues as to what adult men and women did when they were alone.

Her stoic, straitlaced mother, Britannia, should have been the person to provide the necessary details, but she'd never divulged any specifics, and Caroline would have died before inquiring. She and her mother had never gotten along, and often Britannia was so unpleasant that Caroline wondered if her mother hated her.

Their conversations were stilted, awkward affairs, filled with chastisement and reprimand. As to the topic of amour, if Britannia alluded to it at all, it was to hint at beastly masculine drives that could only be satisfied by females of the lower classes, but the cryptic comments shed no light on the subject.

What—precisely—were the foul activities that men relished? Caroline was so anxious to know. When she and her mother were so different, Caroline was positive that if it was something Britannia abhorred, Caroline would probably like it very much.

She'd been kissed exactly once—by Ian—and she wasn't sorry. It had occurred at John's Wakefield estate. She'd been depressed about John's refusal to wed, and she'd been unable to sleep and wandering the halls. Ian had been doing the same.

Not only had he kissed her, but he'd touched her all over. Even now, these many months later, she still quivered with excitement whenever she recollected how splendid he'd made her feel. With the slightest encouragement, she'd jump at the chance to engage in a similar scandalous pursuit.

Over on the bed, his lover was on her knees and straddling his lap. She arched her back, the motion thrusting her bosom up and out, and Ian clasped her breasts, his thumbs grazing her nipples.

Caroline's own nipples responded, but she wasn't surprised. On that one, improvident occasion, Ian had caressed them, so she was aware of how sensitive the taut nubs could be. They throbbed in a rhythm with her pulse, rubbing her corset in a fashion that was disturbing. She was breathless with anticipation, as if Ian were massaging *her* instead of his partner.

He eased the woman forward and—stunning Caroline to her very core—he wrapped his lips around the rosy tip and suckled like a babe. The woman purred and cooed, savoring the indecent gesture.

Caroline was transfixed, the mysterious feminine spot between her legs growing relaxed and wet. In agony, she stuffed a knuckle in her mouth and bit down, stifling a groan of astonishment.

Oh, how would she ever look him in the eye now that she'd seen his lips on that . . . that . . . ?

She shook her head in disgust, once again eager to sneak away, when Mr. Romsey piped up from inside the room. He was watching them? They didn't care? How sordid! How peculiar!

"Are you finally awake?" he queried.

"Barely," Ian replied.

His lover chuckled in a sultry way and chimed in, "I can vouch for the fact that he's very, very awake."

She glided her hips across Ian's loins, and she leaned over, so that she was facing in Mr. Romsey's direction—and Caroline's, too—and Caroline instantly recognized her.

Rebecca Blake! The notorious, lethal Black Widow!

She was beautiful and young—only twenty—and she'd already buried three husbands. This shrew, this vulture, this . . . this . . . murderess was who Ian had chosen to slake his manly lusts?

Caroline was amazed that he was alive and possessed of sufficient vigor to misbehave.

But then, she uncharitably mused, *he isn't married to her. She likes to kill after she's wed. Not before.*

Mrs. Blake grinned toward Mr. Romsey, like the cat that had swallowed the canary. She braced an arm behind her neck, and ran a hand down her front, seeming to taunt him with what he couldn't have.

At the indiscreet pose, Ian scowled. "Don't tease the lad."

"But it's so entertaining," she pouted.

"It's all right," Mr. Romsey claimed. "She can preen all she wants. I'm not interested in what she has to offer."

"Liar," Mrs. Blake bristled.

"Ooh," Mr. Romsey mocked, "such a tiny woman, such an enormous temper."

She frowned, as if contemplating assault, but Ian grabbed her by the waist to keep her from lunging.

"Enough!" he scolded, and he pushed Mrs. Blake to the side and sat up, moaning and clutching his scalp. "I have the worst hangover in history. If I'm forced to listen to you two bickering, I'll have to go out in the alley and shoot myself."

"He started it," Mrs. Blake complained.

"Enough!" Ian repeated, shouting this time, which had him moaning even louder. "You two make me feel like I'm your nanny." He flopped onto the pillow and peered over at Romsey. "What do you want?"

"You have a visitor."

"Who?"

"I'm sure the lady in question would rather I not reveal her identify to your . . . *friend.*"

"A lady!" Mrs. Blake interjected. "Who would dare call on you? Everyone ought to know better. Have you a secret paramour?"

"Are you serious? You constantly wear me out. How could I have the stamina for anyone else?"

"Good. If you were cheating on me, I'd have to kill you—which would be such a waste." She stroked Ian's chest, but he was irritated, and he shoved her hand away.

"Cease your games," Ian snapped at Mr. Romsey, "and just fucking tell me who it is."

Caroline was shocked by his rough language. She'd never previously heard the term, and was confused as to its definition, but she was certain it was an epithet. What had happened to him?

In the years she'd known him, he'd been restrained, cultured, and refined. Yet now, he was drinking to excess, consorting with dubious characters, and using profanity. He was so different that if he'd suddenly sprouted wings and flown away, she couldn't have been more surprised.

Mr. Romsey approached the bed, coming into Caroline's line of sight. He wasn't disturbed by the naked couple, and Caroline imagined he'd witnessed similar displays on numerous occasions. He bent down and whispered something—probably Caroline's name—in Ian's ear.

"The devil it is!" Ian mumbled. "You're positive?"

"Yes," Romsey responded.

"What does she want?"

"She didn't say."

Ian lay very still, considering; then he snarled, "Tell her to go away."

"Tell her yourself."

"She's such a witch, and I'm in such a foul mood. I can't speak with her. I wouldn't be civil, and if I uttered a harsh word, she'd quake herself to pieces."

At discovering his terrible opinion, Caroline was crushed. She'd often been curious as to what he thought of her, and now she knew. Absurdly, tears flooded her eyes. She'd been taught to hide her emotions, to pretend to be what she wasn't. Men treated her as if she were stupid, as if she were frail and incapable of making a decision.

She wasn't a . . . a . . . witch, as he'd so callously charged. She'd been tutored in modesty, in reserve and protocol. As her stern, rigid mother had frequently counseled, she would endure misfortune and trauma in her life, but due to her elevated station, she would be expected to persevere, to lead and show those who depended on her how to forge on through any adversity.

When the situation called for it, she could be tough and tenacious, and she wouldn't be maligned for what she viewed as her strongest traits.

Rippling with anger, not concerned over who learned that she'd arrived, she tugged off her hood, slapped open the door, and marched in.

The three occupants spun to look at her, gaping with varying amounts of incredulity and consternation.

"Caroline Foster?" Mrs. Blake sputtered. "Why, you little strumpet! Get out of here, or I'll make sure your father knows where you were."

"If you do," Caroline warned, "I'll have a chat with your brother-in-law."

Mrs. Blake was at the beginning of legal proceedings with her latest dead husband's family. They planned to discredit her elderly husband's Last Will so that she didn't inherit a penny.

If her brother-in-law was informed of scandalous conduct by Mrs. Blake, it would add fuel to a very public and vicious feud.

"You despicable wench!" Mrs. Blake hurled. "I ought to scratch your—"

"I told you to wait in the foyer," Mr. Romsey calmly interrupted, as Ian pinned Mrs. Blake to the mattress.

"It's been half an hour," Caroline remarked, advancing on the bed, "and I'm weary of your discourtesy."

Her gaze locked with Ian's, and dozens of scattered and unusual sentiments coursed through her. She was disgusted by his indolence, by his apathy for the things that had previously mattered to him, but she was also delighted, her whole being ecstatic that she was with him again.

She hadn't seen him since their kiss at John's estate. John had severed his engagement to her, so they'd all been fighting, and she'd left without so much as a polite farewell.

She regretted that hideous day, had pondered and ruminated over every wonderful, dreadful moment. Had Ian ever reflected on it, himself? Had he ever lamented over how they'd parted?

"Hello, Caro." His eyes were cold and hard, his voice devoid of emotion.

"Hello, Ian."

"You shouldn't have come. Your father would be upset if he knew."

If one more person mentioned her father, if one more person castigated her for taking a breath without his exalted permission, she might start screaming and never stop.

"I don't care what my father would think."

"Yes, you do," he chided as if she were a child. "Let

me assemble myself, and I'll have a servant take you home."

He was treating her as John always had, as her father and brother always had, as if she were a fragile ninny who was too timid to take a single step without some man first advising her of which direction to go.

A pox on all of them!

A veritable ball of umbrage, she guessed she should be more like Mrs. Blake, ready to lash out physically at the slightest provocation. Perhaps if she threw a few fists and bloodied a few noses, she'd garner some of the respect she so desperately craved.

"I'm not leaving until I speak with you," she threatened, "so I'll meet you in your library in fifteen minutes."

She whirled away and stomped to the door, but at the last second, she glared over at Ian. "Don't make me come back up here, or I guarantee you'll be sorry."

She exited, their mouths flapping like fish tossed on a riverbank. Prepared for anything, she walked to the stairs and headed down.

Chapter Two

B loody hell!"
Ian blew out a heavy breath and studied the ceiling. What was Caro doing? Had her snobbish attitude finally driven her over the edge?

"Of all the nerve," Rebecca huffed. "Ordering you about as if you were a servant! Who does she think she is?"

"She *thinks* she's the daughter of the Earl of Derby."

"So? How can that give her the right to barge in and insult us? You ought to have her whipped."

Jack rolled his eyes and asked, "Shall I go down and toss her out?"

Ian shook his head. Only the worst sort of crisis would have spurred Caro to visit. Simple curiosity, if nothing else, would ensure he met with her.

"No. I'll see what she wants."

"You can't be serious," Rebecca griped. She frowned at Jack. "Send her packing. At once!"

"Yes, Your Majesty!" Jack mocked.

Ian sighed. He possessed a mild affection for

Rebecca, and he enjoyed having her in his bed. For such a young woman, she was an accomplished lover who had few scruples, so she was a splendid paramour.

Her reputation was more awful than his own, so when he'd set out to offend the members of High Society with his abominable character, she'd been the perfect choice as mistress, but he'd hooked up with her before Jack had arrived on his stoop.

His despicable, deceased father, Douglas Clayton, had fornicated from one end of the realm to the other, without worrying over the paternal consequences. Ian had suspected that he had other siblings besides John, but until Jack had knocked on his door, he hadn't stumbled on any.

He was thrilled to have Jack as a new brother, just as he was delighted to wallow in iniquity with Rebecca, but he couldn't stand being in the same room with them. Their mutual dislike had been instantaneous, and they fought like cats trapped in a sack, with Ian stuck between them and having to mediate their petty quarrels.

"Rebecca," he said, "go home."

"I won't!" she declared like a spoiled child. "You can't make me."

"I can, and you will. And you're not to mention Lady Caroline to anyone."

"As if I'd be quiet over this juicy tidbit!"

"You will not speak of it!" Ian warned. "She's risked much by coming to me, and I won't have her besmirched by us."

"Ooh, poor Caroline," Rebecca scoffed. "The little lady needs a champion. How wonderful that it will be big, tough Ian Clayton."

Ian ignored her and turned to Jack. "Have the carriage

readied; then escort Rebecca out—whether she agrees to go or not."

"Lucky me," Jack sarcastically oozed.

"Just do it," Ian grumbled.

"Your wish is my command."

"I won't go!" Rebecca insisted, to which Jack begged, "Let me pick her up and drag her out, would you? It would be so amusing to throw her out on her pretty ass."

Rebecca scowled at Jack. "If you so much as—"

"Jack! Rebecca! Be silent!"

"You are not my husband, Ian," Rebecca reminded him. "I don't have to listen to you."

"And you are not my *wife*, Rebecca, so I don't have to listen to you, either. You're going home. Now!"

She was a female who would push and push, but she was savvy enough to realize when she'd gone too far. She peered at him, at Jack, at him again; then she shoved the covers aside, scrambled to the floor, and stomped toward the dressing room and her clothes in the bedchamber beyond.

Her path led her directly past Jack, who was insolently loitering in the threshold and refused to move as she approached. With her curly red hair flowing to her waist, her fabulous, naked body visible for both of them to see, she was a sight—but she knew it.

She stopped next to Jack, neither intimidated by him nor embarrassed by her nudity.

"Have a good look, my darling boy. Tonight—when you're all alone in your bed—you can picture me and fantasize over what you'll never have."

"I'll try not to get too hot and bothered."

She stepped in, her torso nearly pressed to his. She appeared to be taunting him or testing his mettle. Jack stood his ground and didn't flinch, even when she licked her lush lips and shook her halo of auburn hair in a provocative way so that it shimmered and settled around her.

"Will you dream of me?" she asked. "Or will you dream of . . . sheep?"

"Definitely sheep."

"I thought so. You seem the type."

She exited, and on seeing her go, Ian sighed again.

If she and Jack didn't despise each other, Ian might have played matchmaker. They were the same age, and they'd be a handsome couple. Their divergent qualities were an excellent combination of fire and calm, and though she denied it, Rebecca would like to marry, again. Other than Jack loathing her, he'd be ideal as her spouse. He could rein in her more outrageous tendencies, which Ian—being an ancient thirty-two—would never have the stamina to do.

She was too much for him. All that temper and vitality simply made him weary.

"Are you really planning to speak with Lady Caroline?" Jack inquired, yanking Ian out of his pitiful reverie.

"I suppose I must. Why didn't you wake me when she first arrived?"

"I tried, but you were too hungover. You didn't hear me."

Ian had no comment. Once, he'd have been ashamed of his deteriorated circumstance, but not anymore.

As Douglas Clayton's natural son, sired in a Scottish village when Douglas had been on a hunting jaunt, Ian enjoyed confounding the snooty members of the *ton*. He'd acted the part of the refined gentleman, spending so much time pretending he belonged to their society that he'd actually started to believe he did.

But base blood controls. It was an old axiom, but apropos. He'd been born a bastard, would always be a bastard, and he saw no reason to behave any differently. Since his final, ugly fight with John, when he'd hurt his dear brother so deeply, he'd accepted the fact that he was a scoundrel. No matter how he'd previously striven to prove otherwise, he had no redeeming traits.

He was now a drunkard, gambler, and scapegrace, and he wouldn't lament how his foul attributes had taken charge and were ruling him.

He eased his legs over the edge of the mattress. His head pounded, his stomach roiled, and sweat pooled on his brow.

Jack leapt to his rescue, filling a glass of whiskey and holding it out. At Ian's quizzical glare, Jack explained, "Hair of the dog."

"Marvelous. Just what I need."

Ian swilled the entire thing, shuddered with revulsion, then stood and staggered to the dressing room. He clad himself in trousers and shirt, though he didn't bother to tuck it in or button up the neck. He rolled up the sleeves and—unshaven, unwashed, unshod—he proceeded downstairs.

When she viewed his unkempt state, Lady Caroline would likely swoon, but he cared not. She was the very last person he'd expected to show up at his door. He hadn't invited her, and if she didn't like his disheveled condition, she could go hang.

As if he were an arrow and she his target, he trudged to his library, intrigued as to why she'd visited, but he declined to speculate, for he wouldn't admit to any heightened interest. He would courteously attend her, then send her on her way.

He entered and walked straight to the sideboard and

poured himself a whiskey. The one Jack dispensed had had an enormous medicinal effect, and with another dose Ian was certain he'd begin to feel human.

Caroline was over by the window, trying to ignore him, but as the rim of the decanter clinked on the glass, she whipped around, her disapproval gallingly obvious.

"Honestly, Ian," she scolded, "it's the middle of the day, and that liquor is so potent. I'd like you to at least pretend sobriety while we talk. Must you imbibe?"

"Yes, I must."

He gulped the contents. To spite her, he poured another and gulped it, too. She had a way of tilting her aristocratic nose up in the air, of pronouncing her words with a hint of disdain that nipped at his feelings of inferiority.

Her contempt made him angry, made him want to wound her, which was impossible. She was built of ice; she had a heart of stone.

"I didn't ask you here," he pointed out. "If my habits offend you, leave."

"You're drinking to annoy me."

"No, I'm drinking because I feel like it. Your opinion is totally irrelevant."

"You're being an ass."

"I'm being myself."

"You've changed."

"No, I haven't. You're the one who regularly sniped at me because of my crude conduct. I've merely given it free rein."

Still, her low esteem rankled, and the glass was suddenly heavy as an anvil. He put it on the sideboard, as if that's what he'd intended all along. In a huff, hating her, eager to have her gone, he crossed his arms over his chest and frowned.

"What do you want?"

"I need to speak with you."

"On what topic? And be quick about it. I've things to do and places to be, and I won't waste a single second with you."

She studied him as if he were a curious insect. "What have you to do? Will you continue cavorting with Mrs. Blake? Is she upstairs?"

"What if she is?"

"Really, Ian, should you fraternize with her? She's so unsavory. What's gotten into you? You used to have better sense."

A muscle ticked in his cheek, and he struggled to keep from marching over, tossing her over his knee, and giving her the spanking she deserved.

At age twenty, he'd come to London, paid handsomely by his contemptible father to spy on John, then secretly report on his misadventures. John had thought they were friends, but they never had been.

For twelve accursed years, Ian had ingratiated himself to John so that he could eavesdrop and tattle. He had an incredible knack for betrayal and duplicity, and by deceiving John, he'd become wealthy, but his prosperity was like a weight around his neck, choking him with all that had been lost.

Through it all, Caroline had been a constant. When he'd initially met her, she'd been an irksome adolescent, and he'd watched from the background as she'd grown from a cheery, beautiful girl into a frustrated, fuming spinster.

As she'd waited for John to marry her—something he was never going to do—her smile had dimmed and her demeanor soured, until she'd ended up as cold and unpleasant as her parents or her older brother, Adam.

Ian had tolerated, detested, and lusted after her in equal measure. He'd pined away, silently coveting her, but his attraction had been fueled by envy and resentment.

He was Douglas Clayton's oldest son, but because the philandering prig hadn't wed Ian's mother, Ian was nothing to anyone. John was the heir; John held the title and fortune. The unfairness had eaten away at Ian, had left him bitter over all that John possessed.

Ian had wanted Caroline because she'd been John's. There was no higher motive behind his enticement.

It was a despicable legacy, one that he couldn't bear to recall, and he hated being in her presence. She reminded him of the sins he'd committed, of the ways he'd failed John and himself. He didn't need her strutting in and insulting him for his choices or mode of carrying on.

"That's enough." He walked over and clasped her arm. "Let's go."

"To where?"

"I'm sure this will come as an enormous surprise to you, but I don't have to stand here, in my own library, and listen to you denigrating my acquaintances. You're leaving."

"I am not."

"You are."

He stepped toward the hall, but she dug in her heels and wouldn't budge. He pulled again, but couldn't move her, and he was stunned by her resolve.

She'd always been the most tractable of females. Her submissive nature had driven John to distraction and was the reason he'd refused to marry her.

Ian, too, had frequently chided her over her willingness to please, over her absolute devotion to duty. Her life was a long charade of missed opportunities. She never stood up for herself, stated an opinion, or grabbed for what she craved.

Yet all of a sudden, she was firm and adamant. From where had this new virago sprung? Why had she picked this moment—when he simply wanted her gone—to exhibit some backbone?

"Stop it," he scolded.

"Stop what?"

"You're being obstinate."

"And you're being ridiculous."

"I'm allowed. It's my home, and you're not welcome in it."

"Would you kiss me?"

He faltered and staggered away. "What did you say?"

"You heard me."

"I could swear that you asked me to kiss you, so I couldn't possibly have. Now go."

He pointed to the door, figuring that if he couldn't haul her out, maybe she'd depart on her own, but she didn't. Instead, like the most experienced coquette, she closed the distance between them and snuggled herself to him. Not a smidgen of space separated them, so he could feel every inch of her delectable torso. Her breasts, in particular, were riveting, the soft mounds molded to him as if they belonged there and nowhere else.

"Kiss me," she repeated.

"No."

"Why not?"

"Because I don't like you, so I don't wish to."

"You did it once before," she mentioned, making it sound like a challenge.

"And I've regretted it ever since."

"Have you? Let's see."

Stunning him again, she rose on tiptoe and brushed her ruby lips to his. For an insane instant, he permitted the contact. He'd always desired her, and apparently, neither time nor distance had lessened his fascination.

Why not forge ahead? a diabolical voice goaded. *Why not take what she is offering?*

The urging was so strong that he wondered if Satan, himself, wasn't off in the corner and coaxing him to misbehave.

He lurched away, but she clutched at his shirt, trying to draw him to her, the two of them wrestling over whether to reinitiate the embrace. It was the most absurd, farcical episode of his life, and he would have laughed if he hadn't been so disoriented.

He lifted her and physically set her away.

"Have you gone mad?"

"Occasionally, I feel that I have."

"You can't waltz in here and demand to be . . . be . . . kissed."

"Why can't I?"

"It's just not done!"

"Oh."

She shrugged as if she'd never been informed of the restrictions that ruled her world. Then she sauntered to the sideboard and helped herself to a glass of whiskey.

She drank it! The whole thing! Without coughing or sputtering! What on earth had happened to her?

"Does your family in Scotland brew this?" she inquired.

"Yes."

"It has the most relaxing effect. I may have to start purchasing it for myself."

She turned and was about to pour herself another

serving, when he stomped over and yanked the bottle away.

"Give me that."

"No. You had some. Why shouldn't I?"

"You can't . . . can't . . . *drink*."

"Why?"

"Because—"

The likely replies were all ludicrous: *Because you're a grand lady. Because you're an earl's daughter. Because you're Caroline, and you never have previously.*

All of them were foolish, especially in light of the fact that she was an adult and perfectly capable of deciding how to comport herself.

Hadn't that been his complaint with her? He couldn't abide malleable women, and she'd been the ultimate one. She never took a step her father hadn't authorized, had never put her foot down with John when he'd delayed and humiliated her with a string of mistresses.

With her burst of independence, she was acting precisely as he'd insisted she should, so why chastise? If anyone could benefit from a belt of Scottish whiskey, it was she!

Still, it unnerved him to see such unusual conduct. He'd been complicit with others in treating her as if she were a child, and he couldn't seem to break his peculiar need to watch over her.

With a resounding smack, he set the bottle out of reach; then he leaned in and trapped her against the cabinet.

"What do you really want?" he murmured.

"I told you: I want you to kiss me."

"Why?"

"Because when you did it prior, I liked it very

much. I've been thinking that I'd enjoy having you do it again."

He vividly recollected the rash night he'd kissed her. John had finally mustered the strength to cry off and mean it, and Ian had stumbled on her later, when she'd been wretched and needing solace. Like the cad he was, he'd taken full advantage, kissing her as if there were no tomorrow, as if they were the last two people on earth, but she'd hated it.

How could they have such divergent memories of how the incident had played out?

"You didn't *like it*, Caro."

"I did, too! But it was such a long time ago. I was wondering if it would feel the same."

He scrutinized her, struggling to deduce her objective. She didn't have a spontaneous bone in her body, and she wouldn't risk disgrace by coming to him for a mere kiss.

"Tell me the truth," he urged. "If you're in trouble, just say so. I'll assist you if I can."

He'd always felt close to her, connected in an inexplicable way, so he could sense that she was weighing possible responses.

Eventually, she admitted, "I'm going to be married."

A surge of dismay shot through him, but he tamped it down.

"Congratulations."

"Thank you."

"It's what you always wanted."

"I suppose."

"Who's the lucky fellow?"

"I don't know if you'd be acquainted with him. He's a friend of my father's."

"Your father's?" The Earl, Bernard Foster, was sixty if he was a day.

"Yes."

A sinking feeling crept over him. "Who is it, Caro? Who has your father chosen?"

"Mr. Edward Shelton."

Ian hid any visible reaction. While he'd had no personal dealings with Shelton, he knew *of* the man. He was a rich blowhard, in his sixties, too. Rumor had it that he had a penchant for very young girls, so Caroline was much older than he generally preferred.

Was Caro aware of the gossip? Was that the real reason she'd come?

Perhaps she wanted him to allay her fears, and he was greatly conflicted by what he should say. Was this any of his business? A father always selected his daughter's spouse, and at Caro's level, the decisions were made on the basis of wealth and property that were beyond Ian's ken.

What was it to him if the Earl of Derby picked an elderly pervert to wed his spinster daughter?

Since his fight with John, Ian had eschewed the entertainments he'd previously attended, favoring instead the darker side of London. In spite of his isolation, he was cognizant of the stories that had attached to Caro after her failed engagement, and they hadn't been kind.

John had skated away from condemnation, but Caro—whose mother was so hypocritical in her attempts to appear pious and moral—had been painted with a hateful brush. People had tittered over her icy disposition, and tales had been spread that John had tried to seduce her, but had learned she was frigid, so he refused to have her in his bed.

The frenzy was exacerbated by John's hastily

marrying the very common, very pregnant vicar's daughter, Emma Fitzgerald.

As the news broke, John had absented himself from London, so he hadn't been available to counter the lies about Caro, but even if he'd remained in town, how could he have answered? A gentleman could never reply to such vile accounts.

"I'm sure you'll be very happy," he cautiously began.

"Really?"

"It's what the Earl has arranged for you."

"He claims the scandal will die down if I marry someone else."

"I'm certain he's correct."

"Are you?"

"Caro, if you find the match repugnant, you don't have to go through with it." Was that what she'd come to have him say? "This isn't the Middle Ages. He can't force you."

"I know, but if I don't agree, what will become of me?"

"You'll continue to live with your parents—as you always have."

Even as he voiced the remark, he recognized that it would be a horrendous outcome for her. Her parents were unbearable and unlikable. Her mother in particular was petty and vicious, cruel to Caro in innumerable sly ways that Caro tolerated with a quiet dignity. They treated her like a feeble half-wit, and she'd endured the dubious fate for twenty-five years. How could she face more of it?

"Do you know Mr. Shelton?" she inquired.

"No."

"But you understand men and their desires."

"Well . . . yes."

"Will he demand a lot of kissing?"

"Most likely." He grinned, trying to lighten his comment. "Husbands seem to enjoy that sort of behavior."

"But I was wondering . . . that is . . ."

They'd arrived at the crux of the matter. Whatever was driving her, it was about to be revealed, but he wasn't keen to be apprised of what it was. Still, he'd once been her friend, and he liked to believe that he'd retained a spark of humanity and would aid her merely because she needed him to.

"What is it, Caro? You can ask me anything."

"I'm curious as to what else I'll be required to do." She glanced away, embarrassed at her naïveté, at her lack of sexual knowledge.

"Oh . . ."

"I don't have anyone with whom to discuss marital obligation, but I don't think I can marry Mr. Shelton. He's so old, and there's just something about him that's . . ." She trailed off, unable to explain what she sensed in the man. "I don't know what's expected of me, but whatever it is, I can't provide it to him."

"Speak to your father."

"I tried, but he won't listen. So I thought that if I . . . that is . . . well . . ."

"What, Caro?"

"I want to be ruined."

"Ruined!"

"Yes, and I want you to be the one who does it."

Ian gaped at her. "I was correct: You've tipped off your rocker."

"Why would you say so? Can you look me in the eye and tell me I should go through with it? Can you look me in the eye and tell me it's for the best?"

"How can my opinion signify? It would be a waste

of breath. In the end, you'll do as your father has commanded."

"What if I didn't?" she bravely retorted. "Mr. Shelton wants a virginal bride, and if I'm not one, he'll refuse me."

Her vehemence was intriguing and confounding. It was odd for her to be so adamant, to be plotting against her father and fiancé. While Ian didn't want her to be afraid or to worry, when her spouse was to be Edward Shelton she was right to be apprehensive. Yet the debacle was none of his concern. He did *not* want to be involved in the situation, and he was irked that she'd sought him out to question.

"I'm not the one to advise you, Caro. This is between you and your father."

"I realize that, but . . . but . . . maybe if you could show me?"

He was aghast. "Show you what?"

"How ruination occurs. You're experienced, and I don't detest you."

"I'm so relieved to hear it."

"You're very good at kissing, too. That's what I remember most about you."

Uncomfortable with what she'd divulged, she shifted from foot to foot. Suddenly, she appeared very young, very shy, and against his will, he was so bloody sorry for her.

He, too, recollected every moment of their passionate embrace. It had been magnificent, it had been idiotic, and it had lasted entirely too long, so that, in the intervening months, he'd had too many details to mull. He couldn't get over how perfectly she'd fit in his arms, how sweet she'd tasted, how marvelous it had felt to hold her.

For much of his adult life, he'd been bewitched by her. She'd been his forbidden fantasy, the ultimate and unattainable prize, and he'd loathed himself for his desperate attraction. Once, there'd have been nothing he'd have relished more than to be her savior, but the time when he'd have acted as her champion had passed.

He knew her well. Eventually, she'd come to grips with what her father had ordered. She would do her duty—to King and country and family—and she'd wed Edward Shelton.

In the interim, his fixation with her had scarcely waned. He liked her much more than was wise, and he wouldn't risk dallying with her. It was a recipe for disaster.

"I can't help you," he said. He went to the door and hollered, "Jack! Jack, are you still here?"

He hoped that Rebecca was being her usual recalcitrant self, that she hadn't left, and that Jack was in the house and pestering her to hurry. Shortly, he was proved right as Jack's fleet strides pounded down the stairs.

"What is it?" he inquired.

"Would you see Lady Caroline home?"

Jack peered over at Caro and frowned. "I thought you wanted me to take—"

"This is more urgent."

"I don't wish to go," Caro protested.

Jack was torn over who to heed.

"Take her," Ian quietly insisted.

"Ian!" Caro beseeched. "Please don't make me."

He proceeded to the hall, pausing to gaze back at her. For once, he let his regard shine through. In the past, he'd been so meticulous about concealing it. He was anxious for her to depart with some inkling of how much he admired her, how much he imagined they'd have been grand together if status and circumstance hadn't been quite so important.

Then he hid any fond sentiment, his typical mask of ennui and disdain sliding into place.

"Don't ever return, Lady Caroline," he said. "If you do, the staff will have instructions not to let you in."

He spun and fled, climbing and climbing the stairs, until he was far enough away that he couldn't hear as Jack escorted her out.

Chapter THREE

H ello, Ian."

Caroline was lounged in the shadows of his bedchamber, mostly concealed from view, and as he jumped a foot, she bit down a grin. Four days had passed since their prior encounter, and obviously, he hadn't expected her to return. She was delighted to have surprised him—again.

"For pity's sake," he snapped, "who let you in?"

"None of your servants was about, so I admitted myself."

"It's the middle of the night! You can't be in here."

"I already am."

She rose and sauntered toward him. She'd been waiting an eternity for him to arrive, and she wondered where he'd been. At the theater? Out gambling and carousing? Philandering with loose women?

He was dressed for an evening on the town, and in his fancy suit, with his black hair swept off his head, he was so handsome, so masculine. At being near to him and having him all to herself, her heart fluttered with excitement.

He was perplexed by her advance, and the stunned expression on his face was priceless. He had no idea what to make of her brash conduct, and she was struggling to figure it out, herself.

What had possessed her to sneak out of her father's house? What had driven her to Ian's, where she'd prowled about like a thief?

She had no explanation.

"Is your mistress with you?"

At her audacious mentioning of his paramour, he sputtered with shock. "Do you . . . do you . . . mean Mrs. Blake?"

"Have you another besides her?"

"No."

"She won't be stopping by, will she?"

"No," he repeated.

"Good. I'd hate to have her interrupt."

She reached for the clasp on her cloak, unhooked it, and the heavy garment slipped off her shoulders and fell to the floor. She stood before him in corset and drawers, in stockings and heeled shoes, and naught else.

The decision to wear the scanty outfit had come about after she'd eavesdropped on a maid who'd been giggling over how she'd espied a similar circumstance in another noblewoman's boudoir. Caroline had never heard of such scandalous behavior, but had been electrified by the information.

After her previous visit, when Ian had sent her home, she'd been furious. She was sick of men telling her what to do, and she'd determined that, in the future, whatever advice a male gave to her, she would do exactly the opposite. She intended to be as recalcitrant and stubborn as possible.

She'd boldly entered his residence, and she would use every trick imaginable to entice him into letting her stay.

On seeing what she'd revealed, he gasped. "Have you gone stark-raving mad?"

"Perhaps."

"You've shed your clothes!"

"Yes, I have."

"And your hair is down!"

"It's very beautiful, too, don't you think?"

"No, I don't *think*. What's come over you?"

She took a step, then another, until she was directly in front of him. In the space separating them, sparks erupted, and she was thrilled by the sensation. Maybe she wasn't dead, after all.

"I have a secret to share with you," she said.

"What could you have to say that would interest me in the least?"

"John dumped me over like so much rubbish."

"I know. I was there, remember?"

"He was too busy cavorting with his mistresses to marry *me*, when we'd been betrothed for decades. Yet in a thrice, he married somebody he'd only recently met."

"His wife, Miss Fitzgerald, is actually quite—"

"Shut up, Ian."

"What's your point, Caro?"

"Have you any notion of what these last few months have been like for me?"

"I heard some awful rumors."

"People call me an ice maiden. They titter that I'm a

cold fish, that a man who had me in his bed would freeze to death."

"I'm sorry," he murmured, seeming sincere.

"Because of it, my exalted father is planning to wed me to an aged, faltering acquaintance."

"I'm sorry about that, too."

"I feel used up and past my prime. The sole husband available to me is old enough to be my grandfather." She grabbed his lapels and pulled him to her, their torsos melded all the way down. "Can you even begin to guess how angry I am?"

"No, I can't."

"You're the only man who ever evinced the slightest awareness of me as a woman."

"I assure you that it was a moment of temporary insanity."

"Was it?"

"Absolutely."

"And now, when I've come to you, begging for help, you can't be bothered."

"I'm not the person to assist you, Caro."

"You're wrong. Just about now, you're precisely who and what I need."

"I'm not!" he insisted. "I have no idea why you'd presume to impose on me."

"Don't you? I'm not *cold,* Ian. I'm very, very hot. Once upon a time, you understood that fact, and I've decided you should be reminded of it."

While she'd always considered herself to be tall, he was so much taller, and she had to rise up on tiptoe. She seized his shirt and pressed her lips to his.

He was the only man she'd ever kissed, so she hadn't had much practice and wasn't very adept, but *he* was. In his long and iniquitous life, he'd had plenty of experience in the art of wooing, yet he was still as a statue and refusing to participate. She felt as if she were clutching a piece of wood.

Not even her shocking attire could move him. Perhaps he was the one made of stone—and not her.

"Kiss me back, Ian."

"No."

"I know you want to."

"I don't. I really, really don't."

He stared at her, aloof and firm in his resolve to resist, and the more adamant he appeared, the more determined she became. If it killed her, she would drag a reaction out of him!

She took his hand and placed it on her breast, and the stimulation was so intense that she was surprised her knees didn't buckle. The effect was potent for him, as well.

Whatever restrictions had held him in check, whatever wall he'd erected to keep her at bay, it came tumbling down.

He picked her up and carried her to the bed, dropping her onto the mattress. Then he tumbled down atop her, his body stretched out the length of hers.

She'd never lain with a lover, so she hadn't known how it would be, and she was ecstatic to discover that she enjoyed it very much. He was crushing her in a way that should have been suffocating, but he didn't seem heavy. He felt extremely welcome, and suddenly she was contemplating all sorts of conduct that she had no business contemplating.

"You are playing with fire, Caro," he claimed.

"Fire, hah!" she taunted. "I exposed myself to you

unclad, yet you're completely indifferent. You're naught but a hearth of burnt ashes."

"Am I?"

"Yes, and after my ordeal with John, I'm tired of throwing myself at men who don't want me. Perhaps I should seek my ruination elsewhere. There must be a male somewhere in this accursed city who'd be glad to have me."

"You'd seek another man's *bed*? You are out of your bloody mind."

He dipped down and kissed her, finally giving her the attention she'd yearned to receive. With a groan of pleasure, he molded his lips to her own, and she shut her eyes and reveled.

This . . . this . . . was what she'd been seeking, what she'd craved. This frantic rush of need and hunger was a balm to her weary soul. She didn't want to think or fret. For a short while, she simply wanted to *be*.

He was touching her everywhere, riffling through her hair, down her shoulders and arms. She joined in the fray, exploring as she'd always longed to do. She hadn't realized that a man's anatomy could be so perfect, and merely from caressing him she was growing agitated. There was tension building inside her, tension she didn't comprehend and didn't know how to assuage.

His crafty fingers went to her breasts, and he massaged them, the sensation so delightful that she squirmed and writhed in agony. He clasped the nipples, applying pressure so that her skirmishing increased.

His torso was wedged between her thighs, and instinctively, she flexed against him, her hips working in a rhythm that he instantly matched. His loins were connected to hers, only the fabric of her drawers and his trousers separating them, and she could feel the hard ridge at his center, about which her married acquaintances occasionally whispered.

She hadn't unraveled its purpose, but she was dying to learn more about the naughty rod. How was it used? Why was it necessary?

She hadn't a clue, but she recognized it to be an indication of heightened ardor, so despite how he might snap and bark, he still fancied her.

"You've missed me," she charged.

"I haven't."

"You desire me; I can feel that you do."

"You're mad."

"Quit pretending."

"I'm not."

She tried to reach down and touch what she was so curious to investigate, but he grasped her hand, preventing any examination.

"Let me!" she protested.

"No."

He captured her wrists and trapped them over her head. The restrictive position was thrilling, and it placed numerous sensitive spots into closer contact with his masculine parts.

He slid to the side, his thigh draped across her crotch and holding her down. Without her being aware, he'd loosed her corset, and he slipped under the edge, his palm covering her bosom, bare skin to bare skin.

She gasped and arched up, wrestling to get away, but to move nearer, too.

He shoved at the frilly lace, and her breast popped

free of constraint. Grinning, he was insolent and smug, as if this was what he'd planned all along.

"My, my, Caro," he murmured, "how pretty you are."

His thumb was twirling her nipple, making it ache, making it throb.

"Ian!" She was begging for something, but not for him to desist!

"Is this what you wanted? Is this what you came for? I'm about to give you what you've obviously been needing."

He bent down and took her nipple in his mouth, and he sucked on it as a babe would its mother, though with none of the tender ministration. He was rough and demanding, his teeth nipping at it till she was a thrashing ball of misery.

He rooted to the other, and soon he was shifting back and forth between the two. As he kept on, his hand slithered down her stomach, her abdomen. He fiddled with the string on her drawers, then crept inside, continuing on to her womanly hair and lower.

He spread her nether lips, his fingers gliding into her privates. They seemed to fit just right, to scratch an itch she hadn't known she was suffering. He stroked in and out, the tempo so mesmerizing that her sheath wept with joy at the fondling.

She was embarrassed and tried to press her legs together, tried to dislodge him, but he wouldn't budge.

"You are so ready," he muttered.

"For what?"

"For me, darling. For me."

"What are you doing? I feel as if I might explode."

"You just might," he said, worrying her as to what was approaching.

"Oh . . . oh . . ." she panted. "Stop! Please!"

"No."

"I can't . . . I can't . . ."

"Almost there."

"Where?" she anxiously questioned. "Where are we?"

His thumb flicked out, jabbing at a spot she'd never noted before. He poked at it again and again, as he suckled her nipple with all his might.

She splintered, her anatomy seeming to careen off in all directions. She was flying through the universe, blinded by ecstasy, as if pitched toward a precipice she couldn't locate.

Ultimately, she reached it, and she cried out, then began the journey down, floating forever in a sea of bliss and lassitude that totally engulfed her. She'd been paralyzed, her limbs were rubbery, and she was relieved to be lying down. If she'd been standing, she'd have collapsed in a stunned heap.

She landed, safe and secure in his arms. While she'd had her world shattered, her entire being ripped asunder and rearranged, he appeared relaxed and even a tad bored. How could she have been utterly undone, and he not fazed?

At having reduced her to such a pathetic state, he oozed with male arrogance.

"Are you feeling better?" he queried.

"As a matter of fact, I am."

She was far beyond the day when she'd grovel or shy away.

"What were you hoping to accomplish by coming here?"

"Precisely this, I suppose."

"You *suppose*? Didn't you know?"

"I'm a spinster, for pity's sake. How could I guess what would transpire?"

He flopped onto his back and gazed at the ceiling. With their ardor cooling, she was chilled, and she scooted nearer, seeking his body's warmth.

Her life was so sterile, her encounters with men so stilted and formal that she'd never imagined the sort of intimacy they'd just shared. She wanted more of it; she wanted all he had to give. She was tired of being unloved and unwanted, and she was certain that if she wed grumpy, elderly Edward, she'd be more isolated than ever.

"What should I do with you, Caro?" he inquired.

"Am I still a virgin?"

He sighed. "Yes, you are."

"How would I know if you . . ."

"There's a bit more to it."

"What occurs?"

He sighed again. "May I take you home now? Or is your carriage parked out behind the house?"

He would send her home? Now? After what they'd done? How could he?

Her spirits flagged.

She felt as if he'd opened a door to a secret room she hadn't known to exist. She wished there were a mirror next to the bed. She was positive—that if she stared into one—she'd look different, yet he was exactly the same. How could he be so impervious?

"Do you really want me to go?" she shamed herself by asking.

"No, but what good would it do to have you remain?"

"We could spend a few hours together."

"We don't even like each other. What would be the point?"

He turned onto his side and scrutinized her. His face was an expressionless mask, and she peered into his blue, blue eyes, trying to read his mind.

"We could grow to like each other."

He scoffed. "I doubt it. We've had twelve years. It hasn't happened yet."

"I was engaged to your brother the whole time!"

"Yes, you were." He toyed with a lock of her hair. "Why are you really here, Caro? Tell me."

"I don't know."

"Then lie to me. Make something up."

She struggled with what to say, how to explain, but the words wouldn't come. For a fleeting instant, many months prior, he'd seemed to understand her, had been the only person who ever had.

"I'm so lonely," she eventually replied, humiliated by a flood of tears. "I'm so lonely, and I'm so alone, and I—"

As if he couldn't bear to hear the rest, he kissed her.

His mouth bit into hers, as his fingers wound through her hair. He fought with the strands as if he might yank them from her head. He was angry—either with himself or with her, she couldn't decide.

Finally, as if he'd figured out what he needed, or had reached the end of the road, he gentled and drew away.

"I don't want you to leave," he admitted. "I want you to stay. I want you to stay for as long as you can."

"Are you sure?"

"Yes, I'm very sure."

"I can tarry till dawn."

"I'd like that."

"So would I."

He rolled over and pulled her with him so that she was draped across his torso. He grabbed for the laces on her corset, and they began again.

Chapter FOUR

"Do you ever think about our brother?"

"Which one?"

"Which one do you think?" Jack said. "The exalted Viscount Wakefield."

"Sometimes," Ian admitted.

"Will I ever get to meet him?"

"Why would you want to?"

"Just curious. I'm told I resemble him."

"You're an exact copy—though you've managed to control your baser impulses as Wakefield never could."

Jack smiled, glad his history was obscure. Ian had minimal clues about how Jack had survived his youth, but only those tidbits Jack had felt like sharing.

"Wakefield was a scapegrace?"

"And a cad. And a sluggard, but he thrived on his low reputation. He enjoyed aggravating people, and he misbehaved on purpose. It drove our father to distraction."

"Would Wakefield like me?"

Jack hated the plaintive tone underlying his question. He'd never had a family, so he was desperately pleased that he was with Ian. Ian had offered him shelter from the rough streets of London, but Jack couldn't move beyond his wish to become acquainted with his other brother.

The notion of having another sibling, of his being nearby and easily encountered, disturbed Jack's usually placid demeanor. He wanted to look Wakefield in the eye, to take his measure. He wanted Wakefield to know he existed.

"Why would Wakefield *like* you?" Ian asked, trying to appear stern but failing. "You're a pain in the ass."

"You're too kind."

"Aren't I, though?"

Ian was over by the fire, brooding and staring into the flames, and Jack watched him, wondering what had happened. The past few days, he'd seemed bothered, quieter and more pensive, as if he was weighed down by a heavy burden.

They were brothers, but hardly more than strangers. As Ian occupied himself with women, drink, and wagering, they stumbled along, with Jack doing his best to provide friendship and counsel on the lighter issues of life. But he wouldn't dream of giving advice on an important problem, nor was he certain advice would be appreciated.

Suddenly, Ian spun and started for the door. "I'm going out."

"Now? But it's almost midnight, and it's raining cats and dogs."

"I just need to . . . to . . ."

"You don't have to explain. If you want to go, go."

"Rebecca is here. She's upstairs, having a bath. She's waiting for me to join her."

"You don't care to?"

"I guess I don't."

The news was odd. Rebecca was a great beauty, and even though she was a crazed witch, Jack couldn't conceive of any man shunning the chance to bed her.

He let out a low whistle. "If you leave, she won't be happy."

"I don't imagine so."

Ian was shifting from foot to foot, anxious to be away, and Jack waved him toward the hall. "Just go. I'll deal with her."

"You're sure?"

"Positive."

"She can be a handful."

"She's a wee mite. I'm not afraid of her. I'll see her home—if I have to bind and gag her to get her there."

Ian chuckled, his expression relieved. "Thank you."

"You're welcome."

"I owe you one."

He rushed out, as Jack murmured, "Your debt has already been paid a hundred times over."

Dawdling, he contemplated Rebecca. She'd be nude, hot and slippery all over, and at the realization, his cock stirred, which made him grin. She was Ian's mistress, and he wasn't such an ungrateful wretch that he'd take what Ian considered his own, yet he often caught himself lusting after her.

What healthy male wouldn't? She was sin incarnate, a walking, talking erotic fantasy. Frequently, he viewed her naked and doing all sorts of things she oughtn't, and he always tried to act nonchalant, as if he wasn't affected, but it was difficult to pretend indifference.

With that mouth and those eyes, she should have been locked up in a distant convent or prison, where sane, normal men wouldn't have to gaze upon her and be bewitched by lechery.

He went to the stairs and climbed, more eager than he should have been for the pending fracas. He loathed her—for her avarice, for her vanity, for her loose morals—but he garnered an enormous thrill from their sparring. She was a vixen and she-devil, wrapped in a pretty package, and there was nothing quite so entertaining as goading her into a temper.

He entered Ian's bedchamber and proceeded to the dressing room, pushing the door open and marching in. Her back to him, she was reclined in the tub. Her knees were spread wide, and she was sipping on a glass of Ian's whiskey and smoking one of his cheroots. Her lush red hair dangled over the rim and hung to the floor.

Expecting Ian, she glanced over her shoulder, a sultry smile on her ruby lips, but when she saw him, her mood instantly soured.

"Didn't anyone ever teach you to knock?"

"No."

"Were you raised in a cave?"

"I've heard it said that I was."

"I'm not surprised." She spun around, ignoring him. "Get out of here. I'm enjoying myself, and I won't have you pestering me."

Infuriating her to no end, he approached and sat on the edge of the tub. He could see into the water, and he struggled not to gape at her perfect breasts, her tantalizing nipples. He snatched the cigar and snuffed it out; then he took her whiskey and downed the remaining contents.

"You rat!" she protested. "Give me that."

"You're finished."

"I am not."

"You are. Ian's gone out."

"What?"

"He's gone out."

"To where?"

"I haven't the vaguest idea. He asked me to take you home."

"But . . . but . . . I just arrived."

"And now you're leaving."

"I don't wish to go."

"It's not up to you."

"You may have imposed on Ian's affluence and good graces, but this is not your bloody house."

"It's not yours either, princess."

"I don't have to listen to you. You managed to fool him with your false claims of a common paternity, but I'm not so easily duped. He's such a smart fellow. How did you convince him you were brothers?"

"I cast a spell on him. When I was younger, I traveled with a caravan of gypsies, and they showed me how, so be careful, or I'll cast one on you, too."

She frowned and studied him, clearly wondering if a hex was imminent, and he liked that he could keep her off balance.

He wasn't ashamed of his antecedents, but he wouldn't defend them to people who could never understand. His sudden appearance as Ian's brother had fomented tons of gossip, but he never discussed his history or answered the charges that were slyly voiced.

He had to give her credit: She had the courage to level her accusations to his face, rather than behind his back as most were wont to do.

His mother had been a gentleman's daughter, tossed out by her parents after the notorious aristocrat Douglas

Clayton had impregnated her. Jack had indistinct memories of her, but while she'd lived, their life had been one trial after the next, and he recollected it as a period when he was always hungry and cold.

After her death, on a sodden, wintry street in York, he'd been a boy all alone, and he'd gotten by as best he could. He actually *had* traveled with gypsies, with a circus, with a troupe of theatrical players.

Through it all, he'd kept a letter from his father to his mother, as well as a stained baptismal certificate. On a blustery autumn day, as he'd loitered on a London corner, he'd been weary and starving and questioning the reasons he continued on. He'd made a few inquiries, had learned Ian's address, and had knocked on his door.

His brother had read the two tattered documents, then had welcomed him to stay for as long as he liked. It had been as easy as that, but he wouldn't explain as much to Rebecca Blake.

Her world was one of wealth and privilege. She'd never missed a meal or huddled in an empty stairwell to get out of the rain. She'd wed and buried three rich husbands, and each of them had left her money, yet she constantly mentioned that she was broke, when she had no notion of what true poverty entailed.

Her last spouse's family had proposed a settlement, which she'd refused, demanding much more, and it was obvious she was wrangling to have Ian as her fourth husband so that she could latch onto his fortune, too, which seemed so silly.

She had more than enough, yet she was never satisfied.

"Let's get you going," he said.

He reached down and pulled her up, but the tub was

slippery, and she toppled to the side. There was nothing he could do but catch her. She landed in his arms, every damp, shapely inch of her sprawled across him in a provocative way. Her bare bosom was crushed to his chest, her lips a hairsbreadth from his own, and for a stunned moment, they froze, then a wave of madness swept over him, and he kissed her.

He didn't ponder Ian, or her relationship with him, didn't consider her prior dead husbands, or what he viewed as her greedy behavior. He simply forged on.

She was hot and wet, and she smelled so good, and he dragged her across his lap. His cock swelled to an enormous size, and he grew so aroused that he worried he might spill himself in his trousers.

The placard of his pants was all that separated him from paradise and, pushed beyond his limit, he flexed into her. He wrestled to get nearer, as she was doing the same. She hissed and bit, clawed and rasped, offering him her breast, and he seized it in a frenzy.

When she was urging him to feast, how could he fail to oblige her?

He cupped her between her legs, and he felt as if he'd been jolted by lightning. Frantically, he ripped at the buttons on his pants, yanked his phallus free, and impaled himself in her sheath. He thrust once, again, again, and he came in a torrid rush, but the ecstasy quickly waned.

He pressed his forehead to her nape and struggled to calm his breathing. Sanity returned, and reality sank in for both of them.

"Oh, my God!" she muttered. "What have I done?"

She leapt away and stood before him, a naked, quivering ball of wrath.

He stood, too, so that they were eye-to-eye and toe-to-toe. He wanted her again, already.

"I'm not sorry," he said.

"I am!"

"I didn't hear you complaining while it was happening."

"Then you weren't listening very closely. Ian will kill me."

"Probably."

"Don't you dare tell him! If you do, I'll kill *you*!"

He laughed. "I'm shaking in my boots."

"You tricked me! You seduced me against my will!"

"Liar."

He shoved her to the wall, and he leaned in and sucked on her nipple as he fingered her down below. His thumb found her clit, and he touched it once, twice, three times, and she came to high heaven, screaming with bliss, her knees buckling so that he had to hold her up lest she fall to the floor in a heap.

He smirked. She was so damned sexy, and he was so titillated. They were like two combustibles stored in the same shed. The smallest spark had ignited a maelstrom.

"You're laughing at me!" she correctly charged.

"I can't help it. You're easy and loose, and apparently, I'm no better. We're quite a pair."

"Speak for yourself."

She stormed out, and he tarried in the quiet, and as reason reasserted itself, he was aghast.

He'd betrayed his brother, had jeopardized the only stability he'd ever known, merely to climb between the thighs of a tempestuous vixen he could hardly abide. What had he been thinking? How could she—how could any woman—be worth so much?

He plopped into a chair, his chin in his hands, wondering how he'd ever make it right.

※

Y ou will go downstairs—immediately!—and you will be your usual, charming self throughout the entire meal. Am I making myself clear?"

Britannia Foster, Countess of Derby, glared at her recalcitrant daughter.

"My headache is unbearable," Caroline claimed.

"So? Why would a little discomfort keep you from your duties?"

"I don't feel like socializing."

"How can it signify? Mr. Shelton will be here any second. You must be in place to greet him, as is proper and expected."

"No one will notice if I'm not there."

"*I* shall notice," Britannia said. "You've caused sufficient scandal, and I won't stand for your instigating more."

"How have I caused scandal?" Caroline demanded. "I did everything you asked. I waited and waited for John to marry me, yet he cried off. How can his decision be my fault?"

"If you'd enticed him—as any well-bred girl could have accomplished—you'd have been wed long ago." She pulled herself up to her full height, her portly form hovering over Caroline where she huddled on the bed like a sick, whiny child. "You must face the facts: You have no feminine attributes for a man to enjoy. By deigning to wed you, when you are damaged goods, Mr. Shelton has thrown you a lifeline. If you are to have any kind of future, you must seize the chance he's so graciously provided."

"Must I?" Caroline snidely inquired.

"Yes, you must."

From the moment her husband, Bernard, had announced the match, Caroline had been unruly. With each passing day, she grew more intractable, which was so out of character. She'd always been so obedient and submissive.

Britannia was so anxious for the nuptials to occur that it was difficult to conceal her glee over Caroline's fate. When Wakefield had finally spurned Caroline, Britannia had been elated. She'd grabbed the opportunity to have her greatest wish come true.

Revenge against Edward Shelton had driven her for decades. It fueled her crazed ambitions for Caroline—the child she'd conceived in shame, the child she loathed—and fed a secret yearning that was so extreme it bordered on madness.

A few whispered comments to Bernard had sent him racing to Edward with a proposal. Now, with Britannia's scheme so close to fruition, she wouldn't be denied simply because Caroline didn't like Edward.

No woman of their station was ever allowed to wed for love—herself being the prime example of how dreams could be dashed—and she would have her way. She always did. Caroline would be Edward's wife, no matter what. Edward would pay the price Britannia was determined to extract.

"You're trying my patience," she snapped. "Get up, calm yourself, and get down to the parlor. You will join us—in ten minutes. If you don't arrive, I shall return and take a switch to you. Perhaps if I beat some sense into you, you'll remember your obligations to your family."

She stomped off, barely able to keep from striking out. More and more, she felt out of control with rage, her temper bubbling so vehemently just beneath the surface that she could scarcely function.

At age fifty-five, she was a frumpy matron who hadn't aged well, who was trapped in a marriage she abhorred. She was obese and homely. Her jowls sagged, her eyes were beady, her lips taut with disapproval of everyone and everything.

She'd never been beautiful, had never had the allure or polish that other debutantes had so effortlessly exhibited. She, herself, had been a spinster, waiting for her cousin, Bernard, to settle down and tie the knot, a feat which he hadn't chosen to effect until he was thirty and she twenty-five.

Her spouse had been selected for her, and she'd had no say in who it would be, so she had done her duty. But as she'd suspected, her decades with him had been a trial of endurance.

She hated him and the two children she'd spawned. Her eldest, son Adam, was heir to the exalted Derby line, but a spoiled, stupid oaf. Her youngest, daughter Caroline, was ungrateful and brainless, suitable as fodder for the marriage market and naught else. The two offspring had ruined her life and represented her failure to find happiness, and she yearned to wreck their lives as they had wrecked hers.

She tromped down the stairs, and as she reached the foyer, she steeled herself for her pending encounter with Edward. Due to her responsibilities as hostess, she'd welcome him politely, yet during the interminable evening she'd be roiling with animosity.

She detested him and Bernard, but she was so adept at hiding her actual sentiments that they never noted the severe level of her dislike.

Breathing deeply, she was ready to enter, to entertain, when she espied Bernard, dressed in coat and hat, and about to sneak out without her being aware that he'd left. Her fury flared.

"Bernard!" she sharply summoned. "What do you think you're doing?"

He whipped around, irked at having been caught.

"What is it, Britannia?" He sighed, acting the part of the downtrodden husband that he played so skillfully.

She huffed over, sorry that she wasn't holding a pistol, that she hadn't murdered him years earlier. "We have guests coming for supper."

"No, *you* have guests coming for supper. I've told you to stop including me in your frivolous soirees."

"Edward will be here!" she fumed. "You know how obstinate Caroline is being. We must present a united front, so that she understands she has to follow through."

"Caroline will do as I've bid her. She wouldn't dare defy me. Now if you'll excuse me—"

"I don't excuse you."

"Well, that's too bad, for I have no intention of tarrying. Good night."

"Where will you be?" she challenged, weary of pretending to be the blind, contented wife.

"I'm off to Georgette's," he boldly replied. "Where would you suppose?"

"Don't use that harlot's name in this house."

"You asked; I answered. If you don't want the truth, don't press."

"You shall not go!" she hissed. "I will not tolerate it! I will not be humiliated with Edward about to arrive."

"I love her," he ridiculously, tediously claimed, "and I plan to marry her. You have to accept the inevitable. This farce of a marriage is over—as it should have been long ago."

"You're mad. I've spoken with an attorney. There is not a church or court or peer or king who would grant you a divorce from me."

"We'll see," he enigmatically mused as if he had something up his lying, deceitful sleeve.

He marched out, abandoning her in the hall as if she were a servant. She watched him go, yearning to chase after him, to yank him inside, but she didn't. Short of tying him to a chair, she couldn't make him stay.

He was still a handsome man, with a full head of hair and tall, slender body. Women lusted after him, and he returned their affection. She couldn't tabulate how many affairs he'd had, but they'd all been fleeting. Until now. Until Georgette.

He might believe that he would run off with the little hussy. He might assume Britannia would stand by and be shamed to infinity, but he was dead wrong.

She would kill his precious Georgette; then she'd kill him. And she wouldn't bat an eye.

Her expression grim, she proceeded to the parlor, braced to brazen it out before her guests.

꧁

Hello, Edward."

"Hello, Brit," Edward said, using the nickname she hated. It was a petty slight, meant to remind her that he knew her well and she had no secrets. "How have you been?"

"Fine," she retorted, which was a huge fib. She was the most miserable person he'd ever met.

"I missed Bernard at supper."

"He was called out at the last minute. On important business."

They both recognized the statement to be false. Bernard was a carousing roué, yet he and Britannia strutted around as if they were the epitome of a happily married couple. She was such a contemptible hypocrite, and all of London tittered about her behind her back.

At having voiced the lie, her lips were pursed like a prune, and he could barely stifle his distaste. She was such an unlikable woman, and he abhorred that his pending nuptials forced him to fraternize. Once the ceremony was concluded, and there was no further need to feign familial harmony, he'd make it a point never to see her again.

Poor Bernard! The pitiable fellow would never be shed of her, and Edward was so glad that Bernard had ended up with her rather than himself. When they'd all been younger, it had been amusing to toy with her, to fake devotion and act as if he might steal her from Bernard, but Edward never would have. She was simply too unpleasant for words, and over the intervening decades, nothing had occurred to change that fact.

Across the room, Caroline slipped out onto the verandah, and he remarked, "Caroline seems out of sorts."

"Of course she does. She despises you." Sarcastically, she added, "Can you imagine that?"

"Bernard and I have decided on the union. Her opinion is irrelevant."

"Yes, it is."

Her tepid assurance didn't calm his anxiety. While

Caroline had previously been the most docile of females, she'd recently grown surly and curt. Edward had no idea what was eating at her, but he wouldn't brook any feminine hysterics, nor would he permit her to refuse him.

From the day she'd been born, he'd plotted as to how he could wed her, and he'd impatiently waited until she was twelve to first approach Bernard. He'd said no, insisting he would honor the betrothal to Wakefield. After Wakefield had tossed her over, Bernard had come crawling back. He'd begged Edward to save her from disgrace, and Edward had smugly consented.

He preferred young, pure girls, and with sixty years of living he'd wed and survived five child-brides. None of them had been more than fourteen at the time of the ceremony, so Caroline was much older than he'd typically have selected. Yet, he delighted in the realization that he'd finally gotten what he wanted, that she hadn't been able to escape him.

Despite her advanced age, he would have an enormous amount of fun teaching her her marital obligations, and he was eager to start.

Still, she'd been behaving so erratically, had even dared a few caustic comments as they'd chatted before supper. With her being so much more mature than most brides, it was conceivable that a modern notion had lodged in her flighty head and she supposed she didn't have to obey her father. The prospect had Edward unsettled.

"I presume you've told her," he tentatively broached, "that she has no choice in the matter?"

"Don't worry. I shan't allow her to embarrass us more than she has."

"I didn't think you would."

"If I have to drag her to the altar, you'll have her in the end. You may count on it." Her smile was almost eerie in its resolve.

"You're awfully determined."

"Yes, I am."

"Are you jealous? Is that why you're pushing so hard for the match?"

"Jealous! Of . . . of . . . Caroline?"

"Doesn't it bother you that I'm going to have *her*, when I wouldn't have *you* all those years ago?"

"Don't be ridiculous. It's ancient history. I never reflect on it."

"Don't you?"

"No, I was too foolish to know any better. It was a passing fancy."

"Really?"

He chuckled, aware that levity would infuriate her.

She'd been Bernard's impetuous, wretched wife, who'd been desperate to be rescued from a marriage she'd dreaded. Edward could easily have stolen her away, but he hadn't been serious. Even back then, she'd been a fat, obnoxious harpy.

"Don't lie, Brit. If you had to do it all over again, you'd run off with me in a heartbeat."

"You flatter yourself, Edward."

"Do I?"

"You're the most inflated, vainglorious man. I never could abide you."

At the insult, he felt free to hurl one of his own. "I wonder if Caroline will be interesting in bed, or if she'll take after her mother. You always were cold as snow under the blankets."

While there was no love lost between them, it was a horrid remark, even by his low standards.

She gasped and strangely contended, "I'll have my revenge. You'll see."

"What revenge?" he scoffed. "About what are you babbling?"

"Beware, Edward. Beware! Your sins are about to come home to roost."

There was a bizarre gleam in her eye, and for the briefest moment, she appeared quite mad. Then the peculiar interlude concluded, and she stomped off.

He watched her go, and he actually shuddered, an icy shiver slithering down his spine, as if he'd been cursed.

Unnerved, he laughed off the odd episode and went in the other direction. It was time to speak with his fiancée, time to remind her that he was in the room and expecting her to attend him.

He walked to the verandah, hoping he would catch her strolling in the dark. Caroline needed a taste of masculine passion, and he was just the man to provide it.

Chapter FIVE

"Would you pass the tea?"

"But of course. Would you like a biscuit?"

"That would be marvelous. You're too kind."

Ian scowled back and forth at Jack and Rebecca. He'd been in the dining room with them for twenty minutes, and neither had uttered a harsh word. They were being disgustingly solicitous, and there had been so many polite exchanges that he wanted to gag. What on earth had come over them?

He was too hungover to figure it out, and he couldn't abide having to observe as his brother and mistress behaved like imbeciles. As he'd drunk and gambled till dawn, and was fairly sure he'd lost a thousand pounds, his patience and mood were exhausted.

Anymore, he seemed determined to part with every farthing of the blood money he'd received from his father, and if he kept on, he'd be poverty-stricken. Was that his plan? If he ended up destitute, how could penury be beneficial? Especially now that he had Jack to consider.

He glared at Jack. "What is your name?"

"My name?" Jack asked, confused.

"Yes, your name! Your name! I thought it was Jack Romsey."

"You know it is."

"Really? From how you're acting, I could have sworn someone sneaked in and took your place."

"How am I acting?"

"Like a fucking pantywaist. Stop it. You're annoying me." He turned his attention to Rebecca. "And as to you . . ."

At his sharp tone, her fingers shook, and tea sloshed over the rim of her cup.

Appearing meek and guilty as hell, she stared at her plate. "What will you do to me? Just tell me; I can't bear the suspense."

He had no idea what she meant. "What will I *do* to you? For what transgression?"

Her relief was palpable. "Well . . . for . . . nothing. For nothing, at all."

"Are you feeling all right?"

"I'm fine," she insisted, and she stood. "I was going to invite you for a ride in the park, but I . . . ah . . . recollected a previous appointment. I'll come by tomorrow."

As she hustled out, he frowned and muttered, "I don't understand women."

Jack was suddenly in a hurry, too. "I remembered that I have to . . . to . . ."

"Are *you* feeling all right?"

"Just dandy. Why?"

Ian studied him, finding it curious that he looked guilty, too. "No reason, I guess."

"You don't need me for anything, do you?"

"No."

"Then I think I'll . . . I'll . . ." He blushed a bright red.

"Jack?"

"Yes?"

"Get out before I throttle you."

"Am I bothering you? I'm so sorry! I shouldn't have—"

"Jack! Please!"

His brother's irritating mouth snapped shut, and he slithered out, leaving Ian to fume and ponder in the quiet.

He leaned forward, his elbows on the table, his head in his hands, and the worst wave of melancholy swept over him.

What was he doing, carousing to excess? The wagering and inebriation were bad enough, but he was so out of control that he was trifling with Caroline, and he had no qualms about the possibility of discovery. His lack of conscience was so at odds with the man he'd once been that the changes were alarming.

He was bent on destruction, punishing himself by destroying every good thing he'd built in London over the prior twelve years, but castigation was stupid. Some deeds were too heinous to be forgiven, and he could never fully atone for how he'd betrayed John. So why keep trying?

In the middle of his morose reverie, a female voice said, "Hello, Ian."

"Hello, Caro." He sighed and glanced up.

After his night of insanity with her, he'd given

strict instructions to his staff not to let her in again. Yet here she was, like a painful toothache. Would he have to fire someone so the servants would heed his edict?

"How did you gain entrance?"

"I simply walked in. How would you suppose?"

"Have you ever heard of knocking?"

"Why would I? You've told your butler to refuse me."

"Yes, I have. You can't keep coming here!"

"Why shouldn't I?"

"You'll be caught. There'll be a big fuss."

"Maybe I don't care if there's a fuss."

"Yes, you do."

"I'm about to be married," she reminded him, the news like a punch in the gut. "No one's concerned as to where I am or what I do."

"That doesn't mean your father wouldn't have a fit if he knew."

She closed the door, sealing them in. "My wedding is set for March fifteenth."

Her citing of the date was extremely distressing, but he couldn't figure out why it would be. Blandly, he inquired, "Is it so soon?"

"Four weeks away."

"It certainly is."

"Have you any comment on the situation?"

"What would you like me to say besides congratulations?"

"Would you imagine I'll be happy with Mr. Shelton?"

"Since when did your kind ever marry for happiness?"

"My *kind*? Honestly, Ian, where do you get your absurd notions?"

"From status-conscious snobs like you."

She shot a reproving glare. "So what is your opinion as to my pending nuptials? Will my union with Mr. Shelton be one long romantic adventure?"

He couldn't see any reason to lie. "No. It will be quite awful."

She chuckled, though miserably. "You've always been so brutally frank. It's a most infuriating trait."

"I aim to please."

"Were you aware that Mr. Shelton is thirty-five years older than me?"

"Is it that many?"

"My mother claims the age difference is a boon."

"How could it be?"

"She says I'm nervous and fickle, and I'll benefit from his steadying presence."

"Your mother is an idiot."

"It's two in the afternoon," she mentioned, switching subjects, "and you aren't dressed."

"No, I'm not."

"You're falling apart. What's happened to you?"

It was a question he'd asked himself a thousand times.

"You can't keep visiting," he scolded.

"Why not?"

She marched to the sideboard, and he watched—flummoxed—as she passed up the food, but helped herself to some of his uncles' whiskey.

He was aghast. "Have you become a drunkard?"

"I don't believe so. Why?"

"Whenever I see you lately, you have liquor in your hand."

She grinned. "I have, haven't I?"

"Yes, and I don't like the transformation."

She shrugged. "I don't care."

Her reply aggravated him, which was silly. His primary criticism of her had been that she was too cautious. Now, as she was spontaneous at every turn, he was irked. Why couldn't he be glad?

She approached the table, and just as he assumed she'd sit in the chair next to him, she snuggled herself onto his lap.

"Caro!"

"What?"

"What are you doing?"

"I'm sitting on your lap."

"You have to stop being so forward."

"Why?"

"Because . . . because . . ."

"Aren't you the one who urged me to be more impulsive?"

"Well . . . yes."

"I've merely decided to heed your advice, and I'm giving my passionate character free rein. What's wrong with that?"

"What's *wrong* with it? I'll tell you what's wrong with it. It's . . . it's . . ."

"I missed you," she blurted out.

He'd missed her, too, but he'd never admit it. "That's as may be, but it doesn't imply that you can—"

She kissed him! Directly on the mouth!

Her fingers were in his hair, her breasts pressed to his chest. His body reacted as vehemently as could be expected, his cock rising to the occasion, and he was so conflicted.

He'd always desired her, and she was throwing herself at him. Why not catch her? What objective was served by restrained conduct?

He couldn't conceive of a single one.

She'd begged him to ruin her, though he was positive she wasn't serious. She was unhappy and fretting over her marriage, but he was sure—when push came to shove—that she'd go through with it. She simply needed to feel more secure as to her marital obligations, and a few evenings earlier he'd given her a hint as to what would be required. Why not continue with his lessons?

When he was working so hard to establish himself as a bounder and roué, what could be more fitting than to seduce the very prim and proper Lady Caroline? He could go some distance down the sexual road, without actually deflowering her.

If they were discovered, what was it to him? Apparently, she was prepared to risk her reputation, and *she* was the one who had everything to lose. With the exception of his new relationship with Jack, he was possessed of so little that mattered. If she was eager, shouldn't he oblige her?

So far, he'd dawdled like a statue, unwilling to join in, and his anatomy made the choice that his common sense couldn't render. He seized control of the embrace, pulling her nearer, as he caressed her shoulders, hair, and back. He clasped her hips, situating her delectable bottom so it was nestled to his inflamed loins. With each shift of her torso, she rubbed across his phallus, making him groan, making him ripple with lust.

"You've taught me something about myself," she murmured.

"What is that?"

"I adore kissing."

"I can tell."

"I think I have a knack for it, wouldn't you agree?"

"Oh, yes. You definitely have a knack."

With a renewed fervor, he captured her mouth, and he was stunned by how natural it seemed to dally with her. He felt as if he'd been kissing her forever, as if he'd been created specifically for kissing her and no other purpose.

Goaded to recklessness, he draped her over his arm and nibbled down her neck, to her bosom. He fought with the bodice of her dress, then eased a breast free. He licked the aroused tip, as she arched and struggled against the potent stimulation.

"Oh, Lord, yes," she breathed. "Touch me just like that! Don't stop!"

"You've become a wanton."

"Do you mind?"

"Not a whit. I find it quite grand."

He'd often suspected that she was an inferno of buried passions, and he was delighted to be proved correct. How lucky he was to have stumbled on her when she was ready to misbehave!

He sucked on her nipple until her hips started to flex, then he reached down and pressed on her mons with the heel of his hand, but the gesture provided scant relief.

She was beginning to comprehend the pleasures of the flesh, so she knew what her body craved, and he was elated to give it to her. However, they were lounged in a chair in the dining room. He wasn't positive if Jack and Rebecca had departed, and he had no clue as to the location of any of the servants. Someone could walk in on them, and while he wasn't concerned over being observed, he was certain she'd be mortified.

He drew away and straightened her clothes, then he stood her on her feet, and he stood, too.

She frowned. "What are you doing? We can't quit!"

"Let's go up to my bedchamber."

"Will we engage in the sorts of activity we attempted the other night?"

"That was my intent. I'm hoping to have my wicked way with you."

"Then by all means, let's go to your bedchamber."

As if they were adolescent sweethearts, he linked their fingers and led her toward the hall. She'd grown so brazen that she willingly followed, content to leap off any cliff he suggested.

He grabbed for the knob and opened the door, when he literally bumped into Rebecca.

Suddenly and without warning, he was positioned between his mistress who was extremely jealous and Caro who was . . . was . . . Well, he couldn't describe what she *was*. The scene was hideous, and he hadn't a clue how to wiggle out of it.

Like a beast, he stepped away from Caro, pretending no heightened affection. It was the only satisfactory resolution, but still, he could feel her stiffen, could sense that she perceived the insult.

"I thought you'd left," he said to Rebecca, struggling to sound casual.

"I was curious if you'd like to . . ." Rebecca paused as she saw Caro. Her gaze narrowed, her brain whirring as she tried to deduce what Caroline's presence indicated. On the spur of the moment, he couldn't devise an acceptable response.

"What are you doing here?" she asked Caro.

"I might ask you the same question," Caro rejoined, "but then, we both know the answer, don't we?"

Rebecca's hot temper sparked. "I have every right to be here if I wish. Ian and I have an understanding."

"Ian and I have an understanding, too," Caro maintained, being deliberately enigmatic.

Rebecca gasped and shifted her malevolent glare to Ian.

"Explain yourself," she demanded.

He had no idea why he was meeting with Caro, couldn't justify it to himself, and most especially couldn't justify it to Rebecca.

"It's not what you think," he pitifully asserted.

"Isn't it?"

"We're old friends," Caro chimed in, imbuing the comment with too much innuendo. Where had she obtained this aptitude for feminine wiles?

"What are you doing sniffing around Ian?" Rebecca challenged. "Be gone! At once!"

"I'm not ready to leave."

"Ladies," Ian interrupted, "if I might—"

"Shut up, Ian," they snapped in unison.

"Ian," Caroline kept on, regal as any princess, "I'd like to finish our discussion. Would you arrange to have Mrs. Blake escorted out?"

Rebecca scoffed. "As if Ian could order me to do anything! I'm a widow and—as opposed to you—I'm permitted to act however I please."

"I'd forgotten you were a widow in *mourning*," Caro mused. She rudely and critically assessed Rebecca's bright red gown.

"I'm sure it will come as a surprise to someone

as pious and perfect as yourself," Rebecca retorted, "but I'm *not* in mourning. My late husband was a violent boor and not entitled to any lingering respect from me."

"Actually"—Caro was giving as good as she got— "I'm not surprised in the least. How many husbands have you killed? Five? Six?"

"Now you've done it," Ian muttered.

"I didn't kill any of my husbands!"

"That's not what I hear."

"Is it my fault they keep dropping dead?"

"You always seem to be with them when it happens. Some of us find it a tad too coincidental."

"I don't know why they keep dying!"

"Don't you?"

Caro stared her down, appearing greatly harassed, immaculate, and without fear of harm. She regarded Rebecca as if the ferocious, incensed woman were a queer bug that ought to be squashed.

"Jack!" Ian called. "Jack! Are you here? Come help me!"

Shortly, Jack hurried toward them, and in an instant, he discerned the awkwardness of the situation.

"Rebecca," he said, "why don't I see you home?"

"I don't need a boy to show me the way," she fumed, her livid gaze locked on Caro's. She spun and stormed out, halting at the last to hurl over her shoulder, "Lady Caroline, I wonder if Mr. Shelton knows where you are."

Caro was unperturbed by the threat. "Why don't you speak with him? I'm positive he'd be eager to chat with an individual of your stellar character."

For a split second, Rebecca looked as if she might

engage in some of the homicide for which she was so notorious, so Jack blocked her and dragged her away.

Ian watched them go, yearning to trot off after them. At the moment, he'd like nothing better than to be relaxing in a gentlemen's club and enmeshed in an amiable game of dice. He'd be surrounded by sane, rational men, the company of whom he enjoyed and understood.

The dust settled, and Caro broke the jarring silence.

"Well, that was unpleasant."

"It certainly was. I'm sorry."

"Are you?"

"Of course I am."

The ice queen had returned with a vengeance. She was coldly furious, but only a person who knew her intimately—such as himself—could detect it.

"In the past," she charged, "you castigated me because I held my tongue in ugly circumstances, or because I was calm in the middle of discord. Were you implying I should be more like Mrs. Blake? Is she the sort of female you relish?"

There were a dozen replies he could make as to why he persisted with Rebecca. He liked her fire and sass, her spirit and audacity. She was wild in life and wild in bed, and in light of his current attempts to regularly offend others, it was enormously entertaining to observe as she thumbed her nose at Caroline's society, but he doubted Caroline would appreciate any candor on the topic.

"I've known her a long time, Caro," he quietly stated.

"Have you?" She smiled the frosty smile that could set grown men to trembling. It was her mother's smile, her aristocrat's smile, her wealthy, spoiled earl's daughter smile.

"Good-bye," she said.

She tried to step around him, but he moved into her path, a hand on her waist.

"I don't want you to leave. Not when you're so angry."

"I'm not *angry*."

"You can't lie to me. I know you too well."

"No, you don't. You don't know me, at all. Nor do I know you." She yanked away so that he wasn't touching her. "Occasionally, I'm lonely and frightened, and I allow my low feelings to push me into foolish predicaments. I sit in my empty bedchamber, and I pine for you, and I convince myself that you're missing me, too. I forget that you have an entire existence that doesn't include me—just as I have one that doesn't include you and never will."

"That's not true, Caro. We're old friends. You said so yourself."

"I didn't mean it," she cruelly retorted. "I apologize for pestering you. It won't happen again."

"You haven't been a bother. You're welcome to stop by whenever you like."

"Don't start being kind to me. Courtesy doesn't become you."

She walked down the hall, toward the rear door, and he called, "Wait, Caro. Let me take you home."

"I can find my own way—as your mistress can. I'm not helpless and never have been. No one seems to realize that about me."

Then she was gone, and he slumped against the wall.

It had been the worst afternoon of his life, and it

wasn't even three o'clock. If he had a hundred years to try, he wouldn't be able to fix this for either woman.

He proceeded to the dining room, poured a whiskey, and began to drink.

Chapter SIX

Remove your hand before I break your arm," Rebecca warned.

Being his typical, annoying self, Jack didn't heed her command.

"I'm not afraid of you," he blustered.

"You're not?"

"No."

"Let me demonstrate why you should be."

She'd been an orphan raised by distant cousins—who'd had six boys. They'd all been bigger and meaner. She'd learned the hard way how to scrap and brawl, how to defend herself and win.

She whipped around, ready to bloody his nose, when she came face-to-face with his fabulous blue eyes. In the past few days, she'd been haunted by those eyes, and she didn't want to be gazing into them now. They were too piercing, too astute, and they seemed to delve through muscle and pore, down to the center of her miserable black heart.

"What will you do, Rebecca?" he taunted. "Will you fight the entire world?"

"If I have to."

"I'm not the enemy."

"You couldn't prove it by me."

She couldn't bear having him so close, and she stomped to her carriage and climbed in.

She was still trying to figure out what had transpired between them in Ian's dressing room. Jack had come upstairs to inform her that Ian was gone, he'd aggravated and insulted her, and the next thing she knew, she was riding him like a mare in heat.

After the life she'd led, she had few scruples and even fewer reasons to behave, yet she was very committed to Ian. He was a generous, attentive lover, and he'd been kind to her when no one else had shown an ounce of concern. For his stalwart devotion, she owed him gratitude and fidelity, yet Jack had merely glanced in her direction and she'd succumbed like a harlot.

She'd betrayed Ian! Ian whom she adored! Ian whom she hoped to marry! And she'd done it with his penniless, exasperating brother! Had any woman in history ever committed a more heinous act?

As she recollected her treachery, she blushed with shame, which was saying a lot. She never regretted, never apologized or lamented. As a single female, she had to survive as best she could, and if others didn't like how she carried on, she didn't care.

She'd been wed at fourteen, at sixteen, at twenty. Her three husbands had been brutal swine, who weren't missed. The first two had left her meager inheritances that barely paid the bills. The third had been a money-grubbing miser, who'd died with plenty of cash in the bank, but she doubted she'd receive a penny of it.

She was no fool, and she understood how the world worked. She had no influential acquaintances and no power. Despite how long she bickered with her brother-in-law, he would end up with it all, so she had to marry Ian. No other man would have her, but what if he found out what she'd done? There was a limit to what he'd tolerate, and having sex with Jack crossed any acceptable line.

She couldn't justify her crazed rush to fornicate with Jack. She didn't even like Jack!

With how he'd slithered out of nowhere and ingratiated himself to Ian, she remained unconvinced that they were siblings, and she loathed that Ian was so fond of him. Her grip on Ian's affection was tenuous, so she didn't want to share him with anybody.

What had she been thinking? How could she continue visiting Ian? How could she wed him? Her conduct with Jack would forever be a wedge between them, a secret she couldn't divulge.

Desperate to be away, she pounded on the roof of the coach, signaling the driver to hurry, when Jack climbed in behind her.

He paused to peer up at the other man and said, "Mrs. Blake is going home. Take your time arriving, would you?"

He winked! The bastard! The driver would suppose that she'd deliberately planned to be sequestered with Jack, and rumors would spread.

Did Jack want stories drifting to Ian? Was he completely deranged?

"Get out of here!" she hissed, but the horses took that moment to pull, and the carriage lurched forward. Jack tumbled onto her, his weight pushing her onto the seat. In a thrice, she was flat on her back, and he was sprawled on top of her. Down below, his cock was erect and prodding her leg.

They hadn't been secluded for two seconds and he was aroused, which indicated that he desired her again, that their initial encounter hadn't been a fluke. Every feminine part of her rejoiced.

What was the matter with her? Had she no integrity? No honor? People often whispered that she possessed no conscience or morals. Were they correct?

"Ah!" she shrieked. "Are you mad? Get off me!"

He chuckled, but ignored her, so she batted at his shoulders and chest, and he seized her wrists and pinned them over her head.

The position provided even closer contact. Her entire front was stretched out and crushed to his, and her traitorous anatomy was in heaven.

She increased her struggles.

"Desist!" he ordered.

"Not till you move!"

"As if I'd move with you punching at me like a lunatic!"

"If you didn't deserve it, I wouldn't be punching you!"

He kissed her.

At the feel of his delicious mouth touching her own, she melted like butter, her limbs growing rubbery and limp. For the briefest instant, they wallowed in the sweetness. It seemed so natural and right; then he stiffened and jerked away.

He slid to the opposite seat, scowled, and insisted, "I didn't mean to do that."

She was still half-dazed and, as if waking from a dream, she blinked and blinked. Then reality crashed in, and she sat up and pressed herself into the corner.

"I didn't mean to do it, either."

They glared, each blaming the other, when it had been more of a spontaneous combustion of ardor. What had come over them? They were like a pair of rutting dogs.

"Look," he started. "I've been thinking about the other day."

"And . . . ?"

"I said I wasn't sorry, but I was mistaken. I'm very, very sorry that it occurred."

"Why? And as a woman who's regularly accused of violent behavior, might I suggest that you be extremely cautious in your reply?"

If he claimed he hadn't enjoyed it, if he contended it had been all her fault and none of his own, she couldn't predict what she'd do.

"Ian is my brother," he stupidly reminded her.

"Yes, he is."

"And you're his mistress."

"That, too."

"What we did was wrong."

"Yes, it was," she agreed.

"I feel terrible."

"So do I."

"And I was thinking—"

"About what?"

"We have to tell him."

"*Tell* him! Are you insane?"

"I can't abide that we've betrayed him, especially when he's been so kind to me. The truth is like a tough piece of meat stuck in my throat."

She wasn't swallowing it down too well herself, but she couldn't imagine admitting to the tryst. There were some men who didn't care if their mistresses had other lovers, but she was positive Ian Clayton wasn't one of them. They'd never discussed the terms of their arrangement, but they didn't have to.

While he didn't demand much from her, fidelity was the least of what was owed. He'd been a loyal friend, through many trying ordeals, yet she'd repaid him with perfidy.

She shook her head. "We can't confess."

"We have to, Rebecca."

"We do not! It was a reckless whim. Though I can't figure out why, we're suddenly experiencing a physical attraction."

"That's putting it mildly."

"It was heretofore unrealized by us, but now that we're aware of the danger, we'll simply be more vigilant."

"We'll pretend it never happened? We'll sweep it under the rug?"

"Yes."

"How will we accomplish this feat? I live with the man! Whenever I turn around, I bump into you. Am I to ignore you?"

"Yes," she repeated.

"What if I don't wish to ignore you?"

"What are you? A beast in the field that must copulate at the drop of a hat? You have to learn to control your base impulses."

"I'm a healthy, red-blooded male. It's not that easy."

He shot her such a potent, torrid look that she felt it down to the marrow of her bones. She stifled a shudder, glad for the shadows of the carriage so he couldn't see how he affected her.

"You're also an adult," she persisted. "You may suffer

from passionate urges, but that doesn't mean you have to act on them."

"Is that right?"

"Yes, that's right."

He scoffed with derision. "You really are a cold one, aren't you?"

The charge stung, but she refused to let him know. "I'm called the Black Widow. Did you presume my reputation was unearned?"

"Yes, actually, I did."

"Then you're a fool."

"I guess I am."

"I'm fond of Ian," she said.

"You suppose I'm not?"

"I won't have him hurt by our folly."

"So it's better to lie to him?"

"Yes, it is."

Her harsh words had wounded him, but it couldn't be avoided. He shouldn't have any illusions about her.

They were the same age, but compared to her and what she'd endured, he was a babe in the woods. Just then, he appeared so young and troubled, and she yearned to reach across the space that separated them, but she didn't dare. She was so tempted, but she couldn't risk another inferno. She stared the other direction instead, pulling at the curtain and studying the passing street.

She could feel him watching her, his elevated regard like a silky caress, but she forced down the need to revel in it. She had to maintain the distance between them, and she raised the only topic that mattered.

"Why does Lady Caroline keep showing up on Ian's stoop?"

"I haven't the foggiest."

"How often has she been by?"

"I can't say."

"You must have some idea."

"I'm not Ian's nanny," he snapped. "It's hardly my job to track his guests."

"But she's betrothed to Edward Shelton. Why is she visiting Ian?"

"How would I know, Rebecca? You might as well ask me how many drops of water there are in the Thames."

"He hasn't confided in you about her?"

"No, and even if he had, I wouldn't tell you."

She knew she should let it go, but Lady Caroline's behavior had her rattled. "They've been acquainted a long time, but she hasn't previously prevailed on his friendship. Why now?"

"She must want something from him," he allowed. "Perhaps it has to do with our brother, Lord Wakefield. Wakefield's termination of their engagement wasn't very graciously done. Ian knows Wakefield better than anyone. Perhaps there are issues unresolved, and she's seeking his advice."

If Lady Caroline had come to Ian for *advice*, Rebecca would eat her bonnet!

"Have you met Wakefield?" she inquired.

"No. Have you?"

"Yes."

"What's he like?"

"He's a wealthy, indolent aristocrat. What would you imagine?"

"If I called on him"—he was so ridiculously optimistic—"would he grant me an audience?"

"I doubt it. His wife might, though. He married down, and she has a penchant for commoners."

"Really?"

"Ian and Wakefield used to be so close," she mentioned, intent on gleaning any detail that might explain Lady Caroline's motives. "I've heard that he and Ian quarreled, that their rift is irreparable. Do you know the basis of their fight?"

"No."

"I plan to marry Ian," she bluntly stated, wanting Jack to be very clear as to her ultimate goal. "Were you aware of that fact?"

"He doesn't love you."

"So?"

"Then why would you?"

"How about to have a roof over my head and food on the table?"

"You already have a home—with a fine roof and a fully stocked larder."

"Maybe I want a grander roof," she said. "Maybe I want tastier food."

"Why are you so greedy?"

She bristled. "Until you've walked in my shoes, you have no right to judge."

"I've been poor all my life, but it's never made me prostitute myself simply to receive a few fancier baubles."

"Bully for you."

He assessed her, his gaze contemptuous. "Wouldn't you like to be valued as something more than a pair of tits and an ass?"

"What an absolutely cruel thing to say."

"Why is it *cruel*? Aren't you preparing to sell yourself—again—to the highest bidder? I'm merely speaking the truth."

"No, you're not. Your cock is hard, and I haven't

tended it, so you're angry, and you're trying to provoke an argument."

"Is there some reason I should be pleasant at the moment?"

The conversation had deteriorated to its usual juvenile level, which wasn't surprising. They had no capacity to fraternize like normal human beings. The carriage was stalled in traffic and, his disgust with her obvious, he reached for the door, anxious to jump out and leave her to her own devices.

Absurdly, she was hurt that he'd go, and she could barely stop herself from grabbing onto his coat and begging him to stay.

He stared at her, his blue eyes digging deep, making her fidget with his keen scrutiny. He seemed to be cataloguing her features, as if seeing her for the very last time.

"I have to inform Ian of what we did," he quietly announced. "I can't live with myself."

"You are mad!"

"I'm sure you're correct."

"Have you considered the consequences? He might throw you out of his house. Or disavow your kinship. He might . . . might . . . challenge you to a duel!"

"Whatever he might do, my punishment would be warranted," he said with an inherent dignity that belied his humble origins.

"It was just a hasty tumble in the dark," she insisted, denying its import. "You're making too much of it."

He blew out a heavy breath. "The more I listen to you talk, the more I realize it's not worth keeping a secret for you."

"If you tell him, I'll kill you. I swear it."

"In light of the gossip about you in the community, is that a threat you should hurl?"

"Will you get it through your thick head? I don't know why my husbands keep dying!"

"I thought you said your reputation as the Black Widow was well deserved."

He opened the door and leapt to the street, and the crowd swallowed him up.

She leaned against the squab, praying that he didn't mean it, that he'd keep his big mouth shut. If he tattled, what should she do?

Chapter SEVEN

"Oh, my goodness!" a female voice gushed. "Ian Clayton! Is it really you?"

Ian stared down the dark street to where a woman was leaning out the window of a fancy carriage that was parked in front of a restaurant.

A grinning and very pregnant Emma Fitzgerald—make that Emma Clayton, Lady Wakefield—maneuvered the steps of the vehicle with the help of a footman, and she approached from down the walk. Her figure was limned in the light cast by the carriage lamp. She was big as a house and beautifully attired in an emerald dress that set off the auburn in her hair and the rose in her cheeks.

He wasn't surprised that she'd shunned a conservative wardrobe and had done nothing to conceal her delicate condition. She was experienced in midwifery and considered birthing to be normal and respectable. On seeing her again, he tamped down his delight, embarrassed to have it revealed.

He hadn't spoken with her since he and John had argued, since Ian had left Wakefield Manor and never talked to John again, save to threaten his very life if he failed to do the right thing and marry the Emma he'd ruined. Ian had suspected that he'd eventually run into her, but the encounter had arrived too soon, and he wasn't positive how to act.

Luckily, John wasn't present. Ian had no desire to converse with the disreputable bounder, and he would have hated to place Emma in an awkward situation.

Jack was standing next to him, the two of them on their way to join Rebecca at the theater. They'd quarreled as to whether Jack would attend, too, so they weren't in the best mood to greet Emma.

Something was eating away at Jack, something important and troubling, but Ian wouldn't probe for what it was. Jack would blurt it out when he was ready. There was no use pestering him.

Still, for reasons Ian didn't comprehend, he wished he hadn't brought Jack along. Emma would confide to John that they had another brother, and Ian didn't want John to know.

Jack had a childlike infatuation with John, and he was intrigued by all that John symbolized as far as their noble heritage. Absurd as it sounded, Ian was terrified that John would steal Jack away. John was a dynamic and charismatic individual, and with Jack being Ian's only kin, Ian couldn't bear to share him. Not with John. Not with anyone.

"Hello, Lady Wakefield," he said as she neared, and he bowed.

"*Lady* Wakefield!" She laughed and peered around. "Whenever I hear that title attached to my name, I automatically presume the person is referring to someone else. You knew me when I was Miss Fitzgerald. I think that means you should call me Emma."

"Hello, Emma."

"How have you been?"

She took his hands and squeezed them, and he couldn't resist her friendly charm.

"I'm fine."

"John and I have missed you so much. We chat about you every day."

At the tidings, he suffered the silliest spurt of gladness, but he ignored it. She was the ultimate diplomat, and he was certain she was lying. John would never have mentioned him. Their last fight had been too hideous, the basis of John's dislike too shameful and too appropriate. There could be no reconciliation.

Emma spun toward Jack and asked, "And who is your handsome companion?"

Huddled in the shadows as they were, it was difficult to see Jack clearly. With his blond hair and blue eyes—that were an exact replica of her husband's—his resemblance to John was uncanny.

She clutched a fist over her heart and muttered, "Oh, my Lord."

Ian reached out to steady her. "What is it?"

"Is he . . . is he . . . John's son? I had no idea. Does John know?"

"No, no," Ian hastily soothed, "he's not John's son. You can't tell here in the dark, but he's much too old."

"Oh . . . well . . ." Her pulse slowed, her composure reasserting itself.

"I'm sorry. It never occurred to me that you might make such a shocking assumption. This is Mr. Jack Clayton Romsey."

Jack bowed, too. "Lady Wakefield, I'm so pleased to finally meet you. I apologize for any distress."

Emma frowned at Ian. "A Clayton cousin?"

"A brother," Ian gently said.

"A brother! John will be thrilled." She turned her radiant smile on Jack. "What is your story, Jack? May I call you Jack?"

"I'd be honored, milady."

"Why do we know nothing of you? How did you come to be living with Ian?"

Ian explained, "He showed up on my stoop a few months ago."

"Really? Just like that? What a splendid conclusion for both of you."

"I had a letter," Jack stated, "that my mother gave to me when I was a boy, and I always kept it. It was from my father."

"How very romantic!" Emma beamed.

As if a silent signal had been sent, she glanced over her shoulder. A man had exited the restaurant, and Ian and Jack espied him at the same time.

"There's John now. John!" she summoned her husband. "You won't believe who I've found."

Though he was only twenty or thirty feet away, the true distance between them was as vast as an ocean. John pulled up short and glared at Ian, but didn't speak.

"Who's that?" Jack inquired. "Is it Lord Wakefield?"

"Let's go, Jack," Ian said. He grabbed the younger man by the arm and tried to drag him away.

Jack shook him off. "I want to be introduced."

"Jack! Come on!" Ian insisted more sternly.

"Don't be ridiculous," Emma scolded. "Of course you'll stay and meet him."

"I'm fond of you, Emma," Ian quietly replied, "but don't put yourself in the middle of this. You don't belong there."

"Nonsense! Whatever concerns John, concerns me, too. He's not angry, and the two of you will not continue this idiotic feud. Not if I have anything to say about it."

"It's not about anger, Emma. It was perfidy and betrayal, pure and simple."

She glowered at John, then at Ian, but neither of them had moved an inch, and she marched to John, ready to do what, Ian couldn't guess. Emma was like a force of nature, positive she could bend everyone to her will, but not in this case. His conduct toward John was beyond forgiveness.

It was the most humiliating interval of his life, and he wasn't about to tarry and be given a cut direct that would have had High Society gossiping for ages. Not by John—whom he'd loved so dearly. He wouldn't be able to bear it.

"Come, Jack. Let's go." His brother didn't budge, and Ian repeated, "Jack!"

Ian whipped away and hurried off, taking an opposite route from where Lord and Lady Wakefield were furiously whispering, and he didn't peek over to see if Jack had obeyed his command to depart. If Jack had remained behind, if he'd loitered like a sycophant, hoping for Wakefield's notice and blessing, Ian would be crushed.

He rushed around the corner, and for an instant, he thought John bellowed, *Ian, wait!* but he was certain his fevered mind was trying to switch fantasy into reality. He didn't stop.

Momentarily, Jack caught up to him. With Jack torn between the sibling he didn't know and the one he did, familiarity had won out, and Ian's relief was so great that he was amazed his knees didn't buckle.

He was terribly undone by the encounter, but he

didn't want Jack to perceive his upset, and as Jack sidled nearer, Ian's face was an expressionless mask. Only the shaking of his hands provided any indication of how seriously he'd been affected.

They walked on, proceeding toward the entrance to the theater.

Finally, Jack broke the awkward silence. "Lady Wakefield seems very nice."

"She's wonderful," Ian agreed.

"What did you do to Lord Wakefield that caused your fight?"

"Nothing."

"Liar. Tell me. It can't be that ghastly."

It was on the tip of his tongue to confess. He'd never apprised anyone about that awful night, about the horrid accusations that had flown, or the painful information that had been revealed. He was wretched, keeping it all in, acting as if none of it mattered. As he tried to gamble himself into poverty and drink himself into oblivion, the truth was eating him alive.

"It's water under the bridge," he mumbled, incapable of justifying.

Recognizing that he'd get no answers, Jack sighed. "Will Rebecca be joining us?"

"She said she would. Why?"

"I'd just as soon not sit with her."

"I've purchased a box, so she'll be there. She's too much of an attention-seeker to miss the opportunity to have all of London gawking at her."

"That's what I was afraid of."

"Do me a favor," Ian snapped.

"What?"

"Don't make a scene. I'm not in the mood for any of your antics with her."

"I know how to behave in public," Jack bristled. "Regardless of what you think, I wasn't raised by wolves."

In a snit, he stormed off. They were outside the theater, and he waded into the crowd and vanished, making it a perfectly bad ending to a perfectly bad day.

Ian was still reeling from his earlier spat with Rebecca and Caro. Rebecca would get over it. She was too bent on marriage, and she'd persuade herself to forgive him. As to Caro, she'd never speak to him again, and the prospect was more troubling than it should have been.

At his loss of her esteem, coupled with his stumbling on John and Emma, he was completely disordered, barely able to put one foot in front of the other. As he climbed the steps into the building, he was incredibly self-conscious, feeling more isolated and more alone than he'd ever been.

With his disposition being so foul, the notion of enduring a tepid comedy was abhorrent. He almost turned to leave, but he'd invited Rebecca, so he started up the stairs to his box. He trudged toward it, when the horde split, and he was face-to-face with the Earl of Derby's party.

The Earl, himself, wasn't present. It was the most open secret in the city that he rarely consorted with his wife, so it was the Countess, with her only son, Adam, as her escort. Behind them, appearing miserable and oddly mismatched, were Caro and her fiancé, Edward Shelton.

Shelton was lumbering and obese, his gray hair thin and balding, and he was much older than Ian recollected. In stark contrast, Caro looked like a shiny angel. She was dressed in a silvery gown that shimmered when she moved, the sapphire trim enhancing the blue in her eyes, making them seem larger and more luminous. Her blond hair was swept up in an intricate chignon, a few ringlets dangling on either side to accent her beautiful features.

Her cheeks were flushed, her back ramrod straight, and she was trembling slightly, giving him the distinct impression that she was furious.

Had her mother said something vile? Or had Caroline and Shelton been quarreling? Shelton had his hand on her arm, guiding her through the melee, and Ian suffered the most virulent surge of jealousy.

His head flashed with disturbing images of Caro's wedding night, of fat, perverted Edward pinning her down and ravaging her as she pleaded for mercy.

The vision was so clear, and so disgusting, that Ian could scarcely keep from racing over and yanking Shelton away. He couldn't stand to have Shelton touching her, couldn't stand to know that—very soon— Shelton would have the right to do whatever he wished to her.

Her wedding was a month away, and Ian felt ill just from considering what it would mean. Caro had been betrothed to John for years, and Ian had stoically accepted the circumstance. Despite the demands of both fathers, John had had no intention of ever marrying her, so she'd been safely single. But now, jolted by the hard evidence that she was engaged to someone who was prepared to follow through, he was too distraught for words.

He wanted to burst into the middle of the family gathering, wanted to force them to acknowledge his existence. He never approached them in public, for he refused to give them the chance to snub him. Previously, due to his kinship with John, they'd been coolly courteous, but since John's split from Caro, they were overtly hostile. He avoided them like the plague, but suddenly, he was determined to talk to Caro, to witness some hint of affection that would tell him he still mattered to her.

It was folly, it was insanity, his rage being all out of proportion to the situation, but he couldn't put it aside. He marched over, bold as brass, and insinuated himself in front of Lady Derby, coming so near that she would have had to knock him down in order to skirt around him.

"Good evening, Countess," he said.

"Mr. Clayton," she replied with a regal nod.

As if he were vermin, she stepped by him and into the box, with Adam pausing to hold the curtain for her.

"Adam," Ian said, "how have you been?"

"It's *Lord Silverton* to you," Adam growled as if they hadn't been cordial for the past decade, and he, too, swept in, leaving Ian alone with Caro and Shelton.

"Hello, Caro." He inappropriately used her nickname, daring her to comment.

"Mr. Clayton." She imbued the greeting with the same amount of disdain exhibited by her mother.

"Aren't you going to introduce me to your fiancé?"

"No."

He was accustomed to their rebuffs and pretensions, but still, it hurt him, and he chuckled nastily. "You Fosters are such a bunch of snobs. Don't your necks get tired from sticking your noses so far up in the air?"

At the slur, she bit down on a caustic retort, which had him eager to rattle one loose.

"I say," Shelton interrupted, "we don't have to stand here and be insulted by the likes of you."

Shelton urged Caro along, and Ian had to physically restrain himself, lest he reach over and punch the man.

"Who are you, sir?" Ian persisted. "I had assumed you were her fiancé, but I believe I'm mistaken. Aren't you her grandfather?"

People were eavesdropping, and they tittered and guffawed. Malicious gossip would fly for days, and he was shocked that he'd instigate so much trouble. Obviously, he'd been spending too much time with Rebecca and absorbing her spiteful habits.

"You're an ass, Mr. Clayton," Caro responded. "You always have been."

She waltzed away, Shelton tagging after her, the curtain of the box fluttering shut, but sealing them in as firmly as if it had been made of iron.

He dawdled, like a beggar on the street, and he was so bloody tempted to storm in after them, to throw things, curse at them, and continue the despicable scene, but it occurred to him that his indignation was absurd.

He wasn't concerned over what Caro elected to do. He never had been. If she chose to bow to her father's dictate and wed an aged reprobate, what was it to Ian?

Feigning nonchalance, he tugged on his coat and shrugged to the onlookers.

"I can't wait to see the children they produce."

He shuddered dramatically, igniting another round of titters. Then, as if he hadn't a care in the world, he walked on to his own box and climbed in.

Neither Rebecca nor Jack had arrived, and his initial impulse was to head home so he could fume in private.

The brief exchange had pushed him to a dangerous precipice where he wasn't anxious to linger. All his life, he'd grappled with the class distinctions forced on him by his bastardry. He'd coveted and begrudged, but had valiantly fought against his envy and resentment. He'd told himself that he'd moved beyond it, that it no longer had the power to wound as it had when he was younger. But he'd been fooling himself.

The old feelings of impotence and inequity surged to the fore, and he yearned to smash through every wall that had ever been constructed to keep him from joining the exalted ranks of the aristocracy. He was suffocating on an injustice he didn't deserve and couldn't battle.

He wanted to rail and shout, but he'd never let the horrid members of the *ton* realize how grave his distress. They were watching him, giggling and pointing when they thought he couldn't see.

Off to his right, Caro's party was ensconced in their seats, sitting like glum statues, refusing to fuel the fire of rumor Ian had sparked.

He tarried through the first act, then the second, all eyes upon him to learn what he might do. The third act began, and he slipped out and raced down the stairs and into the cold, wet night.

His mind in turmoil, his emotions careening with fury and desolation, he glanced in both directions, wondering where to go next.

Chapter EIGHT

"**W**ho's there?"

Caroline peered into the dark shadows of her bedchamber. Her maid had left a candle burning, and the flame sputtered. A storm was brewing, an odd burst of winter thunder reverberating through the house. The door to her balcony cracked open, the curtains fluttering, her nightgown billowing out.

"Who's there?" she asked again, and like a ghostly apparition, a man stepped across the threshold.

He was attired all in black, rain dripping from his hair and shoulders, and she bit down a squeal of fright.

"Lock the door," he commanded, as he came into view.

"Ian," she murmured, astonished.

For him to have scaled the bastion that was her father's mansion, to have risked danger and ruin merely to be alone with her, was too marvelous and too terrifying to be true. Was he insane?

"Get out of here!" she hissed.

"No."

"You're not welcome."

"I don't care."

"I won't speak with you—not after how you behaved at the theater."

"Lock the door!" he repeated.

Approaching until they were toe-to-toe, he reached over and spun the key, sealing them in. Then he pushed her against the wall and fell on her like a starved beast. There was none of the courtesy or finesse he'd exhibited during their previous trysts. He was livid, teeming with rage and passion, so agitated that she was alarmed by his intensity.

He seized her mouth in a torrid kiss, his hands on her breasts, his thigh wedged between her legs. His lips were icy, his fingers, too, as if he'd tarried in the dastardly weather for hours, waiting for the moment she'd enter her room.

He lifted her, her bare thighs wrapped around his waist, so that she was splayed wide, their intimate parts connected, igniting a fire low in her belly. She'd planned to ignore him and send him away, but she was surprised to find that his rough handling was exactly what she needed. She scratched and clawed at him, fighting to get nearer.

She was blazing with an ache she wanted him to assuage, but footsteps echoed in the hall as her brother climbed the stairs and headed for his own room.

Ian yanked away and glared at her, seeming to accuse her for Adam's passing by, and he clamped his palm over her mouth so that she couldn't call out.

As if she would! The last thing she would ever do was summon assistance, for she could never justify his furtive arrival.

Her brother walked on, without breaking stride,

without having a clue that his sister was being ravished a few feet away. As he retreated, Ian carried her to the bed. He dropped her onto the mattress and crawled on top of her, and he kissed her again, being fierce and unrelenting, demanding that she return his ardor with an equal fervor.

"Don't ever pretend that you don't know me," he growled.

"I hate you!" she seethed.

"I don't care if you hate me," he declared. "Just don't snub me—before your mother and her snooty friends. I can't bear it when you do."

It was the must stunning confession she'd ever heard. He always contended that he held her society in contempt, that her position meant nothing to him.

Obviously, he'd been wounded by her disregard, and she yearned to shake him. How was she supposed to have responded to his galling public advance?

He was the one who'd thrust himself at her mother, when he was aware of how she would react. He'd been an insulting boor, which, in her opinion, was his condition most of the time. Had he expected Caroline to leap to his rescue? If so, he was completely deranged!

"What do you want from me?" she asked, though in a whisper.

"I don't know."

"Why are you here?"

"I can't begin to explain."

"You must have some idea."

"I had to see you." He appeared bewildered, as if his actions were incomprehensible to him.

"Give me one reason I should let you stay. Give me one reason I shouldn't scream bloody murder and bring the servants running."

"I want you," he said. "I've always wanted you."

"Have you?"

"You know I have."

She scoffed. "I know nothing of the sort. You've never been anything but snide and critical."

"That's because I'm mad about you and you drive me berserk with your ridiculous conduct."

"If you're mad about me—as you claim—you have a funny way of showing it."

He slid off her and onto his back, an arm flung over his eyes as he wrestled with private demons. She watched him struggle, and she was overcome by the strongest urge to soothe and comfort. It was a lover's inclination, a wife's inclination. She felt so at ease with him, as if they'd lain like this, sharing secrets in the dark, a thousand occasions prior.

"What is it, Ian?" She caressed his chest, his heartbeat discernible under her hand, and it was the most superb sensation in the world.

After a lengthy pause, he admitted, "I bumped into John."

"What did he say to put you in such a state?"

"We didn't speak."

"Really?"

"No."

There'd been gossip of a terrible quarrel, that John had ordered Ian out of his home and his life. While the rift was occurring, Caroline had had her own problem—that being her failed engagement of twenty-four years—so she'd been too wretched to worry about the stories. But now, she couldn't help but wonder what had caused their discord. Ian had always thought that John treated her abominably, and an awful suspicion dawned: Had she been the catalyst?

"Would you like to tell me about it?" she inquired.

He chuckled, but sadly. "No."

"It wasn't on account of me, was it? I'd be very upset if the two of you were fighting about me."

"It wasn't because of you."

"Then . . . why?"

He gazed at the ceiling, and she had just started to think he'd confide in her, when he rolled onto his side and drew her into his arms.

"You can't marry Edward Shelton. He's depraved in a manner you don't understand."

"He's my father's friend."

"I realize that, but their relationship doesn't preclude his having strange tendencies."

"As far as I'm concerned, all men are peculiar."

"It's more loathsome than that. He's perverted in his tastes, extreme in his pleasures."

"Then he'll hire whores to tend his base needs."

"You can't marry him, Caro. I won't let you."

"It's none of your business, Ian."

"It is! I don't want you hurt—as he will definitely hurt you."

She was humored by his apprehension. Did he suppose she had a dozen other choices, that she was a magician who could pull a different future out of a hat?

"And what would become of me if I didn't wed Mr. Shelton?"

"Demand that your father find you someone else."

It was her turn to chuckle miserably. "Haven't you heard what people are saying about me? Rumor has it that John seduced me, that I'm a soiled dove."

"We both know that's a lie."

"So? The facts don't matter. No other man will have

me. My father scrounged to the bottom of the barrel and stumbled on Mr. Shelton. There is no one else."

"Then . . . then . . . continue on as you have been, living with your parents."

"Till when? Should I stay till I'm thirty? Fifty? A hundred?"

"You're being flip, while I'm being serious."

"My father doesn't want me in his house any longer."

"Nonsense."

"It's true," she divulged. "I eavesdropped when he was arguing with Mother. He's tired of supporting me."

"You can't marry Shelton." He was beginning to sound like a broken clock that kept chiming the same hour.

"And you shouldn't persist in your liaison with Mrs. Blake. Will you stop?"

"No, I won't. Don't be absurd."

"I'm mentioning it because I'm jealous of her."

"You are not."

"I am, and I'm not too proud to tell you. But how about you? What is the real basis for your objection to Mr. Shelton?"

"I've told you: He's exceedingly dissolute."

"And that's it?"

He couldn't look her in the eye but stared somewhere over her shoulder. "Yes, that's it."

"Are you sure you have no *personal* motive? Because if you did, this might be the moment to inform me."

"And what would you do? Would you cry off on your betrothal? Would you leave Shelton waiting at the church and run away with me?"

"I might surprise you. Don't forget: I came to you, begging to be ruined."

"And *I* told you that I wouldn't do it."

"So change your mind. Alter my fate."

At the bold declaration, her pulse raced. Her life had been so steeped in ritual and ceremony that she'd never envisioned another ending.

What if she declined to do as her father bid her? What if she cast caution to the wind? Would the Earth cease spinning? Would the sun not rise in the morning sky?

"You don't really want it to happen, Caro," he gently said.

"I might," she insisted, "if you gave me a good enough reason."

"You'd never follow through," he replied. "I know you too well. You'd never shame your family."

He was correct, but she didn't want him to be. She liked to imagine herself as spontaneous and brave, able to defy her father and march away from her marriage without a backward glance, but she wouldn't. She'd been trained from birth to value and preserve the traditions of status and class, of wealth and privilege. To expect her to believe that a different path was possible, he might as well ask her to believe that the ocean was red or the grass blue.

She smiled and admitted, "You're right in saying that I would never go off with you, but I'm not married yet."

"No, you're not."

"I have this month stretching ahead of me. I don't want to wed Mr. Shelton without learning what it was like to be with you."

She was amazed by her proposal, but suddenly, it seemed like the only feasible solution, as if she'd been planning to do this from the very first.

"Will you give me this piece of yourself?" she inquired. "Will you grant me this gift that I shall treasure all my days?"

❧

I an frowned, struggling with what his answer should be.

He'd always deemed her the most beautiful woman he'd ever met, and with her on her bed, her hair down and attired in her nightclothes, he was even more astounded by her perfection. The dim glow of the candle accentuated her creamy skin, her flawless features, making him ache, making him yearn to give her what she wanted. But should he?

A month was such a short interval, and when the sole purpose of the affair was a fleeting dalliance, was it worth the bother?

They'd have to tiptoe about, would have to plot and scheme so that they weren't caught. Their trysts would be furtive and brief, their occasions for consorting minimal and dangerous.

The slightest whiff of association would bring disaster. Her parents would never let him wed her as a reparation. She'd be shipped off in disgrace, to a rural estate or convent, and he'd never see her again.

Rebecca would be enraged, spurred to commit murder, which—considering her history—was no small concern. Jack would be disappointed by what he'd view as despicable conduct, and his attitude toward Ian as an idolized older brother would fade.

Yet, if Ian forged on, he would have thirty magnificent days with Caro. Each morning—for an entire month!—he'd jump out of bed, excited that she might be able to sneak away, that they might be together for a few minutes or hours.

Silly as it sounded, being with her made him happy, and when he'd always been so alone and unwanted, when contentment was so elusive, the chance for a temporary reprieve was enticing.

Could he agree? How could he not?

"Thirty days," he murmured.

"Yes."

"I can make you no promises."

"Nor can I make any to you."

"We'll have to be very careful."

"That's putting it mildly."

"And I shall have to practice restraint—in my manly drives."

"Don't you dare!"

"You must go to your marital bed a virgin."

She sighed. "I suppose I must."

"I'll ensure that you do."

"Before we're through, will you at least advise me as to what the loss of my virginity entails? I'd like to have some idea as to how it occurs so that I'll know when it happens."

"You'll definitely know."

"How?"

"It's a very physical endeavor."

"What is involved?"

His cheeks flamed bright red. He had no notion of how to explain the ordeal. He had sex with women who were aware of what was required, and he couldn't imagine describing the details. She probably wouldn't believe him anyway. It would seem too odd.

"I'll show you as much as I can. We can come very close without actually progressing to the end."

"Marvelous."

"Yes, it will be. No regrets, Caro."

"Nary a one, Ian."

He began kissing her again, and he was nervous as a lad with his first girl. Now that they'd decided to philander, he was so worried about pleasing her.

The rage he'd suffered at the theater had waned, and it had been replaced by a determination to make her happy. When their affair was concluded, and they went their separate ways, he wanted her to be glad for what they'd done.

He deepened the kiss, his tongue in her mouth, his hands on her breasts. He molded and shaped them, plucking at the erect nipples, but he couldn't stand that she was hidden from him. He fussed with the tiny buttons on her nightgown, but they were so difficult to open, and he quickly lost patience.

"I have to have you naked," he told her.

"Naked! Well . . ."

He was demanding too much, too soon, but he felt as if he'd been waiting all his life to be with her. He clasped the neckline and rent the garment down the middle.

"Ian! You can't be tearing off my clothes!"

"Why not?"

"My maid will suspect what I've been doing."

"Burn it in the fire when we're finished."

At that moment, he was so aroused that he didn't care about such petty matters as clothes or a servant's opinion.

He yanked at the ruined fabric, pushing it to the side so that her front was exposed. He studied her nude torso, his hot attention drifting across her chest, her mons, her thighs. His loins lurched with potent delight, keen to be nearer, to explore in ways he oughtn't.

"You're so pretty, Caro."

"Do you think so?" She flushed a charming shade of pink.

"Oh, yes. So pretty—and all mine."

He fondled her breasts, and at his touching her, bare skin to bare skin, she hissed and arched up, trying to escape, but to offer more of herself, too.

"This is how I want you," he stated. "I want you naked and aching for me."

"Oh, that feels so good."

"And it's about to feel even better."

He abandoned her mouth and blazed a trail to her bosom, his hungry lips eager to nurse at her nipple. He suckled, being hard and rough, keeping on till the tip was raw and inflamed; then he moved to the other and proceeded to do the same.

"Let me show you something," he said.

"What?"

"You'll see."

"Tell me!"

"No."

"Beast!"

"Always."

He continued down, nibbling her tummy, her abdomen. As he arrived at her womanly hair and prepared to delve inside, she raised off the pillow and glared at him.

"What are you doing?" she asked.

"I'm going to kiss you here."

"You are not."

"I am."

"Ian!"

"Be silent. You wouldn't want anyone to catch us like this, would you?"

"No."

"Then be quiet."

She flopped down, as he wedged himself between her thighs, planted so firmly that she couldn't shove him away. He parted her nether lips, his tongue lapping at her most secret spot, and her protests ceased.

He held her down, inflicting bliss, until she was moaning and forgetting where they were and what they were about.

"Hush!" he scolded. "Someone will hear."

"I can't help myself."

"You have to."

"Just finish it! I can't bear this torment."

"All in good time, my little beauty. All in good time."

"If you don't hurry, I shall have to kill you."

He laughed and took pity on her, dabbing at her sexual nub, once, again, and she came in a rush, a scream of pleasure billowing out. He grabbed the pillow and pressed it over her face to stifle the noise, but still, it was noticeable.

As she spiraled up, he froze, his ear toward the door. If anyone had been walking by, they'd have noted the commotion, but no one was there, and he breathed a sigh of relief.

He hated that this was how it would go. They would flirt and seduce, would trifle and tease, but they would be courting danger at every turn. When the passion they generated was so remarkable, the perils didn't seem fair.

She climbed to the peak and was floating down as he nuzzled up her body. He kissed her, and as she grinned and kissed him back, he decided that she was worth every risk.

She pulled him close and whispered, "You are so wicked."

"I try my best."

"I want to do it again."

"I'll bet you do."

"I want to do it all night."

"You can, milady."

"I love it when a man lets me have my way."

He gazed down at her, and the strangest sensation swept over him. He felt as if his heart didn't fit under his ribs, as if he was smiling—but on the inside. It had to be joy. There was no other sentiment that matched the queer, quivery feeling racing from his center to his extremities.

He rolled onto his back, with her draped across him.

"Let me show you something else," he said.

"I can hardly wait."

He reached for his shirt and started in on the buttons.

Chapter NINE

"I sn't that Father?"

"No, it isn't."

Britannia ignored Caroline and stared straight ahead, refusing to glance down the street, for she was aware of what she'd see.

"I'm sure it's him," Caroline persisted. "There. In front of that tea shop."

"You're wrong."

As far as Britannia knew, neither of her two children had a clue that the Earl was a lying, cheating scoundrel. It was a shame she'd sought to hide at all costs. She turned in the opposite direction, forsaking her trip to the milliner's. Caroline had no choice but to spin and follow.

"The weather is so dreary," Caroline complained. "I could use a hot refreshment. Shall we join him? I bet he'd be surprised."

I bet he would be, too, Britannia sourly mused. "We aren't chasing strange men into culinary establishments.

Honestly, Caroline, what's come over you? Would you hurry along?"

Caroline was keeping up, but barely. "I thought you wanted to buy a new hat."

"I have a headache, so we're going home."

"Who's he with?" Caroline was gaping over her shoulder, trying to unravel a mystery that wasn't a mystery, at all. "Why . . . it's a girl. I don't know her, though. Isn't she a pretty little thing?"

"Well, that certainly proves it's not your father. He wouldn't be off gallivanting in the middle of the afternoon. He has meetings with his land agent all day."

They arrived at her carriage, the footmen loafing and unprepared for her sudden reappearance. They jumped to attention and lifted her in. She pressed her bulky form against the squab, soothed by the dark confines, the soft feel and smell of leather.

Caroline was outside and still staring behind her, and Britannia snapped, "Caroline! Don't stand there gawking like a scullery maid. You're making a spectacle of yourself. Get in."

"In a minute, Mother."

"If you are not in this carriage in five seconds, we shall drive off without you."

"I'm coming; I'm coming."

Caroline's irritation was clear, so the footmen would have noted her pique, which would have them gossiping over Britannia's having raised a disrespectful daughter. Britannia was so angry that she yearned to lumber out and beat Caroline to a bloody pulp. Only the prospect that others might see kept her planted in her seat.

Something was bothering Caroline, and Britannia

was sick of her moods and sass. One moment, she'd be smiling and happy, another miserable and morose. Had she heard the rumors about Edward? Was she reconsidering?

Caroline climbed in and settled herself, but she continued to peek out the curtain.

"Mother?"

"Yes?"

"Does Father have a . . . a . . . mistress?"

"Don't be ridiculous."

"But what am I to think?"

"It wasn't the Earl!"

"Who was that girl with him?"

"Be silent!"

"But—"

"I don't have to sit here and listen to your rude insinuations." She started to tremble, her wrath bubbling up like soup in a pot. "If you mention the topic again, I shall slap your mouth."

The threat was sufficient. Caroline's curiosity was retracted and refocused inside the coach.

After a painful interval, she insolently inquired, "Do you ever regret marrying Father?"

"What a ludicrous question. Of course I don't."

"Are you satisfied with your life?"

"I'm perfectly content." Her face was so brittle, she was amazed it didn't crack.

Out of the blue, Caroline said, "I don't want to marry Mr. Shelton."

"So? No woman ever wants the man who is selected for her. You'll grow to tolerate him."

"I can't go through with it. Would you speak to Father?"

"No."

"Please?"

"No."

"I can't do it."

"Your wishes have no bearing on the situation."

"Why can't I have an opinion? I'm the one who will have to live with him. Not you. I've heard terrible stories."

"They're not true."

"How can you say that when I haven't told you what they are?"

"It doesn't matter what they are."

Caroline studied her as if seeing her for the very first time, and in the worst display of sentiment, tears welled into her eyes.

"You don't care about me, do you?" Caroline accused.

"Don't be absurd. I'm your mother."

"You don't like me; you never have."

Britannia glared, her patience exhausted. If Caroline was determined to drag them into a mire, then Britannia would oblige her. As calmly as if they were discussing the weather, she replied, "No, I don't. Not really."

"Why not? Am I so unlovable?"

"You were a difficult child, Caroline."

"How? How was I *difficult*? I did everything you ever asked. For years, at your insistence, I pursued my fruitless betrothal to Wakefield, and now, I've accepted this odious arrangement with Mr. Shelton, and I never once objected."

"Do you assume that makes you a saint?"

"Yes, that's precisely how I feel: Saint Caroline. I'm about to be sacrificed at the altar of your peculiar whim. You seem so bent on my marrying Mr. Shelton. Why are you?"

"Your father has decided on it."

"You and Father were arguing one day. He said he's weary of supporting me. Was he serious?"

"What do you suppose?"

"Was he?" Caroline pressed.

"Yes."

"If I backed out of my betrothal, would you let me continue residing with you?"

"No. I'd cast you out. You'd be disgraced, shunned by the entire world."

"I don't want to end up like you," she rudely pronounced. "I'll speak with Father, myself, about canceling the engagement."

"Yes, by all means," Britannia sneered. "Talk to him. Boast of how recalcitrant and ungrateful you've become. I'm sure he'll be delighted to have you tell him all about it."

"He's fond of me."

"Is he?"

"He'll listen."

"No, he won't. He's a selfish man—the most selfish I've ever known. You're naught but a bother to him, and if you presume differently, then you're a fool."

Declining to quarrel further, Britannia shut her eyes, pretending to doze, though her reflections were in turmoil.

Caroline *had* to marry Edward. There was no other choice.

All those years ago, when Edward had seduced Britannia, she'd believed his lies and had yielded to him, but he'd acted with malicious intent. At the liaison's conclusion, he'd waltzed away without a second thought, and Britannia had been left to suffer the consequences of his feigned regard—for twenty-five years!—while he'd suffered no consequences for his wicked deed, at all.

Well, revenge was a hearty meal, and Britannia had waited forever to dine on her feast of vengeance. With her scheme so close to fruition, she wouldn't be denied the chance to use Caroline to extract punishment. She had to see the expression on Edward's face when she informed him of what he'd actually done by marrying the girl who'd always been there—right under his nose.

Caroline would be his bride—whether she wished it or not—and if she was getting cold feet, it was time to move things forward. The wedding date wasn't set in stone, and perhaps it would be wise to hold it even sooner.

She nodded with satisfaction. Caroline would be wed before she knew it, and in the interim, Britannia would watch her like a hawk. The child was spewing strange ideas, and Britannia had to discover why.

Nothing and no one could be allowed to interfere with Britannia's plan.

※

G ood-bye, darling."
   "Good-bye."
   "You'll talk to her, won't you?"
"The moment I arrive home."

Bernard smiled at Georgette, his latest in a long line of infatuations. He'd been in love so often, with so many pretty girls, but for some reason, she'd captured his fancy in a way none of the others had.

He didn't understand why he was so obsessed with her. He'd bribed her with gifts and courted her like an attentive swain, but she wouldn't succumb to his advances, and the more she resisted, the more he desired her. She was like a grand prize, being dangled just out of reach.

She was petite and slender, a waiflike creature, with beautiful brown hair and big brown eyes. She made him feel manly and strong, capable and indispensable to her happiness. When she gazed up at him, as she was now, looking innocent and adorable, so in need of his help and protection, it was difficult to refuse her anything.

"If you don't get the divorce arranged," she mentioned, "I'm not certain my mother will let you keep visiting."

"Why not?" The old bat was constantly hovering, so there could be no impropriety.

"She claims gossip is spreading."

The notion infuriated him. Why couldn't people mind their own business? His peccadilloes were his own private affair.

"What is being said?"

"Well, that you aren't sincere in your affection."

"Of course I'm sincere. How can you doubt me?"

"I don't! But Mother is afraid that you'll tire of me, and after you go, my reputation will be ruined. I won't be able to show myself in Polite Society ever again."

"I'll take steps to begin the legal proceedings at once."

Her grin lit up the room. "Do you promise?"

"Yes, I promise."

She threw her arms around his neck and gave him the sweetest peck on the lips. At having her slim, tiny body crushed to his, he pulled her nearer and deepened the kiss, his hands roving over her, his lust instantly out of control.

She submitted until he grazed her breast; then, breathless and overcome, she yanked away.

"Please, Lord Derby," she protested, "you know I can't."

"I know. Forgive me."

"It's torture, having to wait and wait for you to be free. I can't bear it."

"I can't, either. I'll speak to the Countess again."

"Will you?"

"Yes."

"You're too kind to me."

"And I'll be even kinder in the future." He gave her a parting, fatherly kiss on the forehead. "Now I must be off."

"Will you be by tomorrow?"

"Most definitely."

She escorted him to the door, waving merrily from the stoop till he was out of sight. The second he could no longer see her, he started missing her.

He couldn't go on as he was. Georgie was so vivacious and fun, and she made him feel twenty years old, like a young buck on the prowl. His world was all boring duty, all tedium and monotony, but when he was with her, he forgot his responsibilities.

He couldn't abide the thought of returning home, of sitting through another stuffy supper with Britannia. She'd be nagging. Caroline would be glaring at him, bitter over her pending nuptials. Adam—who'd discovered Bernard's passion for Georgie—would be piously reproachful of Bernard's late arrival.

He wanted to be separate and on his own. He would

give the management of the estates over to his attorneys. Then he'd send Adam abroad so he didn't have to observe his surly face. He'd hurry Caroline's wedding to Edward, and he'd divorce Britannia.

There would be no one to interfere, no one to chastise or condemn. He and Georgie would be together at last!

***

"Is he gone?"

"Yes, thank the Lord."

Shaking with relief, Miss Georgette Lane walked to the sideboard and downed three quick brandies, indulging her tendency to over-imbibe; then she went to the foot of the stairs as her mother, Maude, plodded down.

"I didn't think he'd ever leave," Maude muttered.

"Neither did I."

"Did he bestow any trinkets?"

"Not today."

"But you were with him all afternoon!"

"I know."

"Cheap bastard."

"No, he's not."

Georgie defended him by holding up her hand to display two of the rings she'd received prior, but her mother wasn't impressed. Whatever Lord Derby opted to give, greedy Maude whined that it should have been more.

It had been Maude's idea to split off from their traveling troupe, to try to make a new start—through swindle and vice—in London. How could they have guessed that Lord Derby would present himself as such an easy mark? And so fast, too!

Georgie was weary of the entire wicked charade.

"I suppose he felt at liberty to fondle and poke, though," Maude complained.

"Doesn't he always?"

"You didn't let him do anything relevant, did you?"

"No. He touched my breast; then I acted all panicky and made him stop."

"You're the most convincing virgin."

"That's what *he* presumes I am."

"Keep it that way."

"I'm trying my best."

Georgie hated her part in their scheme, but was willing to persist all the same. Ages ago, she could have yielded and become his mistress, but Maude had done a thorough investigation of the perverted codger. He was a fickle fellow, whose attention was prone to wandering. The trick was to keep him coming back, to keep the gifts and promises flowing. If she could snag Derby, the rewards would be indescribable.

"I don't understand men and their penchant for girls," Maude was saying. "You're so skinny, and your chest is so flat. He should just find himself a boy."

"I don't believe he's partial to boys," Georgie replied.

"What the hell is he looking for then?"

"You said it yourself: He wants to be young again. He assumes that having a youthful bride will change everything."

"Stupid fool."

Maude proceeded on into the parlor and poured herself a brandy, while Georgie stared out the window in the direction the Earl had gone.

Would he really shame his wife with a divorce? Would he break up his family, stun his friends, horrify his children? Would he do something so terrible—just for her?

It was the most preposterous notion imaginable, and the man was an idiot to even consider it.

"There ought to be a law," she mumbled; then she went to join her mother for another stiff drink.

Edward Shelton climbed out of his carriage, his hat pulled low to shield his identity, and he scurried through the gate and was swallowed up behind a hedge. Since it was a dark night, and a disreputable section of town, the chances of his stumbling on an acquaintance were slim to none. Yet, a person couldn't be too careful. His peers would ignore many bad habits, but not all of them.

He rapped on the door, using the secret knock the madam had devised, and immediately he was ushered to a private salon.

With his wedding to Caroline only a few weeks away, his lust was at a fevered pitch. There were so many things he wanted to do to her, so many things he wanted to teach her, and his fantasies were driving him wild with anticipation.

He was still furious that she'd evaded him when she was small. With her big blue eyes and silky blond hair, she'd been like a perfect, porcelain doll. Throughout her childhood, he'd tried to steal a brief grope or kiss without her parents knowing, but he'd never been able to lure her away.

Though it was aberrant and foul, the undeveloped female body excited him. His whole life he'd grappled with the scurrilous urges, but they were too powerful to fight, and he'd ceased his struggles to control them.

Caroline was much more mature than he liked, but she would—if he was lucky—birth many, many daughters who resembled her, and he'd have them in his home and available to enchant him for decades to come.

Everything had the most wonderful way of working out for the best!

The madam appeared. She was a malodorous, buxom woman, whom he couldn't abide, but she knew her business. Nothing surprised or shocked her, not even his most depraved requests.

"What'll it be, sir?" she queried.

"I'd like a tiny girl, with rosy cheeks and rosy lips—like a little doll. I want the youngest you have in the house, but she shouldn't be too experienced. I want to scare her a bit."

"I think I have someone you'll enjoy very much," the woman said without hesitating.

Edward handed over a purse full of money, and the woman hurried off to fetch the child of his dreams.

※

I have to tell you something."

"What is it?" Ian snapped at Jack.

"It's a confession."

"I'm not in the mood."

Ian was reeling from the prior night's encounters. Too much had transpired in too short a time. He'd finally bumped into John, but he'd been too much of a coward to walk over and offer the apology that was owed, or beg for the forgiveness that was craved.

He'd met Caro's family at the theater and had allowed her mother to hurl public insults. The altercation had tossed him into an abyss of despair, and for hours he'd hovered outside Derby's mansion, in the rain and the wind. He'd wrongly entered Caro's bedchamber and dallied with her till dawn, sneaking out after the cock had crowed.

He felt drained and confused. He hadn't slept a wink, was grumpy and exhausted, and the last thing he wanted to do was have a philosophical chat with Jack.

"Can't it wait?" he asked.

"No. I should have spoken up days ago."

"Very well. Sit down."

"I'd rather stand."

"Sit!" Ian gestured to the chair opposite. "I'm not about to strain my neck glaring up at you while you blather on and on."

"All right, if you feel I must."

"You must."

Jack plopped down, and he stared at the floor, unable to begin.

He seemed very young, very unsure. He carried himself so well, was so reliable and courteous, that Ian frequently forgot his true age. Just then, he looked so much like John, so much like the captivating, insolent rascal who'd gotten himself into so many jams and who'd always come to Ian for advice and assistance.

Ian couldn't remain angry, and his ire faded.

"What is it?" Ian repeated more gently.

Jack hemmed and hawed, then admitted, "I had sex with Rebecca."

"You what?"

"I . . . I . . . had sex with Rebecca."

"You did?"

"Yes. I didn't mean to. It just . . . just happened."

"How does sex just *happen?*"

"It was sort of an . . . an . . . accident."

Ian wanted to laugh, but didn't. He wasn't positive what he'd been expecting, but it wasn't anything close to this. He was very still, studying the boy, trying to figure out how he should react.

He wasn't upset—when he probably should have been. He wasn't hurt—when he probably should have been. He didn't feel betrayed or let down, so what should be his response?

He and Rebecca had a different relationship that was incomprehensible to others. They were both on a reckless course, circumstances causing them to behave badly, so they were a good match. They understood each other. Neither condemned the other for lapses in judgment, just as neither hoped for improved conduct. They were friends; they were cordial; they were excellent together in bed.

"Jack," he started, "Rebecca is my mistress."

"I know; I know."

"She and I have an arrangement."

"I know that, too."

"Yet you proceeded anyway."

"Yes." He peeked up. "I realize that this is where I'm supposed to apologize, but I'm not sorry."

"You're not?"

"Well, I'm sorry that I deceived you, but I'm not sorry for what I did with her. I liked it very much, and I won't lie to you."

"I see."

"It was actually quite spectacular," he muttered.

"I don't need any details, Jack. I've fornicated with Rebecca on many occasions. I'm aware of her numerous charms."

Ian sighed. For the life of him, he couldn't decide what was best. He couldn't have his brother copulating with his mistress, yet he didn't want to be shed of either of them. It was difficult to acquire a suitable paramour, and he wasn't in the mood to search for a new one. Obviously, a brother was irreplaceable.

After a lengthy silence, where Ian mulled and stewed, Jack urged, "Say something."

"I'm curious as to what I should do, and I'd love to hear your opinion."

"I guess you'd be entitled to kill me."

"That seems a little dramatic."

"Or . . . or . . . you could throw me out. I packed a bag—just in case."

"Is the situation likely to reoccur?"

"I'm not certain. The first time was more of a collision, if you will, but if the same kind of opportunity crept up on me . . ." He blushed and cleared his throat.

"Have you discussed this with Rebecca?"

"Oh, yes."

"What was her suggestion?"

"She said that if I confessed, she'd murder me."

He sighed again. "She oughtn't go about making such spurious threats. People misconstrue her intent."

"I told her the exact same thing." Jack frowned, then inquired, "Do you imagine she was serious? Should I watch my back?"

Ian scoffed. "She didn't murder her husbands. At least, I don't believe she did. I've often wondered about the second one, but the other two were very elderly. They dropped dead of their own accord."

"So I'm safe?".

"She won't kill you, but she'll definitely get even."

"I was afraid you'd say that." He rose and shuffled his feet. "So . . . should I fetch my bag?"

Ian didn't have to ponder the question, for he'd known the answer before Jack asked it. He couldn't carry on without Jack. Their lives had rapidly grown inseparable, intertwined like two strands of a rope. Ian didn't want him to ever leave.

"No, I don't want you to go."

"Are you sure?"

"Absolutely."

"Thank you."

"You can't have sex with Rebecca again, though."

"I know."

"Maybe you two should avoid each other?"

"I'll see to it."

"I'd appreciate it if you would. And if you find yourself contemplating another *accident* with her, I'd be obliged if you could tell me right away."

"I will," Jack promised, and he scurried off.

Chapter TEN

"Father, may I speak with you?"

"No."

Caroline stared at her father, imploring him as he proceeded toward the door.

"It's important."

"I'm on my way out, Caroline."

"Please?"

"Oh, all right." As if she were the greatest burden in the world, he blew out a heavy breath and stomped into the nearest parlor. "I can spare you five minutes, so whatever it is, be quick about it."

She longed to shake him. How could the entire course of her life hang in the balance of five measly minutes?

"It's about my engagement," she started.

"What about it?"

"I don't wish to marry Mr. Shelton."

"So?"

"I need you to call it off."

"Call it off?" He was aghast. "On what grounds?"

"You may use any basis you like. I just want it over."

"Are you insane?"

"No. I simply can't be his wife. You never asked my opinion; you just forged ahead. I'm twenty-five years old, and I ought to have been consulted."

"Where did you come by such a ludicrous notion?"

"It's not ludicrous," she insisted. "Many fathers confer with their daughters on such a weighty issue."

"Not *this* father. This isn't some fantasy in a story-book where females are allowed to act however they please. This is England. I am the Earl of Derby, a peer of the realm, a friend of the King. You'll do as you're bid, and you'll do it gladly."

Desperate to be away, he peeked at the clock, and she tamped down her frustration. Why couldn't she be clear? Why couldn't she make him understand?

"You can blame it all on me, and I won't say a word."

"How very big of you!"

"Mr. Shelton can explain the split any way he likes."

"Oh, he can, can he?"

"Yes."

He rolled his eyes and spun away. "I don't have time for your nonsense."

"When will you have *time*?"

"I never will," he said. "You're marrying Edward and that's final. I suggest you prepare yourself."

Then he was gone, and she dropped onto the couch, listening as he stormed out. An image flashed in her mind—of the pretty brown-haired girl she'd seen with him outside the tea shop.

Had he raced off to be with a mistress who was young enough to be his granddaughter? The prospect—of his being too busy to help her merely because he'd rather be off philandering—was so galling that she was enraged.

Her request to end the arranged marriage was the first occasion she'd ever stood up for herself, and he couldn't be bothered to heed her complaint, let alone aid her in facilitating a resolution. Perhaps with all the meekness she'd displayed over the years, it was beyond him to take her seriously.

She glanced around the ornately furnished room, and suddenly she felt as if she was suffocating on the accouterments of her boring, privileged life. Her family had money, status, and power, but when they were all so miserable, what good was any of it?

She had to escape, if only for a few hours, and she knew precisely where she'd go. She had to be with Ian. When she was with him, her problems faded away, vanishing in the haze of the passion and desire he generated.

She hastened to grab a cloak and sneak away, but as she hurried to the foyer, the door so close to being reached, she bumped into her mother.

"Have you seen the Earl?" Britannia inquired.

"He left already."

"Left! But he just arrived. I didn't have a chance to speak to him. Where was he going?"

"I assume he was off to visit his paramour."

"I have no idea who you mean," Britannia huffed. "Did he mention when he'd return?"

"I wouldn't expect him back anytime soon."

Caroline was stunned by the contemptible remarks flowing from her lips. It was as if she'd opened her mouth and another woman's comments were being voiced.

She'd never been so angry, and it was fabulous to be furious and lashing out. She'd always let others treat her as if she were stupid, as if she hadn't a brain in her head. She'd done everything—everything!—they'd asked, yet they repaid her with scorn and indifference.

She skirted by her mother and walked to the door.

"Where are *you* going?" Britannia demanded.

"Out."

"I don't give you permission to leave."

"I don't care."

She scurried away, the mansion like a prison gate that could swing shut and trap her if she didn't dash to freedom. It was very cold, an icy rain falling, the frigid air bracing.

Like a madwoman, she gaped about, then sprinted to the street, and she ran and ran until her neighborhood of stately mansions disappeared and she began to see shops and pedestrians on their daily errands.

On the corner, there was a row of rental cabs, and she went to the nearest one, tossed coins to the driver, and clambered in without assistance.

Shortly, she was at Ian's house, and she leapt out and marched to his stoop.

She was frantic to be with him. Their ardent interludes were the only thing that made sense, the only thing that seemed genuine. She felt as if she were weightless, floating away, and that he was a tether to all that was normal and real. If he didn't seize hold of her, she might fly off to some distant, unknown place and never return.

She knocked and knocked, but no one answered, so she barged in. Luckily, at the same moment, he was coming down the hall. He halted and frowned.

"Caro?"

"Yes."

"My goodness, did anyone see you? It's broad daylight. What are you thinking? What's wrong?"

"My mother hates me," she said in a rush, sounding

desperate and crazed, "and my father is having an affair, and I can't marry Mr. Shelton, but no one will help me. I don't know what to do. I just had to be with you."

If he sent her away, she couldn't predict how she'd react. When she'd fled from her mother, she'd needed a refuge, and he'd been the only choice.

Like a blind woman, she stumbled over, and she collapsed toward him, relieved that he caught her. If he hadn't reached out, she'd have plummeted to the rug.

"You're soaked through," he chided, though kindly.

"I had to get away from them."

She pressed herself to him, her nose buried against his chest. He was so warm, so sturdy and reliable, and she could have tarried there forever, safe and secure in the circle of his arms.

He took her hand and led her up the stairs to his bedchamber, and she followed along, perfectly content to do whatever he wanted. There was a toasty fire burning in the grate, and he guided her to it. She stared into the flames, mesmerized, as he removed her cloak; then he sat in a chair and drew her onto his lap.

"Calm yourself," he murmured, "and tell me what's happening."

"I can't marry Mr. Shelton."

"I'm thrilled to hear it."

"I want to be happy. That's all I want."

"It's so difficult to achieve, isn't it? Happiness, I mean."

"Yes, so I talked to my mother. I told her that I refuse to end up like her. She's so forlorn and angry."

"She definitely is."

"I want something better for myself, but she said I have to wed Mr. Shelton."

"So you spoke to your father?"

"But he wouldn't listen, either. He was eager to be with his mistress, so he was too busy to discuss it."

"He has a terrible reputation for that sort of thing."

"So this girl isn't the first?"

"No, not the first."

"I didn't know! My world is disintegrating before my very eyes! Everything I believed about my family is false."

"Have you ever stopped to consider that it might be *you* who's changing? Perhaps they're exactly as they've always been and you're simply seeing them more clearly."

"Perhaps," she allowed.

"I'm proud of you."

She was amazed. "You are?"

"I recognize how hard it is for you to stand up to them." He kissed her temple. "I'm glad you came to me."

"So am I."

"How long can you stay?"

"For as long as you'd like. No one will notice if I'm late getting back."

"I doubt that's true."

"I suppose you're right." She sighed. "I should probably be home by dark."

He smiled. "Then I suspect we shall have a lovely afternoon."

She smiled, too. "I suspect we shall."

❧

Come with me."

Ian eased her to her feet.

"To where?"

"Let me show you."

He'd just staggered out of bed, and a bath had been delivered, so the water would still be hot. She was freezing, her garments damp, her hair wet, and his initial order of business was to warm her and dry her clothes.

He couldn't get over the fact that she'd visited him, in the middle of the day—without hesitation or concealment—which indicated that the scene with her parents must have been appalling. He'd imagined that life with the Earl of Derby was unpleasant, so he wasn't surprised by her story, but it pained him that she was hurting.

He peeked in his dressing room, ensuring there were no servants lurking; then he drew her inside.

"What's this?" she said.

"Honestly, Caro, you must have seen one. It's a hip bath."

"I know *that*," she retorted. "I assume one of us is about to bathe. Is it to be me? Or you?"

"You."

"Are you going to watch?"

"Yes. I intend to wash you, too." He grinned wickedly. "If you're really nice to me, I might even join you."

"In the tub?"

"Yes."

"Are you telling me that men and women actually carry on this way? Together and in the open, where any servant could stroll in?"

"It's quite common, and a favorite pastime of mine." At realizing how much he'd revealed about his disreputable character, she glowered, and he hastily added, "Not that I've ever done such a thing with a female."

"Oh, of course not."

"I'm a veritable saint."

"Absolutely," she wryly agreed. "How could I be twenty-five years old and not have learned these secrets?"

"Don't ever regret being sheltered."

"I used to presume it beneficial"—her sizzling gaze took a deliberate, inquisitive meander down his torso—"but since becoming involved with you, I've changed my mind."

"I have that effect on people. The more you get to know me, the worse you'll behave. I guarantee it."

She chuckled and spun around. "Unbutton my gown."

He proceeded methodically, stripping her as if he were a lady's maid. He could have lingered and enjoyed the endeavor, but he wanted her naked. He removed her dress, petticoats, shoes, and stockings, and he paused to take them into the bedchamber, to drape them over the chairs in front of the fire.

At seeing her belongings scattered about, he was much more pleased than he should have been, and when he returned to her, he was frowning.

"Why are you scowling?" she asked.

"Because I like having you here."

"My presence makes you grumpy?"

"Very."

"I don't understand men."

He nestled himself to her backside and peered over her shoulder, tantalized by how her breasts pushed against her corset. She was so beautiful, and she was all his.

He untied her laces, dragging the blasted contraption away; then he yanked off her drawers, and in a thrice, she was nude. He wrapped his arms around her and ran his palms down her stomach and thighs, and she shivered, but he was fairly sure it wasn't from desire.

"Let's get you in the tub," he urged, and he held her hand as she climbed in.

She slid down, hissing as she immersed herself. There was an extra bucket of hot water on the floor, and he dumped it over her, earning a squeal of irritated delight; then he pulled up a stool and sat next to her.

She was relaxed and content, and at the sight, he was overcome by the oddest impression that she'd finally arrived right where she was meant to be. His heart did a funny flip-flop, jerking in his chest, until he actually rubbed the center, massaging away the ache.

"You're scowling again," she said, laughing.

"I'm trying to figure out how rapidly I can have you in my bed."

"Is that your plan?"

"Oh, yes, that's my plan."

"You have a very fiendish mind."

"I can't deny it."

"I'm not complaining."

He snatched up a cloth and swished it; then he swabbed it over her body, stroking it across her shoulders and bosom, down her tummy and between her legs.

Though she was a spinster and a virgin, she'd abandoned her prior reticence. Events had made her more reckless, more eager to experience the mischief he initiated, so she did nothing to slow him, which was incredibly titillating. His cock was so hard that he wondered how he'd stand.

"Are you feeling better?" he inquired.

"Oh, yes."

"Have I vanquished your chill?"

"Like a knight in shining armor."

"Marvelous. Out you go."

He helped her rise and step out; then he grabbed a towel and dried her.

"You didn't get in with me," she protested.

"That's because I'm so impatient to lure you to my bed, instead."

"Will you join me next time?"

"Most definitely."

At the notion that she was already contemplating a *next* time, his heart made that silly fluttering motion again.

He was so happy when she was near, so miserable when she wasn't, but he wouldn't focus on the peculiar sentiment. He wouldn't like her more than was wise, wouldn't moon over her when they were apart. If he did, he'd start to dream about a future that could never be, which was the height of folly.

They'd been acquainted forever, and he knew her well. Though she was currently distressed over her betrothal, in the end she would relent. If he began to hope she'd do anything else, he'd drive himself crazy.

He folded the towel around her, tucking the corner between her breasts, and he led her into his bedchamber. They tumbled onto the mattress, and Caro was as comfortable as if they'd been lovers for years rather than days.

He rolled on top of her, and as he kissed her he was stung by the realization that he never wanted to let her go, so his journey to insanity was complete.

He wasn't looking for a mistress—he had one of

those—and he wasn't looking for a wife. He especially wasn't looking for a wife who was the daughter of one of the most powerful families in England. He would never pursue such a negligent path, but at that moment, when she was warm and fragrant and snuggled beneath him, any wild conclusion seemed possible.

Needing to feel her flesh pressed to his own, he yanked at his shirt, tugging it off and tossing it on the floor. Then he pulled her towel away, exposing her to his avid scrutiny, and he lay atop her again, both of them moaning with pleasure as bare skin connected.

He nibbled down her neck, across her chest, and he suckled at his leisure. His sexual stimulation was painful, his poor, neglected phallus begging for mercy.

He groaned with dismay.

"What is it?" she asked. "Are you injured?"

"No, but I'm so aroused that it hurts."

"Really?"

"Yes."

She grinned. "You're suffering because of me?"

"Yes, you wench."

"Fabulous. How can I soothe your ache?"

"You can't."

"Why not?"

"Well . . . there are . . . we are . . . I am . . ." He still wasn't able to explain the mechanics of fornication. It was simply beyond him.

"Why are you embarrassed? Are you telling me that you can philander with ease, but you can't talk about it?"

"Some things are better in the demonstrating."

"So demonstrate." She flung her arms wide, like a virgin about to be sacrificed.

"No."

"Why?"

"Because I'd have to remove my trousers and have you touch me."

"What a grand idea! Let's try it." She wiggled out from under him, ready to undress him against his will.

"No," he said again. "If I take off my pants, there's no predicting what I might do."

"You'd be spurred to further misbehavior?"

"Yes, and a man can become too provoked, to where he can't control himself."

"Have I suggested you control yourself?"

"You're to be wed soon, Caro."

"Not if I can help it."

He continued as if she hadn't interrupted. "So we can't do anything that might harm you at the start of your marriage."

She shoved him onto his back, her glare imperious and irked. "I hate it when you treat me like a child, and I'm tired of waiting for you to get on with it."

"One of us needs to keep a level head."

"I don't see why. So far, we've broken every imaginable rule. Why restrain ourselves now?"

"Because we must."

"Ian?"

"Yes."

"Do be silent."

She came up on her knees, and she hovered over his crotch, making quick work of the buttons on his trousers, and he dawdled like an imbecile and let her have her way. He should have stopped her, but his anatomy seemed to have cast a spell on his tongue, and he couldn't utter a single word of protest.

She drew the fabric away, baring him to his haunches, and she sucked in a surprised breath.

"My, my," she murmured, "would you look at that!"

"We're built differently—in our private parts," he managed to grind out.

"I know. I've listened to women gossiping."

As if she were a tot that had discovered a new flavor of candy, she proceeded to explore. She squeezed and caressed, each innocent stroke shooting through him like a bolt of lightning. Her thumb grazed the sensitive crown, his limbs jerking in response as sparks of desire flowed from his loins outward.

"It's very large," she mentioned.

"It can be—when I'm excited."

"Such as now?"

"Yes. I'm definitely excited now."

"Wonderful."

He reached down and positioned her fingers, wrapping his hand around hers and guiding her in the appropriate rhythm. She was a willing, adept pupil, who instantly grasped what was required, but the stimulation was too extreme.

He'd intended to be patient, to let her tease and play, but he'd been goaded to madness. His lust spiked, his seed surging to the tip and demanding release. He slapped her away, when she didn't understand why he would.

"What's the matter?" she queried. "What did I do?"

"I need to come."

"I don't know what that means."

"You don't have to *know*. Just hold me."

"Like this?"

"Yes."

She hugged him as he stretched out, his phallus pressed to the soft skin of her belly. He thrust once, again, and again, and he emptied himself against her stomach. A potent orgasm carried him away, and as he spiraled up he worried that he'd never find the peak.

Finally, it crested and he tumbled down, joyous and laughing and happier than he could ever remember being. He landed in her arms, so glad to be with her, so glad he'd taken the chance.

As he struggled to slow his frantic pulse, she chuckled and said, "What on earth was that?"

"That, my darling, Caro, was a very dramatic example of male sexual ecstasy."

"*Dramatic*, was it?"

"Oh, yes."

"And what is this?" She dabbed at the spot on her abdomen where he'd spewed himself with such relish.

"My seed."

"What is it for?"

"It's a sign that I was pushed beyond my limit."

"It erupts from the tip every time?"

"Only when I'm very satisfied."

"So I take it that you were?"

"Yes, you minx. But it can also plant a babe."

She scowled. "How?"

He slipped his fingers into her sheath. "When my rod is very erect, I can shove it inside you—here."

"Inside?"

"Yes, and if I would spill myself while I was there, I could leave you with child."

"You're joking."

"No."

"What happens when you simply discharge it on my stomach?"

"Nothing. It's very pleasurable."

She appeared very smug. "Can we do it again?"

"If you give me a minute to catch my breath."

"But I'm ready now."

"A man needs a bit of a break in between."

"Spoilsport," she pouted. She fondled his cock, which was sated and half-erect. "You're not very hard."

"But I will be very soon. Just you watch."

He rolled her onto her back and started in again.

Chapter ELEVEN

"You lousy bastard."

"What? What did I do?"

Rebecca stormed into Jack's bedchamber and slammed the door. He'd just bathed, so his hair was damp and swept off his forehead. He was attired solely in a pair of tight-fitting trousers that delineated every muscle on his fabulous body, but she refused to be distracted by how marvelous he looked.

"You tattled to Ian," she seethed.

"Yes, I did."

"I told you not to."

"I couldn't keep such a terrible secret," he piously declared. "It was eating away at me."

"What about what I wanted?"

"What about it? Ian is my brother, and you are . . . are . . ."

"What am I?" she demanded when he couldn't finish. "And I must warn you that if you're about to refer to me in a derogatory fashion, you might wish to reconsider. I'm very, very angry."

She reached into her reticule to retrieve a small pistol, and she aimed the short barrel right at the center of his black heart.

"Are you mad?" he snapped.

Not intimidated in the least, he stomped over, stopping directly in front of her. He didn't grab for the weapon, nor did she lower it. A stony, awkward impasse ensued.

"I take it the rumors are true," he taunted.

"What rumors?"

"You're a man-killer."

"Only when the *man* in question needs killing. Then, I don't have the slightest qualms."

"Really?"

"Yes, really. Take another step and you'll see what I mean."

She didn't want to murder him, but after the humiliating encounter she'd just endured with Ian, she'd decided that Jack should pay for the damage he'd wrought. At that moment, death seemed like a dandy price to extract.

She hadn't visited Ian in days, hadn't had sex with him in weeks, when she was supposed to be his devoted mistress. Their separation unnerved her, had her fretting over whether his attention was waning.

She'd come to his home, dressed for seduction, but she'd been rebuffed. Not only had he been uninterested in a tryst, but he'd claimed that they should break off for a bit and let their ardor cool. He'd even hinted that perhaps they should split for good.

When she'd pressed him as to why, he'd informed her of Jack's confession, but she hadn't felt he was being entirely candid. There were other issues driving him, issues that had nothing to do with Jack. Ian had changed, was happier and more content than he'd ever been. Something had happened that went beyond her misbehavior, and she had to learn what it was, but in the interim, she had to deal with Jack.

He was such an insolent, imperious creature, and he needed to be put in his place. Hence, the pistol.

She waved it at him. "I'd like to hear one reason why I shouldn't kill you."

"Because I'm awfully partial to living?"

"You'd best think up a better response."

"Do you actually expect me to believe you'd shoot me?"

His disdain made her even more irate. "Yes, that's precisely what I expect you to believe."

"Give me that thing before you hurt yourself."

He laughed! The bastard laughed as if she were some wee bug who wouldn't harm a fly.

Didn't he understand anything about her? She had to marry Ian. She wouldn't be poor, wouldn't be forced into another violent marriage. When she was a girl, her cousins had wed her to the first reprobate who'd asked. They'd treated her as if she were a prized cow, and they'd received a pretty penny for their efforts, too. Then she'd been sold again, and a third time, until she'd grown old enough to avoid their machinations.

She would never again be in a position where her finances and physical safety were at risk, yet he stood there chortling as if her problems were a joke.

Her fury spiked.

"Shut up, Jack."

"I'm sorry, but I can't help myself. You humor me in too many ways to count."

"Shut up!"

He lunged, and without thought or deliberation, she

squeezed the trigger just as he knocked her to the floor. They both landed with a painful thud, and she tried to crawl away, but he stretched out and pinned her down.

The room was filled with smoke, the smell of gunpowder heavy in the air, the loud explosion making her ears ring. She gaped about, hoping to discover that she'd hit him, but with how tightly he was restraining her, she was fairly sure she'd missed.

Wasn't that just her luck! She'd fired at point-blank range, and the arrogant ass was still breathing!

Over his shoulder, she could see where the ball had struck the plaster. He stared at it, too, aghast at the damage.

"You've blasted a hole in Ian's wall."

"Yes, I have, and if I had a second round, I'd shoot another—only I'd aim more carefully."

"But you've wrecked his wall," he stupidly repeated.

"You ought to be glad."

"Glad!"

"If you hadn't tackled me, I'd have shot you instead. Which was definitely my intent." She struggled against him, wanting to escape his annoying presence. "Let me go."

"No, you crazed vixen. Hold still."

He clasped her wrists over her head, and suddenly every intimate spot was joined, chests, bellies, thighs forged fast. Down below, his cock had swelled in size. He smirked and took a naughty, delicious flex, his gaze metamorphosing from anger to desire in the beat of a heart.

He bent down and kissed her, and before she could command her traitorous body to ignore him, she was kissing him back.

Like two carnal savages, they were wild for each other. They clawed and bit, yanked and pulled, rolling about on the rug and fighting as if they were in a tavern brawl.

He jerked at her skirt, pushed her legs apart, and began unbuttoning his trousers.

"Don't you dare!" she warned. "I won't have sex with you. Not ever again."

"Won't you?"

He'd freed himself from the confines of his pants, and he wedged the blunt crown into her sheath. "You could have killed me."

"I wish I had!"

"You deserve a spanking."

"Hah! I'm trembling in my slippers."

"What you're going to get—is this!"

In a smooth thrust, he was impaled to the hilt, and the feel of him, so hot and virile, sent her into an immediate orgasm.

The pleasure was too extreme, like nothing she'd ever experienced prior, and she screamed in ecstasy. He clamped a hand over her mouth, as he found his own potent end. They came and came, spiraling up, then plummeting down together.

The instant it was concluded, his penetrations ceased, his livid look returning, as if she'd bewitched him against his will.

Footsteps hurried down the hall, as a servant approached to see what the racket had been.

Jack drew away and adjusted his trousers, while she lay there, gawking at the ceiling. He'd tumbled her as if she were a cheap harlot. Her dress was rucked up, her thighs bruised from his forceful incursion, her feminine regions wet and sticky with his seed. She'd never previously participated in such a shocking fornication, and all in all, she felt quite grand. Not that she'd admit it to the conceited oaf.

Across the room, he opened the door a crack and peeked out.

"Yes?" His voice was amazingly calm.

"I heard a loud bang, sir," the butler said.

"A bang?" He was innocence, itself.

"I thought I should check. It sounded like a gunshot."

"Oh, that!"

"There was screaming, too. A woman. Screaming."

Jack leaned nearer and whispered, "Mrs. Blake was here. She was upset. We quarreled."

"So she shot at you?"

"No, no. She threw a . . . a . . . lamp."

"And the scream?"

"She has a temper."

"That she does," the butler agreed. "I've brought a broom. Should I clean the mess?"

"The mess?"

"From the lamp."

"I tidied up myself."

"I see." There was a pause, the butler clearly incredulous; then he bowed. "Very good, sir."

He left, and Jack closed the door with a determined click. He whipped around, as she scrambled to her feet. She spun away, showing him her back as she straightened herself and pretended she hadn't been affected in the slightest.

"A lamp?" she chided, stifling a laugh.

"It was the best I could do on short notice."

He marched over to her, and he stood, fists on hips, glaring down his haughty nose. She wasn't sure what he wanted, what he expected, but she couldn't give it to him. She continued ignoring him as she fussed with her clothes.

Out of the blue, he said, "Will you marry me?"

She froze, panicked; then she shifted away, acting as if the words hadn't been uttered. She strolled about, picking up her belongings.

"Have you seen my earring? It seems to have fallen off. I can't find it anywhere."

"Marry me," he said again.

"No."

"Why?"

She scoffed. "Because I don't like you."

"Yes, you do. You're wild for me."

"I am not. I think you're a horse's ass."

"Are you in the habit," he crudely asked, "of fucking men you don't like on the middle of the floor in their bedchambers? Does it happen often?"

"It was another moment of temporary insanity."

"We keep having a lot of those."

"It doesn't mean anything," she insisted.

"Doesn't it?"

"No."

"What is the real reason?

"For what?"

She turned away, feigning nonchalance, even though her insides were churning, her fingers shaking. His proposal had rattled loose emotions she'd buried. She'd once been a female who'd harbored silly romantic notions about love and marriage, but they'd been extinguished with liberal doses of reality.

Wealth was the only thing that mattered, the only genuine security. If a woman had enough money, she could take care of herself. She didn't have to depend on tepid assistance from an unreliable man.

He laid a hand on her arm, the gesture stopping her in her tracks.

"Rebecca!"

"What?"

"Why won't you have me?"

"Leave it be, Jack."

"I deserve to know."

"You won't like my answer."

"Tell me anyway."

She shrugged him off. "All right. You're poor as a church mouse. As far as I can see, that fact will never change."

She grabbed her purse and started out, eager to be away and wanting the horrid scene to end. He foiled her by beating her to the door and bracing his palm on it.

"Let me out," she fumed.

"We have to talk about this."

"We just did. You didn't like my response—as I warned you wouldn't—so I can't imagine what else needs to be said."

"I love you."

Her stupid heart fluttered. "You do not."

"I do."

"Don't be ridiculous."

He absolutely could not be in love with her! If he persisted with his ludicrous assertion, she might begin to believe him, might assume they could have a future, when she knew how fickle strong sentiment could be. A man's affection never lasted. Jack could declare himself till doomsday, and she wouldn't listen.

She peered up at him. He looked so young, so handsome and confused, and she was overcome by the worst maternal instinct—when she had no maternal instinct, at all—to hug him and tell him that everything would be fine.

At experiencing the impulse, which was so foreign to her character, she was alarmed. He had an odd ability to stimulate her in ways she didn't like, to goad her into doing things she didn't wish to do. Like shooting at him, or having torrid sex on the rug.

It was folly to fraternize, and she had to make him understand that his fondness was grossly misplaced.

"Jack, you're behaving like a virginal debutante."

"Am I?"

"Yes. We've fornicated twice—and I'll be the first to admit that both occasions were overly passionate, but you're letting your emotions run amok."

"How?"

"You've obviously never been informed that sex can stir potent feelings, and it jumbles a person's common sense."

"So if I say I'm in love with you, I'm merely suffering from carnal delusions?"

"Basically, yes."

"Are you supposing you're the only woman with whom I've ever copulated?"

"No, you're much too good at it to be a novice."

"You're right, Rebecca. I'm *much* too good at it, and I know a few things about sex and love that you never will."

She frowned. He seemed to imply that he'd had many, many paramours, and that he'd been in love many, many times. If he was going to aggravate her with maudlin drivel, he at least ought to leave her with the illusion that she'd been his favorite!

"And what have you learned that's so accursedly wise?" she inquired.

"What's between us is very powerful, and we'd be fools to walk away from it."

"There's nothing between us!"

"Liar! Why don't you stick to the real reason you've refused me: I'm not rich enough to suit you."

"That's correct. You're not."

"Why must money be all that matters to you? You have a house and a steady income. Why isn't that sufficient? Why must it always be more, more, more?"

He was so snide, so certain his opinion was the sole one that was valid, and she was infuriated by his callous disregard for her precarious position. What did he know of being an unattached female? What did he know of struggling to make ends meet, of worrying—month after long month—whether there'd be funds to pay the bills?

"You say you love me," she countered, "so prove it."

"How can I? If cash is your prime motivator, I have none."

"So go get some. Ask your brother to endow you with a stipend."

"Ask Ian?" At the suggestion, he was appalled. "On what grounds would I solicit an allowance? Pray enlighten me; I'm dying to hear your reply."

"Have you ever inquired as to why he fought with Wakefield?"

"No, and I wouldn't presume to pry."

"Haven't you ever wondered how Ian obtained his fortune? He's a bastard son—as you are yourself—and he's never worked a day in his life. Yet, he's rich as Croesus."

"So?"

"Rumor has it that he *earned* his money by stealing

FORBIDDEN FANTASY

153

it from Wakefield. He pilfered the Clayton coffers for
years, without Wakefield suspecting."

She'd finally made him angry, and he shook his
head in disgust.

"I won't listen to such vile slander, Rebecca. Not
from you. Not from anyone."

"Ask him!" she pressed. "Ask him where he came
by his wealth! If he embezzled it, then it's ill-gotten
gains. Why shouldn't you have some?" She paused,
letting her terrible words sink in. "If you love me—as
you claim—then that's what you can do. Demand your
share, become affluent, and I am yours."

"You are such a mercenary," he accurately charged.
"I can't believe that you would stand here in the man's
home, that you would sleep in his bed and harbor
hopes of wedding him, but have the gall to level such
despicable accusations as to his character."

"I'm simply repeating the gossip," she coldly said.
"I thought you should know."

"How dare you speak so wickedly of him!" he loy-
ally, tediously stated. "He's been kind to me! He took
me in when I had nowhere to go!"

"So? His kindness doesn't mean he isn't a thief."

With each comment, she felt as if she were stabbing
him with a knife. Any affection had been crushed, and
the worst wave of melancholy swept over her.

By hurting him as she had, she'd relinquished
something remarkable and fine, and she was bereft at
what was lost, but she wouldn't sorrow. She'd set out to
erect a permanent barrier between them, and now that
she had, she wouldn't regret it.

"What will it be?" she nagged. "How badly do you
want me?"

He grimaced with loathing. "As opposed to you, I have my pride. I'd live in the gutter before I'd beg him for a handout."

"Then I guess you'll never have me as your wife, will you?"

"I guess I won't."

He went to the bed, stooped down, and picked up her pistol.

"Don't forget this," he said. "With that temper of yours, I'm sure you'll need it many times in the future."

He opened the door, and she stood there, heartsick, enraged, resolved. She yearned to explain, to justify, to plead for sympathy. It was on the tip of her tongue to apologize, to change her mind and announce that she'd have him, after all, but she spun and walked out without a farewell.

Chapter TWELVE

T here's a hole in my wall."

"I know."

"Were you planning to enlighten me as to how it got there?"

"Eventually."

Ian frowned at Jack and sighed. "The servants inform me that you were arguing with Rebecca. Alone. In your bedchamber. A gun was fired."

"It was."

"And . . . ?"

"She was very angry."

"Are you about to confide that the two of you had another sexual *accident*?"

Jack was silent, staring at his supper plate. Finally, he muttered, "I asked her to marry me."

"So she shot at you? That must have been quite a proposal."

"She didn't appear to care for it," he grumbled.

"You know, Jack, it's not very sporting of you to propose matrimony to my mistress."

"Don't worry; she said *no*."

"And this is supposed to make me feel better? Did she shoot at you before or after she rejected you?"

"Very funny."

Jack went to the sideboard and poured himself a whiskey.

"Would you like one?" he queried.

"I believe I would."

Jack poured another and, looking morose and miserable, he sat again.

"Would you mind telling me what's wrong?" Ian pressed. "Besides the fact that you've discovered Rebecca to be a wild hothead?"

Jack downed his drink. "Why did you fight with Lord Wakefield?"

"With Wakefield? Why would you inquire about him?"

"I'm curious about something I was told."

"What was that?"

Jack gazed around the ornate dining parlor, studying the fancy furnishings, the plush rugs, the silver candlesticks and crystal chandelier.

"Rebecca swears that you're rich because you embezzled from Wakefield. She said that he caught you and that's why you quarreled."

"*Rebecca* said all that, did she?"

"Yes."

"You two are certainly a pair of chums. I don't know why I continue to act as if I'm involved with her."

Jack shrugged, which could have indicated any number of replies, so Ian kept pushing.

"Where did she hear such a dastardly thing?"

"She claims it's being whispered all over London."

"Really?"

"Yes. Is it true?"

Ian's face was an impassive mask. "What do you think?"

"I have no idea."

Ian gulped his own whiskey and stood. "Good night."

"I want to know what happened," Jack declared, "and I want you to be the one who apprises me. I won't have every society rumormonger needling me with stories."

Ian assessed Jack, whom he'd grown to love so dearly. He was glad they'd met, glad that Jack had come to live with him. He couldn't remember what his life had been like before he'd had an exasperating younger sibling, and at the notion that he might have squandered Jack's regard he was unbearably sad.

"It's sort of true," Ian quietly admitted.

"*Sort of?* What does that mean? You either stole from him or you didn't."

There was a lengthy, painful silence; then Jack posed the question that Ian had asked himself on a thousand different occasions.

"What possessed you? Why lose a brother over something as stupid as money?"

Why indeed? "It seemed like the thing to do at the time."

"Don't be flip," Jack scolded. "Not about this. It doesn't become you."

Ian's humiliation rose up, flaming his cheeks with the wickedness of what he'd done. He plopped into a chair. "It wasn't because of the money. John couldn't have cared less about that."

"How odd. Rich men usually obsess about their finances."

"Not John. If he could have, he'd have given it all to

me—the title, the properties, and every last chattel. He didn't want any of it."

"Then what did you do to make him so angry?"

"I earned my fortune, but I didn't deserve it. Our father rewarded me for . . . for . . . spying on him."

"Why would you?"

"John was set to inherit so much wealth, but Father didn't trust him to manage any of it—and with valid reason. Before John married Emma, he was a mess. I was paid to report back, but the funds came from John's estates."

"For twelve years, Ian?"

"Yes."

"That's such a long time."

"I know. Father brought me down from Scotland and arranged for us to cross paths when we were little more than boys—I was twenty and John was eighteen—but I pretended it was a chance encounter."

"Wakefield didn't realize?"

"He never had a clue. So you see, it was betrayal that killed us."

"Shame on you," Jack murmured.

Ian winced, as if the terrible night were occurring all over again. It was all still so vivid in his memory. John had been so shocked, so hurt.

I thought you were my friend, he'd said.

I never was, Ian had lied.

Ian hadn't meant it, but they'd been fighting, and they'd hurled awful remarks that couldn't be retracted. They'd both been wounded too deeply.

He and John had had their ups and downs, and John was renowned for being spoiled and difficult. But Ian had loved him, flaws and all.

He missed John. He missed John each and every day.

"By every measure, Ian, our father was an ass. Why would you help him?"

"I've never been able to explain why I did it."

He'd been young and poor and foolish, and his father had offered him an opportunity to change his life and grow incredibly affluent in the process. Ian had acted as any sane fellow would have, had forged ahead to prosperity and status, but he wouldn't try to justify his behavior to Jack.

There was no way to make it sound acceptable.

Fate had evened things out, though. Early on, Ian had learned that no matter how many dirty pounds he stashed in his bank account, his illicit Scottish heritage guaranteed that he was never welcomed as a full son by his father, never acknowledged as a Clayton child by his father's peers. Only John had enjoyed knowing him, and he'd deceived John at every turn.

"You're not very loyal, are you, Ian?"

Ian watched Jack's esteem fade.

"No, I'm not."

"If you could be so heartless to Lord Wakefield, what might you do to me?"

"It's not the same."

"Isn't it? I assumed you were a different kind of man."

"I've tried to claim otherwise, but my base blood has always controlled me. You should let it be a lesson to you."

"How so?"

"We're Douglas Clayton's illegitimate offspring, and we can't shed the stain of our paternity. We shouldn't pretend to be what we're not."

"That's where you're mistaken, Ian. Douglas may have sired me, but I don't have to be like him. I'm *not* like him."

His sanctimonious pronouncement over, Jack stood and walked to the door.

"Where are you going?"

"I think maybe I should leave."

"Leave . . . my home?" Ian scoffed. "Don't be absurd. How would you get by?"

"I'm sure it will surprise you, but before coming here, I made my own way. I didn't have a fancy house to live in, or delicious food to stuff in my belly, but I never betrayed a soul, and I most definitely never hurt a friend."

"Aren't you a paragon?" Ian maliciously retorted.

"Not a paragon, no. But a stalwart and trustworthy person—always." He started out again. "I don't want to stay here. I don't want to end up so cruel and miserable—as you and Rebecca seem to be."

Ian listened to Jack stomping away, and he felt as if the past was repeating itself, that what had transpired with John was occurring with Jack. He'd split with one brother because he'd been too proud to speak up. Was he prepared to have the same conclusion with Jack?

The horrid prospect jolted him out of his stupor, and he hurried to the hall, just as Jack had reached the stairs and begun to climb.

"Jack, wait."

Jack halted, the distance separating them impossibly wide. "What is it?"

"I never told John, but I was so sorry."

"He's not dead. You could talk to him. You could apologize now."

"He wouldn't grant me an audience."

"What if you're wrong? What if he would?"

The notion dangled between them, but Ian was too distraught to embrace it. Instead, he said what he could, what was absolutely true.

"I don't want you to go. Not ever. And most especially not when you're so angry."

"I don't belong here," Jack insisted.

"You *do* belong. You belong right here—with me."

Jack looked so bewildered. "I don't know what to do, Ian. Everything is so jumbled."

"Sleep on it. Things will seem less bleak in the morning."

"We'll see." He kept climbing.

"Please?"

Ian heard the quiver in his voice, and he hated that he was begging, but if Jack left, what good was any of it? He'd have no one in the entire world, save Rebecca, and having her was worse than having no one, at all.

"Jack!" he snapped, his irritation poking through. "Tell me you'll stay."

"We'll see," his brother said again, and he continued on, as Ian fussed and stewed in his empty parlor.

He paced back and forth, back and forth, and with each trek across the floor, he was more despairing. Why couldn't he ever have what he craved? Why couldn't anything ever go as he planned?

Like a spoiled toddler, he railed against life, against Fate. Every imaginable injustice appeared to have been foisted on him, and he was so weary of battling for every little scrap.

He merely wanted to be happy. That's all he wanted. Why couldn't he be happy? Why was contentment so difficult to attain?

He wanted Caro.

The sudden need flowered in his chest, and it grew and grew until it was blazing like a forest fire.

He'd suffered years of rejection, and he was tired of denying himself. For more than a decade he'd mooned over Caro, and now he was about to stand idly by while her parents married her to Edward Shelton.

What was the matter with him? Why was he so ready to surrender? Why couldn't he fight—just once—for what he desired?

He glanced at the clock, seeing that it was after ten and wondering where Caro was. Had she gone out for the evening? If she was attending a soiree, could he locate her? Or should he risk sneaking into her father's mansion again?

He had to find her, and he marched to the foyer, anxious to grab a coat and hat, to have a horse saddled so he could ride off in search of her. He'd just stepped toward the door, when it opened and—as if he'd conjured her by magic—she slipped in.

She pushed off the hood of her cloak, and she was pale and shaking.

"I had to speak with you," she started. "Is it all right that I've come?"

"You never need an invitation."

He approached and took her hands in his. She was frozen, her fingers icy, and he was sickened to realize that she'd traipsed through the dark London streets to be with him.

"What happened?" he asked. "What is it?"

"After I was with you the other afternoon, my mother was furious."

"I presumed she would be."

"She's decreed that I'm out of control and should be punished. She conferred with my father, and he agreed."

"To what?"

"They've moved up the wedding date."

"When is it to be?"

"A week from today."

❧

I'm here to say good-bye," Caro said.

"Good-bye?"

Ian was aghast, which provided some relief. She was weary of lectures about duty and responsibility, and she'd wanted to converse with someone who would be as appalled as she was, herself. Ian was the only one who would listen, the only one who would commiserate or empathize, so after Britannia had made her vile announcement Caroline had crept away as soon as she was able.

What she truly yearned to say was, *Save me! Help me!* but she didn't, for what—precisely—could Ian do for her?

If she declined to go through with the ceremony, her father would cast her out, and she'd be shunned by society. She'd be disowned, a poverty-stricken female, with no funds and no acquaintances to offer her aid or shelter.

Would she beg Ian to take her in and support her? For how long? In what capacity?

It was ludicrous to suppose he was the answer to her prayers.

"I can't stop by again," she stated, feigning calm.

"Never?"

"With the wedding so near, I'm sure I won't have another chance to get away."

"I see. . . ."

There was a noise down the hall, most likely a servant rambling about, and Ian gestured for silence and led her to the stairs. Without argument, she followed him up to his bedchamber. He shut and locked the door, and as they stood, facing each other, she noticed what hadn't been apparent in the foyer.

He was greatly distressed, himself, perhaps even more than she, so it was a terrible moment to have arrived, but she wouldn't regret her decision.

They had no remaining opportunities where they could be together. After she was married, despite how dreadful it turned out to be, she would honor her vows to Mr. Shelton.

"What is it, Ian?" she inquired. "What's wrong?"

"Everyone is leaving me," he oddly said.

"Everyone?"

"First John, then Jack, now you." He drew her into his arms, and he kissed her with a particular desperation. "I don't want you to go."

With a groan of dismay, he proceeded to the bed. He removed her cloak and tossed it on the floor; then he climbed onto the mattress, urging her down so that she was draped across him. She was still attired in the gown she'd worn to supper, the fashionable neckline cut very low, her breasts practically falling out of the bodice.

With the slightest tug, he freed them and sucked on her nipple, seeming to be soothed by the gentle motion. But as he shifted to the other one, the passion rapidly escalated.

"How long can you stay?" he queried.

"As long as you'd like."

"Till dawn?"

"Certainly."

"I want to make love to you. I want to make you mine in every way that counts."

"I want it, too."

"I don't want to ever forget what it was like."

"Neither do I."

He was unbuttoning her dress, as she worked on his shirt. They jerked and pulled, wrenched and yanked, and quickly they were naked. They stretched out, with her on top.

"I wish there was more time for you to teach me your sexual games," she said. "I feel like there's so much I don't know."

"I've created a wanton."

"Yes, you have."

She relished how naughty they were when they were alone, and as a spinster she'd missed out on many fantastic adventures. Without a doubt, Mr. Shelton would never inspire her to such outbursts of ardor.

It seemed as if a portal was closing, as if she was about to be shut off from the life she could have had if she'd been smarter in her decisions. On this, her last night with Ian, she felt that it was her final chance to be happy, and she planned to grab for whatever bliss he chose to bestow. At the moment, she didn't care about Mr. Shelton or her mother or her duty to her family. For once, she would selfishly revel.

In the morning, when it was over, she was positive she'd rue and regret, but not now, not when her every sinful desire was about to be realized.

He dipped down and nursed at her breasts again; then he meandered lower and settled himself between her legs. She grasped his destination, and she spread wide, welcoming the decadent invasion.

Swiftly, he goaded her to the precipice and heaved

her over, her anatomy convulsing with ecstasy. She struggled to the peak, then floated down—grinning—as he caught her.

He was very tense, his body rigid with unfulfilled lust, and she wasn't certain how to pleasure him. He'd always acted like too much of a gentleman, so he'd never shown her the indecencies she'd been anxious to learn.

"I want you to put your mouth on me," he said. "I want to be inside you at least once before we're through."

"I don't understand what you mean."

He hesitated, then mumbled, "I don't know if we should."

"I'll do whatever you'd like. Tell me what it is."

"It's a whore's trick," he claimed. "It's awful of me to ask you."

"I don't mind."

He shifted up the pillows, his masculine shaft alive and reaching out to her, demanding she tend it.

To her amazement, he clasped it and brushed the tip across her lips.

"Lick me with your tongue," he instructed.

Surprised by the request, she froze, then did as he'd commanded, and she was tantalized by how she'd galvanized his attention. She didn't think she'd ever seen a man quite so focused.

"You like that, do you?"

"Very much." He moaned and flexed his hips. "Open up. Take me like this."

She gazed at him, stunned, but horribly fascinated, too, and she eagerly complied. He tasted like heat and salt, and though he'd mentioned that it was a deed for a harlot to perform, she was enthralled.

He thrust, pushing in, then retreating, giving her a

bit more with each penetration. She could have lain there forever, savoring the depraved escapade, which only proved how low her true character actually was.

She might have been an earl's daughter, but she was thrilled to misbehave like any common trollop. He was transfixed, and she was delighted to confer something he so obviously treasured.

She'd just started to get the hang of it when he shoved her away, and she glared up at him, wanting to keep on.

"What are you doing?"

"I'm too aroused; I can't continue."

"You never let me have any fun," she pouted.

He was in agony, every muscle taut as a bowstring, and he urgently needed the male release that would bring him relief. She snuggled herself to him, assuming he would rub himself on her belly as he had during prior trysts, but he rolled them so that she was on the bottom and he was wedged between her thighs, his rod dropping to her center.

"I want you so badly," he said through clenched teeth.

"Then take me. I am yours."

"My God! Don't give me permission."

"I want it to be you. I want to know what it's like."

He nudged forward so that the end was inserted.

"If I proceed," he warned, "there is a thin piece of skin that's called your maidenhead. I'll tear it."

"Will it grow back?"

"No. So your *husband*"—he could barely pronounce the loathsome word—"will know that you've been with another man."

She thought about Mr. Shelton, about her bitter, resentful mother, her foolish, preoccupied father. They were sacrificing her like an innocent maiden in a savage's ritual. What loyalty was owed?

"I don't care if I'm discovered," she insisted.

"He could beat you for it, Caro. Or divorce you, or kill you, and he would suffer no punishment for his crime."

"I don't care," she repeated. "I really don't."

She pressed herself to him, the crown lodged in even farther. He hung his head, his eyes closed, as if praying for strength.

"I'm so hard for you," he muttered.

"Then take me! Don't make me wait. Don't leave me wondering."

For an eternity, he paused, perched on a cliff of indecision, so she raised the stakes.

"I can't be with you again," she said.

"I know."

"This is our only chance."

"I know that, too." His expression changed, becoming more tender. "If we progress, there's no fixing what we've done. I would hate it if you were sorry later on."

"I never will be."

He studied her, then nodded, and he clasped her flanks and braced himself.

"No regrets, Caro."

"No, none."

He began driving into her, and at feeling him so intimately and unusually located, she had an attack of virginal nerves and tried to wiggle away, but he held her in place.

"Ian, stop!"

"No."

"Can we talk about this?"

"No!"

"Please."

"It has to conclude like this, Caro. Don't you see? This is where we've been going all along."

He flexed and flexed, and he broke through, his cock fully impaled.

"Oh, oh . . ." she breathed, arching up, tears stinging her eyes. "You didn't tell me it would hurt." She forced a chuckle, but it was a miserable sound.

"I didn't want to frighten you."

He kissed her, dawdling and delaying, and gradually, her anatomy adapted. As she relaxed, he commenced again, entering her over and over, and rapidly she was meeting him thrust for thrust.

His passion increased, his penetrations more precise, more resolute, and finally he tensed and emptied himself against her womb. The sensation was magical, and she hugged him tight, wishing they could be together forever, that nothing from the outside world would ever intrude. Her heart was filled to bursting, and she roiled with emotion. She was so happy; she was so sad, and she was experiencing every wild swing of sentiment in between the two conditions.

I love you!

The phrase popped into her mind, and she didn't know why it hadn't occurred to her before. Of course she loved him. She always had and always would.

He drew away, though he was still buried deep.

"Are you all right?" he murmured.

"Why wouldn't I be? I'm not made of glass."

"No, you're not." He kissed the center of her palm.

"I'm so glad it was you." She sighed, reflecting on what they'd done, where it would lead, how it would end. "I'm not a virgin anymore, am I?"

"No."

"I'm glad about that, too."

The lazy night stretched in front of her. He was partially erect, his phallus unsated and ready for another go, and she was curious as to how much effort it would take to encourage him.

"How soon will you be able to do it again?"

"Not soon enough to suit you, you minx."

He laughed, a merry chortle she'd never previously heard from him, and he shifted them so they were snuggled on their sides and grinning like a pair of half-wits.

She traced his lips with her tongue, as she took his hand and laid it on her breast.

"I can only stay till dawn," she reminded him, "so you'd best get busy."

Chapter THIRTEEN

Ian stood by the window and stared out at the horizon that was swiftly growing brighter, the stars fading with the onset of morning. Caro was asleep in his bed, and he needed to wake her and see her safely home, but he couldn't bear to rouse her.

He rubbed a hand over the center of his chest. His heart was aching, and he didn't care for the sensation. They'd rutted like wild animals, and on three separate occasions he'd spilled himself inside her. Throughout the passionate interlude, he'd been so overwhelmed that he hadn't restrained himself, but with sanity and daylight creeping in, he was panicked.

Oh, what was he to do? What if he'd planted a babe?

He couldn't send Caro back to her fiancé and her parents. Yet, how could he keep her with him? The only way would be to marry her. Was he prepared to propose? It was the appropriate remedy, but he couldn't imagine asking her, nor could he envision her accepting.

What had he to offer a woman like Caro?

He had an income that was sufficient for a bachelor, but it couldn't begin to compare to her father's fortune. If she allied herself with him, her mode of living would fall substantially. Could she tolerate such a change? Plus, any union between them would cause a terrible scandal.

He had no lofty acquaintances to stand with them during the tumult. She'd be shunned, cut off from all that was familiar, and the shame would kill her.

Was he worth it? He didn't have to pose the question, for he knew the answer: categorically not.

He went to the bed and eased a hip onto the mattress. She stirred and smiled. She looked rumbled and adorable, smug with her seduction and pleased with what she'd wrought.

"What time is it?" she inquired.

"Almost five."

"I should be going," but she didn't make any move to rise.

"I don't want you to leave."

"I have to. You know that."

She sat up, the blankets clutched to her bosom, her hair spilling about her shoulders. She laid her palm on his cheek, and for a moment, they tarried, neither of them able to speak.

Then she urged him aside and climbed to the floor. In silence, she strolled about, scooping up her clothes and tugging them on as he did the same. Eventually, they were dressed, her cloak fastened, the hood up. There was nothing left to do but escort her out, but they couldn't seem to depart.

He dawdled, awkward as an adolescent.

For the prior twelve years, her presence in his world

had been a constant, and he couldn't let her walk away. Not without a fight. She'd come to mean too much to him, and he couldn't picture a future without her in it.

Did she feel any similar sentiment? Would she be willing to alter the course of her life for him?

He had to know her opinion, and if he didn't seek it now, when it was very likely the only chance he'd ever have, he'd forever wonder how she would have replied.

If she laughed or scoffed, so be it. If she rejected him, so be it. But he had to be certain.

Tentatively, he ventured, "I have something to discuss with you."

"What is it?"

"Don't respond right away. You need to go home and think on it."

"Fine. Just tell me what it is."

"I want you to marry me."

"*Marry* you?"

"Yes."

"Oh, Ian . . ."

She had the most peculiar expression on her face, and he couldn't decide if she was surprised or aghast. She'd been raised to believe that class and status mattered above all else, so she was precisely the sort of female who would wed Edward Shelton simply because of his lineage and without regard to any other factor.

"I can't permit Shelton to have you. Not after last night. Not after how it's been between us."

"But my father has promised me to him," she stressed, as if he'd forgotten.

"I understand that, Caro, but you're no longer a virgin, and we might have made a babe together. When there's a possibility you could be pregnant with my child, I can't let you go."

Her eyes widened with dismay, the startling prospect not having occurred to her.

She frowned. "I hadn't thought about a babe."

"It's my fault," he insisted, refusing to have her feel that she was to blame. He was the one experienced in fornication, just as he was aware of the dire consequences that could result. "I shouldn't have behaved so negligently, but the deed is done, and we have to carry on with circumstances as they're now confronting us."

"I'd have to publicly cry off."

"Yes, but could you marry him, Caro? Could you cuckold him? If you're pregnant with my son, you'd have to pass him off as his. I know you, Caro. You couldn't do it. You're not that kind of person."

"My parents would never agree."

"I'm not asking you to solicit their permission."

"Then what are you asking?"

"I want you to elope with me. To Scotland. We'd have to lie and fabricate stories; then we'd sneak away without informing anyone. Not a maid. Not a friend."

"It sounds so tawdry."

"There's no other way to pull it off."

"I don't know, Ian." As if her head had begun to pound, she rubbed her temples.

"I realize it's an outrageous request. That's why you should reflect on it."

"There'd be a big scandal."

"Yes, there would."

"I'd be drummed out of society. From the instant we proceeded, every door would be shut to me."

"Yes," he repeated.

"My father would disown me. I'd have to relinquish all ties to my family."

"I'm absolutely sure of it." He was being brutally frank, for he couldn't have her harboring any silly, romantic notions about the implications of aligning herself with him.

"The Earl would never release my dowry to you."

He shrugged. "I hadn't expected he would."

"You'd have to support me. Where would we live?"

She glanced around his bedchamber, and he received the distinct impression that she judged it unbefitting of her elevated station. He tamped down his irritation.

"We could return here," he cautiously mentioned, "though we might have to stay away from London for a time."

"Stay away? Why?"

"We'd wait for the gossip to die down—so it would be easier on you."

"Where would we *wait*?"

"We could remain in Scotland, with one of my uncles."

"We'd leave England?" She was so shocked that he might have suggested she journey with him to the moon.

"Yes."

"For how long?"

"I don't know."

"Forever?"

"It would depend on how vicious the uproar. If it never abated, I can't imagine that we'd care to come back."

She nodded, pensive, perplexed.

He was demanding so much from her, was pressuring her to commit to decisions that were totally foreign to her character. No doubt, she'd be happy for a while, but ultimately, the rumors would settle, and she'd be stuck with him. Would she regret what she'd relinquished? If they had to stay in Scotland, cut off from civilization, ostracized by all, how would she survive it? Would she grow to hate him?

"This is such a huge step," she said. "Why would you take it?"

"What do you mean?"

"I know you, too, Ian. Though you work to hide it, you have a chivalrous heart beating in your chest."

"Perhaps," he allowed.

"But why would you assist me? Is it merely your generous nature surging to the fore? Or have you another reason?"

This was the point where he was to declare himself, where he was to fall on bended knee and profess his devotion. It was on the tip of his tongue to claim that he loved her, but did he?

He was suffering from the most insane impulses, his emotions careening between joy and dread. When he was with her, he felt grand, contented in a fashion he'd never been, but did it amount to love?

He had no idea.

If it was no more than heightened lust, it would flicker out quickly enough, and she wouldn't be the only one miserable in her choice of a spouse.

He wouldn't lie and announce sentiment he didn't feel, wouldn't pretend an affection he couldn't sustain.

"We must wed, Caro. It's the right thing to do."

"But you don't wish to marry me. As far as I recollect, you've never wished to marry anyone."

"It's the price I must pay for my carelessness."

The remark was jarring and cold, and it came out .completely wrong. She jerked away as if he'd slapped her.

"I see."

Outside, a bird peeped, the morning chorus of chirping about to commence.

They stared and stared, a thousand unspoken comments swirling between them. He hadn't said what he'd truly wanted to say, hadn't explained very well or offered her any good incentives to agree. He could only hope that—once she had occasion to reflect—she would recognize the wisdom of his plan.

What alternative did she have?

"I'd best get home," she said.

"It would take so long to have my carriage readied. I thought I'd walk you. It will be much faster."

"That will be fine."

He went to the hall and peeked out, certain there'd be no servants about, but still, it was prudent to be vigilant. He linked their fingers, and they tiptoed down the stairs and out into the frigid air. The ground was frosty, their breath billowing about their heads.

She lived many blocks away, and they started off, both of them silent and morose and fretting over what would happen next. The streets were mostly empty, with only a few teamsters making deliveries of milk and coal. He skirted her past the hearty souls, barely drawing a glance, and in minutes they crept around the stables behind her father's mansion.

As he reached for the gate, the first rays of dawn were visible on the horizon.

She rose up and kissed him, and he resisted the urge to pull her close, to hold on to her and never let her go.

There was a strange finality to the moment, as if he'd been through it before and knew that disaster approached. Suddenly, he was overwhelmed by the conviction that he'd never see her again.

He was being maudlin as a schoolgirl, and he shucked off the peculiar fright. He peered over the fence to the house, relieved that the windows were dark, not a candle burning anywhere.

"I must think on this," she whispered.

"I know. If your answer is *yes,* send me a message, and I'll come fetch you. Or you can show up at my door. I'll have a bag packed, and we can leave immediately."

"And if my answer is *no*?"

"Then you need do nothing, at all, and I will wish you happy in your pending marriage. Now go."

She hesitated, looking as if she would say something profound and definitive, but in the end, she swallowed down whatever it had been. She spun and stepped through the gate, and she was many strides across the yard when he was again overcome by the notion that she was going forever.

Softly, frantically, he called, "Caro!"

She whirled around. "What?"

"Don't wait too long to decide."

"I won't."

She walked on, and he watched until she was inside, and he continued to tarry, unable to force himself away. He gazed up at her bedchamber, where he yearned to see the glow of a lamp. He was desperate for the small assurance that she'd arrived, but there was no sign of her.

The sky was growing lighter, the shadows fading, the risk increasing that someone might espy him lurking—like a vagrant or a robber—near the Earl's residence. It was dangerous to remain.

He turned and left.

Rebecca peeked out the window of her carriage. The horse sighed; the driver shifted his bulky form. Both man and animal were hoping she'd either get out or give the instruction to keep on. It was the witching hour she hated most, that lonely period just before dawn when she could never sleep.

At such a forlorn time, she always ended up doing precisely what she oughtn't. Such as she was contemplating now.

She wrapped her fur cloak more tightly over her body, the silky fabric of her ball gown crinkling in the cold air. She'd had too much to drink, had gamboled much later than she'd intended, and any sane individual would have been lounged at home by a warm fire.

Ian's house loomed in the distance, and she was torn over her having stopped by. He'd told her not to, and in view of her misbehavior with his brother, it was the only logical course. Yet she recognized it as the initial stage of his tossing her over, which she couldn't allow.

She didn't love Ian—she'd never loved anyone—but she liked and understood him, and she was determined that they wed.

An image flashed—of annoying, exasperating Jack Romsey—but she pushed it away. She wouldn't be dissuaded. Not by his sexy demeanor. Not by his ludicrous proposal. Not by his handsome looks or fabulous anatomy.

She wanted to marry Ian—she *needed* to marry Ian—and she wouldn't let anything prevent the conclusion she desired.

He had to be reminded of why he enjoyed their

relationship so much. A rough and rowdy bout of fornication would restore his waning affection, and she'd just planned to get out, when his front door opened. She observed, stunned, as he exited with a cloaked woman hanging on his arm.

He was already entertaining another paramour! The bastard!

She was furious, and she frowned, trying to glean the woman's identity, though it wasn't much of a mystery. She hadn't forgotten how Lady Caroline had been slinking around.

Was Ian involved with her? Could he be that foolish?

The pair proceeded on, with Ian so focused on Caroline that he didn't notice Rebecca where she was parked down the block.

She loitered until they were a safe distance away; then she had her driver tag after them. As they approached the Earl of Derby's mansion, her temper flared.

Lady Caroline could have any man she wanted. She was engaged, for pity's sake. Why sniff after Ian?

Ian belonged to Rebecca! How dare Lady Caroline interfere! The little hussy!

They vanished into the alley, and though it was despicable, Rebecca clambered out and sneaked after them.

She hid behind a tree trunk, and she was close enough to see, but not close enough to hear. Lady Caroline kissed Ian on the lips, and they lingered, touching and whispering; then Caroline slipped inside. Ian dawdled, keeping vigil, gazing after her with such unfulfilled yearning that it was almost painful to watch.

Finally, he trudged back to the street. Rebecca huddled behind the tree, not breathing, not moving a muscle, as he passed by a few feet away. She stayed put till he'd disappeared; then she returned to her carriage and climbed in.

The driver urged the horse forward, and they started toward home. She leaned against the squab, her mind racing with what she'd discovered.

Deep down, she wasn't a wicked person, but as the old saying went: All was fair in love and war. And this was definitely war. Lady C. had her own fiancé, and she needed some encouragement to avoid Ian. She'd been warned off before, but obviously, she hadn't heeded Rebecca's advice.

The question now was to figure out the best way to make her pay attention and do what Rebecca wanted.

Rebecca thought and thought, and as the answer became clear, she sighed with resignation. There was really only one choice.

If Lady Derby happened to learn what her darling Caro was doing, how would she react?

It was going to be interesting to find out.

Chapter FOURTEEN

I know who you are, Mrs. Blake."

Britannia stared at the notorious woman. She was very beautiful, but in a deadly way—as three prior husbands had discovered to their peril.

With her lush red hair and her piercing blue eyes, she was very striking, and Britannia thought that men would lust after her like dogs in a barnyard. She was too attractive, and for someone so young, she exuded a sensual air that was disturbing.

Britannia hated her on sight.

"Shall we sit?" Mrs. Blake rudely asked, since Britannia hadn't had the courtesy to suggest it.

"No. I have no idea why I stooped to granting you an audience—curiosity, I suppose—but I intend for your appointment to be extremely short."

As if she hadn't just been insulted to high heaven, the annoying child chuckled. "I guess the gossip is accurate."

"And what gossip would that be?"

"You, Lady Derby, are an irrepressible shrew."

Britannia couldn't remember when she'd ever previously been so offended.

"Get out of my house."

"I'll go in a minute. As you said, this won't take very long."

Blake sauntered to the sideboard and, without invitation, poured herself a drink.

Britannia sputtered with indignation, huffed to the hall, and bellowed, "Jenkins! Come at once! I need you."

As usual, the slothful butler didn't appear, so she stormed over to Mrs. Blake, ready to pick her up bodily and toss her out on the lawn.

"Speak your piece," Britannia seethed. "Then be on your way."

"Won't you join me in a whiskey? You're going to require fortification."

"Jenkins!" Britannia shouted again.

"Very well." Blake sighed. "Do you know where your daughter was last night?"

"My . . . daughter?" The remark caught Britannia off guard. "You mean Lady Caroline?"

"Have you another daughter of which I'm unaware?"

"She was in her bed, fast asleep."

"Was she?"

Blake raised a brow with such aggravating confidence that Britannia could only surmise that whatever the harlot was about to impart would be the truth. There wasn't a person alive who could barge in with such cool poise unless they held all the cards. Not that Britannia would ever let on that she believed any stories.

"I hear that you're set on her marriage to Mr. Shelton," Mrs. Blake mentioned. "In fact, it's rumored that you're so determined it's almost an obsession with you."

"You *hear* many things, Mrs. Blake. I would recommend that you consider the source of your information. When you roll in the gutter, it's common for rubbish to stick."

Jenkins took that moment to haul himself into the parlor.

"You called, Lady Derby?" he inquired.

"Show Mrs. Blake to the door, and if she ever returns, summon the law and have her dragged off as a vagrant."

Blake didn't move. Neither did Jenkins. Then Blake flashed such a wicked grin that Britannia blanched. Whatever would next spew from Blake's mouth was nothing that should be voiced in front of a servant.

"I'll just be off," Blake said. "I merely stopped by to advise that you have Lady Caroline checked by a midwife before the wedding. You ought to be positive that she's . . . well . . ." She halted and giggled, looking so innocent, so lethal. "Mr. Shelton would probably like to know for sure."

Britannia gaped at her, thinking it would be so easy to commit murder, to simply reach over, wrap her large hands around Blake's slender throat, then squeeze and squeeze until the woman collapsed dead on the floor.

"Leave us, Jenkins," Britannia commanded, and the retainer scurried out. Once he'd departed, she demanded, "What are you trying to say?"

"Lady Caroline is having a sexual affair with Ian Clayton."

In her entire life, Britannia had never been more shocked. "Ian . . . Clayton? Douglas Clayton's Scottish spawn?"

"Yes. She's been sneaking to his house, in the

afternoons and evenings, when no one is watching where she's gone."

"You're lying."

"I've seen them with my own two eyes."

Britannia's mind whirled. Why would Caroline do it? Why would she risk so much for an ordinary peasant? But more important, why would Blake tattle? What had she to gain?

"Are you hoping to blackmail me, Mrs. Blake? Is that your game? For if it is, I must tell you that you'll find a very dry well. I won't pay you a penny. You may shout your falsehoods hither and yon, and the Earl and I shall ruin you."

"I'm not after any money," Blake claimed.

"Then what is it? Why have you come? If you're not plotting to spread your filth, what is your purpose?"

"Their liaison must end. Immediately."

"Really? And am I to assume that your motives are purely benevolent?"

"No, I'm being completely selfish."

"In what fashion?"

"Ian is mine," she stated, "and I want her to leave him alone. That's all I want. I'd appreciate it if she's not allowed to meet with him again. Can you handle the situation, Lady Derby? Or will you force me to confer directly with your husband?"

Without another word, Blake spun and left, and Britannia's quaking knees gave out. She sank down onto the nearest chair, wondering what her next step should be.

She'd waited twenty-five agonizing years to orchestrate Edward's marriage to Caroline. The prospect had sustained her through every social engagement where she'd had to observe Edward flirting with others, where she'd had to smile at him and pretend they were cordial.

If she couldn't have her revenge, if it was suddenly snatched from her at the very last second, how would she survive it?

Desperate measures were required. The only question was: What should they be?

$\maltese$

"There you are," Bernard grumbled. "I've been searching everywhere."

"What are you doing home at this hour?" Britannia asked.

"I must speak with you."

"Well, after the morning I've had, I have no desire to speak with *you*."

He ignored her and crossed over to where she was slumped in a chair. She was very glum, but he wouldn't try to ascertain why. She was an impediment to his plans, and he would soon be shed of her.

Britannia was the past. Georgie was the future.

"I must get my affairs arranged," he said. "I'm tired of your delays and arguments, so I'm proceeding with the divorce—whether you're amenable or not."

She scoffed and shot him such a malevolent glare that a frisson of fear slithered down his spine, but he pushed away the absurd reaction. He disliked her, was constantly aggravated by her, but he wasn't—and never had been—afraid of her.

What could she do to him? She was a woman, and a very stupid one at that.

"How typical of you, Bernard, to think only of yourself at a time such as this."

"What do you mean?"

"I've just had the most interesting visitor."

"Why would you bother me with the details of your petty life, Britannia?"

"Tell me what you know about Ian Clayton."

"Ian Clayton? Wakefield's brother?"

"Yes."

"You know him as well as I. Form your own opinion, and don't pester me. Now about the divorce—"

She rose, and she looked menacing in a manner he'd never noted prior. She was big boned and obese, and though he was taller, she seemed to tower over him.

"Tell me about him!" she insisted.

"He's quiet and driven, reputed to be honorable, but I'm told that he quarreled with John and it changed him. His Scottish heritage gives him a dashing air that the ladies consider attractive."

"Would that include your own daughter?"

"She'd never stoop that low."

"Wouldn't she?" Britannia laughed in an eerie way. "She's fucking him."

The crude remark was so abruptly voiced, and so out of character, that he couldn't decide what to make of it. For a brief instant, she appeared quite mad.

"What did you say?"

"You heard me. What should we do?"

"If you expect me to believe she's been having sex with him, you are out of your bloody mind."

"Am I?"

"Yes."

"Shall we call her down and interrogate her?"

"About Ian Clayton? Don't be ridiculous."

He assessed her, worried that she'd tipped off her rocker, which would be just his luck. It was sufficiently

difficult to cope with her when she was merely hysterical and boring. It would be total hell to put up with her
if she was crazy.

"But what if Edward learns of the rumors?" she
nagged.

"What rumors? If your snippy companions are
spreading gossip, I'll sue to shut them up."

"Fine then, I will deal with it myself, but if you don't
like the steps I take, I won't listen to any complaints."

"Be my guest," he magnanimously stated. "You
have my permission to make a fool of yourself in any
fashion you desire."

He started out, when she snapped, "Where are you
going?"

"Where would you suppose? Georgie and her mother
have invited me for supper. Then I'm escorting Georgie
to the theater."

She gasped. "Will you sit with her in our box?
Where all the world can see?"

"It's not *our* box. It's *my* box, and yes, I will."

"If you do, you'll be sorry," she threatened.

"Sticks and stones, Britannia. Sticks and stones.
Georgie is your destiny, approaching like a bad carriage accident. I suggest you prepare yourself."

"What about Caroline?" she hissed.

"What about her? She's scheduled to marry Edward
next week, and she *will* marry Edward next week."

Despite how Britannia whined, she couldn't make
him feel guilty, couldn't make him stay. He was weary
of her, weary of his two tedious children, and he was
moving on to a new and better life.

He whirled away and stomped out, curious as to
why he still bothered stopping at home.

T here's really only one choice," Caroline murmured.

"Did you say something, milady?"

Caroline jumped, having forgotten there was a maid in the dining parlor with her.

"No, nothing," she lied. She glanced at her breakfast plate, her fork blindly pushing the eggs round and round in a circle.

She could elope with Ian, the enigmatic, captivating man she loved. Or she could remain in London and marry Mr. Shelton. She could keep what she had or throw it all away. She felt as if she was perched on a high cliff and about to leap over the edge, when she had no idea how far it was to the bottom.

If she refused Ian, she'd never see him again, and though she'd been groomed to be tough and stoic, she didn't imagine she could survive the loss. Not now. Not when she'd finally realized how important he was to her.

She stood, causing the maid to frown as she stared at Caroline's uneaten food.

"Wasn't the meal to your liking, milady? Shall I have Cook make you something else?"

"No, it was wonderful. I'm so distracted this morning that I'm not hungry."

She raced out and up the stairs to her room. Her first order of business was to escape the house and never return. If she packed a bag, the staff would be suspicious, so she couldn't take anything, and she gazed about, studying her bedchamber.

They were so wealthy it was almost obscene, yet she was leaving with only the clothes on her back: She was abandoning it all for the man of her dreams, like a heroine in a romantic theatrical. When she was ready to give up everything for him, could there be a more striking example of how much she cared?

After donning her cloak and hat, she'd spun to go when panic seized her. What if she was delayed? What if she couldn't get away immediately?

She wanted Ian to know that her answer was *yes,* wanted him to be excited and watching for her, and she grabbed a pen and jotted him a quick note; then she folded it and hid it in her reticule.

Feigning calm, she walked down to the foyer and casually requested that the carriage be brought round. Now that she'd made up her mind, she was anxious to be away, and she loitered in the drive, impatient for it to arrive.

By the time she heard the horse's hooves, she was frantic. The longer she dawdled, the more convinced she became that she would never get away. There seemed to be talons curling around her ankles and trying to drag her inside.

Just as the carriage pulled up, a maid bounded out to announce that her mother needed Caroline to attend her at once.

Caroline gaped at the carriage, at the maid, as she considered climbing in and trotting off, but when so many servants were observing, she couldn't disobey the summons. There was no greater way to draw notice to herself.

She smiled and agreed, even though a strange terror was gnawing at her. With her plans so near to fruition, she was in a wild state. Her note to Ian was like a lead weight in her purse, and she was desperate to have it sent.

She slipped it to a footman, claiming that it was a message from her brother to Mr. Clayton, and that she'd offered to deliver it for him. The servants transported dozens of letters every day, so he would convey it to Ian's home without a second thought.

She went in and proceeded to the front parlor, surprised—but not overly so—when she was advised that her mother was sequestered in her private suite and asking that Caroline meet her there.

Determined to conclude the appointment as rapidly as possible, she rushed up, anticipating that her mother would be prone and suffering from some ludicrous complaint. Instead, Britannia was over by the window and scowling down on the driveway where Caroline had been about to depart in the carriage.

They both froze, and Caroline was positive she looked guilty as sin. Instantly, she reverted to form, masking her expression, slowing the violent beating of her heart.

"Mother, I'm told you wanted me."

"Were you going somewhere, Caroline?"

"I'm off on some errands."

"What *errands* are those precisely?"

Caroline had never been adept at prevarication, so it was difficult to lie with any aplomb. "I have a dress fitting, and the hats I ordered are finished."

"I wasn't informed that you'd purchased any clothes."

"You weren't? So sorry. I'm off to fetch them. May I help you with something before I go?"

She stepped toward the hall, as if to indicate that she was in a hurry. Britannia was silent, but she approached and circled Caroline, providing her with the distinct impression that Britannia was blocking her in. Caroline tamped down her annoyance, recognizing that any display of exasperation would only extend the encounter.

Britannia shut the door, and there was an odd finality to the motion, as if it had been closed for good and would never open again. She glared at Britannia, irked to realize that her mother was very angry, and for once, Caroline was in no mood for any dramatic posturing.

She'd spent her whole life politely listening to her mother's diatribes, and her tolerance for a lecture had vanished.

"What is it, Mother? I can see you're upset."

"To whom did you write?"

Caroline was confused by the query. "What?"

"I was watching you. You gave a letter to the footman. To whom was it composed?"

"I wrote no letter," she fibbed. "It was Adam's correspondence. I was merely delivering it for him."

"So if I question your brother, he will verify your story?"

"Why wouldn't he?"

Britannia advanced until they were toe-to-toe, and she towered over Caroline, making her feel small and exposed.

"Tell me about Ian Clayton," Britannia snarled.

It was the last comment Caroline had expected, and her astonishment registered before she was able to conceal it.

"Ian . . . Clayton?" She pretended to be puzzled. "Wakefield's natural brother? Why would you inquire about him?"

"I had a visitor who's relayed the most intriguing tale."

"Really?" Caroline's pulse thudded with dread. "About what?"

"Confess your treachery, Caroline Foster. I would hear it from your own perfidious lips."

"My . . . my . . . treachery? Honestly, Mother. What are you saying?"

"Are you still a virgin? Or have you squandered your most prized asset on that Scottish vagabond?"

"Mother!"

Half-mad with fury, Britannia loomed nearer.

"Were you aware," she seethed, "that I can tie you down and have a midwife examine you to learn for sure?"

"How could you insult me so horridly?" She tried to seize the offensive, but her indignation was too tepid to be believed. "I scarcely know Mr. Clayton. How could you accuse me of dastardly behavior?"

"So . . . it's your ploy to deny culpability?"

"As I've done nothing wrong, of course I'll deny it."

"Liar!" Britannia hissed, and she drew her hand from the fold of her skirt.

Caroline was stunned to see that Britannia clutched a riding whip, and she lurched away as Britannia struck her across the face. She was off balance, and she stumbled to the side, as Britannia hit her again and again, the blows raining down on her head and shoulders, the force driving her to the floor.

She was on her knees, trying to crawl away, but Britannia was in a frenzy, and there was no escaping her wrath.

"Your base blood has gained control of you," her mother raged. "I knew it would eventually! I knew it!"

"Mother, stop!" Caroline begged, but it did no good.

Britannia was practically foaming at the mouth, spewing nonsense and hurling invectives.

"You will marry your father!" she shouted. "You

will be forever joined to the devil that spawned you. I've been waiting all these years for it to happen, and happen it shall! My shame must be avenged!"

"I'm not marrying Father," Caroline said, hoping to inject some sanity into her mother's rant. "I'm marrying Mr. Shelton. I'm marrying Edward."

"Yes, yes, you're marrying your father!"

Chapter FIFTEEN

Y ou'll marry your father! You will! You will!"
Seeming befuddled and out of her mind,
Britannia babbled the strange remark over and
over.

"No, I'm to wed Edward," Caroline soothed, "just
as you asked of me."

"Edward, yes, Edward," Britannia agreed, the lash
slowing, lucidity gradually creeping in. "You will be
his bride, and the two of you will get what you've always deserved."

The whipping ended, and Caroline struggled to regroup, but before she could, Britannia grabbed her and
dragged her to the dressing room. Though Caroline
fought and kicked, Britannia had the strength of ten
men, and with hardly any effort, she pushed Caroline
into the small, windowless space.

Was she to be confined? Was she to be Britannia's
prisoner?

"Mother! What are you doing?"

"You shan't leave this house till the wedding."

"Don't be absurd. I won't stay in here. You can't make me."

"Can't I? I am your lawful parent, and I have spoken with Bernard as to what should be done with your whoring self. He says the ceremony must go forward, and that I may proceed as I see fit to guarantee that it does. You will never be with your precious Ian Clayton again."

She slammed the door and spun the key in the lock. Then she stomped out, each door of the outer chambers slamming, too. Caroline pounded on the wood and cried for help, but no one dared to assist her, so there would be no rescue.

She was all alone.

❧

Jack trudged toward home, his ears burning with cold, his fingers frozen, his coat too thin for the frigid morning air.

After his hideous fight with Ian, he'd spent the night drinking himself silly, and he was stumbling back with his head aching and his pockets empty, but he didn't feel any better than he had when he'd departed in a huff.

He was disgusted with himself, with Ian, with life in general, and he kicked at a rock, sending it skipping down the street. He was walking through a fancy neighborhood, and he scrutinized the large mansions, manicured gardens, brick drives, and wrought-iron fences. What would it be like to live in such splendor? Were any of the wealthy, indolent occupants happy?

As he strolled by one of the gates, he realized it was the Earl of Derby's property. In no hurry, he studied it, and his curiosity was piqued when the front door opened. He watched, mildly interested in who might exit until he saw Rebecca Blake step out, and he was immediately suspicious as to her motives. What reason could she have for stopping by?

No doubt, she was creating mischief for someone, and it was probably Ian. The petty witch!

Jack was livid. He might be furious with Ian, himself, but that didn't mean he'd stand by and let Rebecca harm him. What was she thinking?

He tarried, keeping out of sight till she'd climbed in her coach, and it approached. The driver tugged on the reins, halting as another carriage went by, and Jack seized the opportunity, grabbing for the door and climbing in after her.

She jumped a foot, and muttered, "What the devil?"

"Hello, Rebecca," he said as he plopped down on the seat across from her.

"My heart nearly gave out. Are you insane? You could have been trampled by the horse or crushed by the wheels."

"I'm too tough to be killed."

"Pity," she cooed.

He lounged, a foot negligently tossed over his knee, and he stared her down, using silence to unnerve her, to make her chatter and spew lies about what she'd been doing, but it didn't work. She ignored him and gazed out at the passing buildings.

Ultimately, he broke the impasse, taking a stab at unraveling her plot.

"How is Lady Derby?"

"She's a royal bitch."

"So I've heard."

The silence grew, and she closed her eyes and nestled

against the squab. She looked wretched, and he wondered why.

Was she having second thoughts? Was she suffering a twinge of remorse?

He couldn't imagine it. She would do or say anything to get what she wanted, and she wasn't concerned over who she hurt in the process.

"How could you?" he finally began.

"How could I what?"

"You tattled to Lady Derby."

For a moment, it seemed as if she'd deny the charge; then she murmured, "Leave it be, Jack. It's none of your affair."

"Isn't it?"

"No."

"Everything about Ian is my *affair*. I'll have to tell him what I saw."

"I was visiting Lady Derby. So what?" She shrugged. "Why must you run to him over the least little difficulty? You're like a whiny child in the schoolyard who rushes to the tutor over the smallest infraction."

"Ian deserves to know that you're scheming."

"Who says I'm *scheming*?"

"You are the worst liar."

"I was merely paying a social call. If you don't believe me, ask the Countess."

She appeared guileless and innocent, and if he hadn't understood her quite so well, he might have been fooled. As it was, he yearned to lean over, to clasp her by the shoulders, and shake her till her teeth rattled.

"You're aware of the type of people the Fosters are. If you've been indiscreet, can you envision what they'll do to Lady Caroline?"

"If she's gotten herself into some sort of trouble, why would I care?"

"Yes, Rebecca, why would you?"

He assessed her flawless features, her curvaceous body. She was so beautiful, and she oozed an animal magnetism that was disturbing and exciting. Too bad the pretty package concealed such a black soul.

She was cold as ice, brutal as a slave master. She had a heart of stone beating in her chest.

Why had he ever presumed himself in love with her? Why had he proposed marriage? He was a kind man, a good man. If he'd had the misfortune to ally himself with her, her malice and wickedness would have rubbed off. Eventually, he'd have started to act just like her.

An expression of relief crossed his face, and she snapped, "Why are you grinning?"

"I just realized how lucky I am that you spurned me."

"I'm so glad I could brighten your day."

"I was thinking with my cock rather than my head. I'd have been miserable for the rest of my life."

"I'm sure you're correct. That's why I refused you."

To his surprise, she seemed wounded by his remarks, which was impossible. She had no conscience. No insult could faze her.

She fussed with the curtain, continuing to stare outside. "I'm marrying Ian, Jack. You must forget any absurd notions you had to the contrary."

He hadn't a clue if Ian would wed her or not. Who could predict what a fellow might do to possess a female like Rebecca Blake?

"What if he's decided to marry Lady Caroline instead?"

"Has he?"

To torment her, he replied, "Maybe."

"If he assumes it will happen, he's mad. It doesn't matter what she's told him. She'll never go against her family. He's chasing windmills."

"Is he? If you're so certain of his intentions toward you, why speak to Lady Derby? Of what are you afraid?"

She fumed quietly, then admitted, "I'm terrified that I'll end up old and poor. I'll do anything to escape such a dire fate."

"I've always been poor, but poverty didn't make me cruel or vindictive."

"Bully for you."

The carriage had stalled in traffic, and with the cessation of movement he felt as if he was suffocating. He was desperate to be away, and he reached for the door, anxious to flee as rapidly as he'd arrived.

"Jack!" she said before he could jump.

He peered over his shoulder. Stupidly, he rippled with a wave of hope that she might have changed her mind, that she'd have him, after all.

What the hell was wrong with him? Had he no pride? No sense?

"What?" he barked.

"I'm sorry."

He scoffed. "No, you're not. You've never been sorry about anything in your whole life."

"I *am* sorry," she claimed. "I never meant to hurt you, but you simply can't give me what I require. Why can't you at least try to understand my position?"

"I understand it perfectly. I believed I was in love with you, but it was a chimera. You're not the person I imagined you to be."

"And what sort of person did you suppose I was?"

"I thought you were vulnerable and lonely and in need of a friend. I thought you might come to love me in return."

"I wouldn't have," she candidly advised. "I've never loved anyone. I couldn't have made you happy."

"On that point, Mrs. Blake, we are in complete accord."

He leapt into the street and walked away without a backward glance.

※

W hat does she want?"

"She didn't say, Miss Georgette."

"Well . . . tell her . . . tell her . . . I'm indisposed and to be on her way."

"I doubt she'll heed me. She's made herself comfortable in the front parlor."

Georgie glared at the butler, and she yearned to scold or berate, but she couldn't blame him for being upset. With the indomitable Countess of Derby having barged in at such an ungodly hour, he was at a loss. So was she. What a disaster!

She sighed. "I'll be right down."

"Thank you, Miss."

"You're welcome."

He scurried away, and Georgie paused at the mirror to primp and preen. By all accounts, the Countess was ugly and horrid, and Georgie was determined that their physical differences be visible and blatant.

She started out, and with each stride, she cursed the Earl. Only minutes earlier, having come home late from the theater, she'd shoved him out the door. He'd been gone such a short time that she hadn't so much as changed out of her gown or brushed her hair.

Why couldn't the blasted man control his wife? Had he any notion as to where the Countess was at that very moment?

How she wished her mother, Maude, had returned from her own evening on the town. Georgie would have liked nothing better than to send Maude to skirmish with the Countess. As it was, she was alone, the servants in bed—except for her beleaguered butler—and she'd had too much to drink. She was in no condition to match wits with the older, richer female, and she hoped there wouldn't be a lot of shouting or threats.

She tottered to the stairs and marched down, struggling to appear calm and sober.

"Lady Derby," she greeted as she breezed in, looking young and gay, as if she hadn't a care in the world, as if the wife of her married suitor visited every day.

"Miss Lane."

"How kind of you to call. Feel free to make yourself at home. Oh wait! You already have."

The Countess had seated herself in a large chair on the other side of the room, so Georgie had to cross to her. The placement of the chair, combined with the Countess's bulk and imperiousness, gave Derby a regal air, as if Georgie should bow to the Queen.

"You there, boy!" the Countess summoned the butler who was hovering in the hall. "Pour us both a sherry. Your mistress is going to need it."

Georgie smiled at him, acting as if liquor had been her own idea.

"Yes, Arthur, please pour us a drink."

Arthur stumbled in, his hands shaking as he went

about his business. Once he'd finished, the Countess glowered at him.

"You may take to your bed. What I'm about to say to your mistress is nothing you should overhear." He didn't move, and the Countess snarled, "Go away, you foolish oaf. I won't tell you twice."

"You may leave us, Arthur," Georgie added more gently.

"If you're sure, Miss?"

"I'll be fine." He hesitated, and she said, "I'll see you tomorrow."

He put the bottle on the table between them, then he raced out, and Georgie sat, frowning at the Countess, till his footsteps faded.

The Countess reached for her glass and gestured for Georgie to do the same, and Georgie seized hers and gulped down the contents. She'd meant to daintily swallow, but she was so nervous that she craved its instant effect.

The Countess was silent and dour, which rattled Georgie even more, though she strove to hide it. If the Countess wanted to glumly tarry, Georgie would, too. Georgie could tarry all night.

Locked in a taciturn battle of wills, she found her glass quickly emptied, and she helped herself to a second serving, then a third. As she swilled them down, the Countess smirked—as if Georgie was behaving exactly as planned.

"I'd been informed," the Countess said, "that you're powerless to resist an alcoholic libation."

"Were you?"

"Actually, I know quite a bit about you."

"How interesting."

"Yes, isn't it? I like to learn as much as I can about my enemies."

"Why would you presume us to be *enemies,* Lady Derby?" Georgie was all wide-eyed innocence, all sweet, youthful sincerity. "We both want the same thing."

"And what is that, Miss Lane?"

"Why, we both want Bernard to be happy."

"No, we don't," Derby scoffed. "I don't want him to be happy, at all. In fact, if he fell over dead, I'd be delighted. I hate him. I've always hated him."

Georgie was frightened by the woman's vitriol, and she regretted having come downstairs. There were limits as to what she'd endure in her mother's scheme to snare Lord Derby, and Georgie's having to dawdle in the parlor with his surly wife was more than she could abide.

"Why are you here, Lady Derby?" Georgie grouched. "It's two o'clock in the morning, and I'm exhausted."

"Are you? Poor dear. It must be so draining to constantly frolic with my spouse."

"It's obvious you know where I've been and who I've been with, so let's not play games."

"No, indeed, let's not."

"If you're begging me to desist, you're speaking to the wrong person. *He* pursued me, Lady Derby. *He* chased after me every step of the way, so if there is something you need to say, I suggest you say it to the Earl."

She deemed it an excellent speech that had put the lofty lady in her place, and she had every intention of storming out in a huff, but though she ordered her feet to depart, she couldn't rise.

"I'm fully cognizant of the Earl's despicable tendencies toward pretty girls," the Countess said, "and I will deal with him at the appropriate moment. In the meantime, there's you to consider."

"I keep asking you what you want, but you won't tell me."

"Won't I? How remiss of me."

"Please get it all off your chest. Insult me in every manner you can, then go away and don't come back. I detest scenes, and I'm eager for this one to be over."

"Would you like some more sherry, Miss Lane?"

"No."

"Oh, but I insist."

The Countess refilled the glass that Georgie still held in her hand, but she didn't need more wine. The container slid from her fingers and thudded to the floor, a dark stain spreading on the rug. Georgie recognized that she should bend over and blot up the mess, but she couldn't.

She wasn't feeling very well. Her head was spinning, her stomach queasy. The room had grown overly hot, the air stuffy, and she had the oddest choking sensation in her throat, as if it was beginning to close.

She was panicked, but couldn't act on her terror.

"Would you go?" she inquired, her words slow and slurred.

"But I haven't finished what I came to do."

"And what is that?"

"I'm here to kill you. Didn't you know?"

Georgie should have leapt up and run away, but her pulse had escalated to an alarming rate, and the obstruction in her throat was strangling her. She was paralyzed in her chair, not able to talk, breathe, or move.

"How . . . did . . . you . . ." was all she could manage.

"It was simple. I'd heard you were a drunkard, so I poisoned the sherry."

The Countess was puttering about, cleaning up after herself. She opened the window and dumped the remaining liquor into the yard.

"We can't have any evidence lying around," she explained, "although I doubt your demise will be investigated. The tincture I utilized is extremely lethal, but it leaves no taste or odor. It will be assumed by all that you over-imbibed to the point of mortality. Given your passion for strong spirits, no one will be surprised."

She flashed a malevolent grin. "Who will miss you, Miss Lane? Will anyone?"

Georgie thought that the Earl might, and Maude would be distressed, but only because the flow of money and gifts that the Earl had showered on them would cease. Sadly, she couldn't think of anybody else who would be concerned.

In an excruciating daze, she watched as Lady Derby lifted her and carried her to the sofa. Georgie was laid out, arranged as if for her funeral viewing, her arms over her chest, her toes sticking up. Then the Countess positioned several empty bottles on the floor so it would look as if Georgie had consumed the entire amount.

The pain in her stomach was agonizing, and she felt as if her belly were being stabbed by sharp knives. She couldn't swallow, and her tongue had swelled to a ghastly size.

Help me! she mutely implored. *Do something!*

The crazed Countess seemed to heed her plea. She reached for a knitted throw and tucked it around Georgie's torso, but the thin blanket was useless. Georgie was shivering so hard, freezing and burning up at the same time.

Convulsions racked her, and through it all, the Countess calmly observed.

"Don't worry," the older woman soothed. "The poison works very fast. It will be over before you know it."

She clasped Georgie's hand and took the ruby promise ring that the Earl had placed there.

"I believe I'll keep this as a souvenir." The Countess slipped it onto her fat finger. "You don't mind, do you? You won't be needing it."

She blew out the lamp, turned, and left, so Georgie had to suffer to the end all alone.

Georgie imagined herself rising up and hurrying after her. She'd advise the Countess of all the ways she was stealing her husband, which had been easy since Lady Derby was an obnoxious shrew whom the Earl hated.

But the reality was that Lady Derby had been correct: The poison did indeed work very fast. After a few more desperate minutes, death was a welcomed relief.

Chapter SIXTEEN

I tried to explain to your father about your whoring, but he wouldn't listen."

Caroline stared at her mother, wondering how someone so obviously crazed could appear so sane. A hint of madness glowed in her eyes, but other than that abnormal glimmer, she seemed as fussy and straitlaced as she'd always been.

Caroline was sitting in a chair, pretending to be very meek, when, in fact, she was terrified and confused and angrier than she'd ever been.

She wanted to scream for help, to bring the servants running, but as she'd discovered from her long night of pounding on the door, they wouldn't cross Britannia. She'd trained the staff well. If she locked Caroline in a closet, if she beat and starved Caroline, nary a one would intervene.

Caroline couldn't count on anyone but herself, so she was alert for the slightest inattention by her mother. The minute Britannia's back was turned, Caroline would sneak out and race to Ian. He would protect her.

After he'd received her letter but she hadn't arrived, what must he have thought? Was he panicked and fretting? At any moment, would he rush to her aid?

Or what if the footman hadn't delivered the note? What if Ian didn't know she'd been intending to come? If she never had another chance to speak with him, if he went on assuming she'd chosen Mr. Shelton, she'd never forgive herself.

She had to get away!

"Your father couldn't focus on business," her mother was saying, "so he told me to handle everything."

"He wouldn't want you to be so cruel, Mother."

"Wouldn't he? Do you really suppose he cares? He's been so preoccupied, sticking his rod in that harlot's hole—"

"Mother!"

"—that he won't notice how I treat you."

"Perhaps we should ask Father to come upstairs," Caroline coaxed, anxious for him to see what had happened.

Britannia gave a sinister laugh. "We don't need your father to solve our problem with Ian Clayton."

"We have no *problem* with Mr. Clayton. I scarcely know him."

"I understand your attraction, Caroline. He's a rugged, handsome sort, and after the Wakefield debacle, you were humiliated. It was only natural that you would seek inappropriate comfort."

"I didn't misbehave with Mr. Clayton," she insisted.

As if she hadn't commented, her mother continued, "I, myself, sought physical consolation in the arms of another man when I had my own pathetic fling."

Her mother had had an *amour?* How very peculiar!

"Did you love him?" Caroline probed, trying to find common ground, trying to lower Britannia's guard.

"Love, bah!" she sneered. "He never came for me, even though he swore he would. I was increasing and frightened and alone."

Britannia talked as if she'd been pregnant with her paramour's child. Had Britannia met him before marrying the Earl? Was she claiming that the Earl wasn't Adam's father? Or had there been no child? Was Britannia so deranged she simply imagined there was?

"It must have been awful," Caroline soothed. "I'm sorry for you."

"Why would you be sorry? I learned a valuable lesson—as you have not—that there is nothing but treachery in the world. Now as to how we'll proceed . . ."

She walked to the window and peered outside, studying something only she could see. She held up her hand, and she was wearing a ruby ring on her smallest finger. Grinning, she looked at it like the cat that had eaten the canary; then she whipped around, her expression cold and stony, once more.

"The wedding will go forward, and your indiscretion will remain our little secret."

"I can't do it for you, Mother."

"Your opinion is completely irrelevant."

"But I—"

"Be silent, Caroline. I'm weary of your protests. I selected Edward for you, and there's no use quarreling."

"And if I refuse?"

"I'll murder your beloved Mr. Clayton."

"What?"

"You heard me: I shall kill Mr. Clayton. I would rather see him dead than let you defy me."

"What an absurd threat." Caroline scoffed. "I've

known you all my life. As if I'd believe you'd . . . you'd . . . *kill* someone."

"You presume I wouldn't?"

"I'm positive you wouldn't. You seem to be experiencing some type of noxious spell, and so far, I've humored you, but I won't listen to any more of your ranting. It can't be healthy. I have to advise Father that you're ill."

Britannia chuckled. "You won't have to notify Bernard. He'll be apprised soon enough."

"What do you mean?"

"I killed his mistress."

"You did not."

"I did."

"When?"

"Last night, while you were locked in my dressing room. I went to her home and murdered her."

"With what?"

"With poison—the spurned woman's weapon. What would you expect? It was extremely satisfying, too."

"You can't be serious."

"Oh, but I am. He'll stop haranguing about a divorce, and when the next pretty girl catches his eye, he'll think twice about becoming involved with her." She gazed at the ruby ring, twirling it round and round on her finger. "If I'd been aware of how easy it was to accomplish, I'd have started doing it years ago. It would have saved me so many headaches."

Caroline's mind reeled with questions: Could her mother actually have done such a terrible thing? Could she have stooped to homicide? Did Caroline know her, at all? From where had this bloodthirsty stranger sprung?

"You're stark-raving mad," Caroline murmured.

"Yes, I suppose I am," Britannia agreed, which made it so much worse. "Now then, let's go down to dinner. After, I'll lock you in again, which is where you will spend every minute until the ceremony."

"I have to tell, Mother," she declared. "I have to tell everyone what you did."

"Who will you tell, Caroline? Who would believe that I—the Countess of Derby—would bother with murdering a strumpet? Your father's had dozens. And don't forget: If you whisper a word of this, I will kill Mr. Clayton. I'm afraid I'll have to insist on it. So . . . you can marry Edward, as I've requested, and your precious Ian will be safe forever. Or you can tattle, and he will be dead shortly. The choice is yours. What will it be?"

She opened the door, gesturing into the hall as if it were an ordinary day, as if they'd been having a pleasant mother-daughter chat.

"Let's go down, shall we? I'm starving."

She strolled out, fully anticipating that Caroline would tag along without argument.

Shaken, stunned, Caroline rose and trailed after her.

❧

Bernard, this came for you. The messenger said it was urgent."

Britannia was holding a sealed note, and Bernard scowled.

"Who is it from?"

"Your latest trollop. Or perhaps her mother. I'm told something has happened and the girl was incapable of writing herself. Isn't she a drunkard? She was probably too intoxicated to pick up a pen."

His heart skipped several beats. "Give it to me."

He snatched it away and tore at the seal. The sentences seemed to swim on the page, and he had to read it over and over before they made any sense.

"Georgie!" he gasped, and he collapsed onto the nearest chair.

"Are you all right, Bernard? Is it bad news? Oh, how I hope it is!"

He skimmed the note again, the import sinking in. "You were there! You were the last to see her alive."

"Was I? How intriguing."

"What were you doing?"

"I tried bribing her to stay away from you—as any rich, sane wife would do. I offered her a fortune, too, but the stupid child refused it. It must have been true love, after all."

She giggled and fluttered her hand over her enormous bosom, and he was shocked to find that she was wearing Georgie's ring. He was sure it was hers!

Could Britannia have . . . ? Oh, he couldn't finish the thought!

"Where did you get that ring?" he asked, aghast but struggling to remain calm.

"This old thing?" She waved it about as if she'd forgotten she had it on. "You gave it to me ages ago. Don't you remember?"

Speculating, horrified, inconsolable, he gawked at her.

His dear Georgie! She'd brought him such joy! Had Britannia been so jealous that she'd been driven to homicide? Was it possible?

"If I ever learn that you were responsible for this atrocity, I'll . . . I'll . . ."

"You'll what?"

It was a valid question. What could he do to her? Who would believe that his countess, his spouse of thirty years, would suddenly commit murder?

"If I discover that it was you," he warned, "I'll strangle you with my own two hands."

"You haven't the nerve."

She spun and left him to stew and grieve all alone.

҂

I an paced across his parlor, his anxiety rising, his worry extreme.

Caroline's letter was clutched in his fist, and he'd read it a thousand times. She'd sworn she was coming so that they could elope to Scotland.

Where was she?

He'd waited all night. He'd waited all morning, but she hadn't arrived, and he didn't know what her non-appearance indicated or what he should do about it.

Should he continue to wait? Should he storm to her father's house and demand to speak with her? Or should he face reality and admit that she hadn't been serious?

Just then, carriage wheels sounded on the street. He raced to the window and peered out, delighted to see the Earl's coach pulling up.

She'd come! She'd come at last!

On pins and needles, he tarried, much too eager for his first glimpse of her, but as the footman lowered the step, it wasn't Caro who emerged.

The Countess lumbered out, and as she approached, his dread spiraled.

What did the visit portend? He steeled himself against disappointment, against the mortification and regret that he was certain the Countess would make him feel.

He stood, gaping and frozen, curious as to how their liaison had been exposed. Had Caro confessed it? Had someone else? Did it matter how the Countess had been apprised? Probably not. The damage was done, and he could only move through the aftermath.

"Hello, Mr. Clayton," she said as the butler showed her in.

"Lady Derby." He tipped his head. "Shall we sit?"

"There's no need. This isn't a social call, and I intend to be brief."

She glanced at Caro's note that he still held.

"Since you obviously know why I am here," she began, "I'll be blunt."

"By all means," he mocked.

"Lady Caroline isn't coming."

He'd already surmised as much, but it hurt to have her voice the truth aloud.

"I've been wondering what happened, so thank you for stopping by."

He gestured to the door, wanting her to grasp that their meeting was ended, but he should have known it wouldn't be easy to get rid of her.

She jeered, "I'm not sure why you had the gall to initiate this affair."

He shrugged, loathing her tone, and determined to aggravate her as much as he was able. "It seemed like the thing to do at the time."

"I understand how your connection to Lord Wakefield has skewed your view of your place in relation to an exalted family such as ours."

"My brother definitely let me run amok. Because of him, I'm always putting on airs."

He was being sarcastic, but she nodded in agreement, deeming him sincere.

"I imagine you thought you'd become rich if you married her. I imagine you thought her father would eventually pardon you and give you some of her dowry."

"It was at the top of my list of reasons," he lied.

"I hate to have you thwarted financially."

"Do you?"

"Money difficulties can make a fellow behave in desperate ways."

"Yes, they can."

"This development could leave you in a fiscal crunch, so I'm prepared to remunerate you for your troubles." She passed over an envelope. "It's a bank draft. Cash it, and the full amount is yours."

He peeked inside, his eyes widening at the large sum. "Why, Lady Derby, this is too much. What am I to assume? You must want something in exchange."

"Of course I do. I'm buying your discretion."

"Well, this should purchase an enormous quantity of it."

"Don't be smart with me. I won't have stories circulating about some ridiculous *amour* between the two of you. Nor will I have you slithering out of the woodwork to ruin her wedding. I'm told you're a pragmatic man, Mr. Clayton."

"I am."

"So you can see how I might worry over your future comments."

"Oh, absolutely."

"I'm simply nipping scandal in the bud."

"Silence is golden?"

"Quite. You'll cash the draft?"

"I'd be a fool not to."

"You certainly would."

"There's just one catch."

She sighed. "Why am I not surprised? What is it?"

"You must tell me why she changed her mind."

"Does it matter why?"

"To me it does."

She chuckled, her disdain oozing through. "She was never going to run off with you, Mr. Clayton. You're aware of the type of person she is. She could no more shirk her duty than she could sprout wings and fly."

"So it was all a lark for her?"

She considered, then shook her head. "No, she had genuine feelings for you, but she wouldn't have acted on them. It was humorous for her to ponder another sort of life, but it was naught but a romantic fantasy."

It was just as he'd suspected. Caro was who she was: the beautiful, spoiled daughter of an earl. She was like an angel in heaven, whom he could adore and worship from afar, but could never have for his own.

He knew better than to have made plans, but still, he was a contrary individual. The more a snob such as Lady Derby put him in his place, the harder he fought to stay where he didn't belong.

"If Caroline is so happy over choosing Mr. Shelton, why didn't she come with you and inform me herself?"

"She has no desire to see you ever again. She'd be embarrassed."

"Embarrassed?"

"Yes. She was fond of you, and she feels terrible about trifling with your affections."

He tried to picture Caro conversing with her mother, saying the words the Countess attributed to her, but he couldn't get the vision to gel.

What if she hadn't said them, at all? What if the

Countess had bullied or punished her? What if Caro hadn't arrived because her mother had prevented her?

As the prospect arose, he suffered the silliest spurt of gladness. He was so thrilled to hope that she hadn't forsaken him, and the obvious conclusion finally became apparent: He loved her. He'd always loved her. How could he not have known?

"Guess what, Lady Derby?"

"What?"

"I have another condition."

"Oh, for pity's sake. What is it?"

"I will take your money and go on my merry way, provided I'm allowed to speak to Caroline myself. I want to hear from her own lips that she'd rather have Edward Shelton than me."

She hadn't counted on him demanding anything so rash, and she turned beet red, her eyes bulging out of their sockets. The temper for which she was renowned began to exert itself.

"You may not see her."

"How will you stop me? London—for all its size—is a very small town."

"The wedding is in three days, Mr. Clayton. I think we can keep you away from her for three days."

"Maybe so, but how will you quell my vicious tongue? If you won't let me talk to her, I'll spread gossip hither and yon. The minute you walk out my door, I'll commence tattling."

"You dare to threaten me, Mr. Clayton?"

She approached until they were toe-to-toe, and she was a formidable sight. A lesser mortal might have been alarmed to witness all that pent-up wrath.

"I'm not afraid of you," he boasted, "so there's no need to bluster."

"Your courage is impressive, but your posturing is a waste of energy."

"Is it?"

"Let me be more clear: You will not see Caroline. You will whisper no rumors. You will do nothing but take the windfall I've offered and slink away to some obscure location where we will never again be bothered by your despicable self."

"As I previously stated, how will you stop me?"

"Even if you wreck her chance with Mr. Shelton, she will never be permitted to marry you."

"Why would you presume you'll have a say in the matter? She's of age. All she need do is escape your clutches and come to me. I'll whisk her off to Scotland and be married to her before you realize she's gone."

"But it will never happen, Mr. Clayton. That's what you fail to understand."

"How have I miscalculated?"

"If she does not wed Edward, we will commit her to an insane asylum."

The possibility was so shocking and so casually delivered that he sucked in a stunned breath before he could mask it. His reaction supplied her with evidence of his most vulnerable spot—which was Caro—and she would use the weakness to his detriment.

"You wouldn't," he tried to claim.

"Wouldn't we? We've already picked out the facility. She will remain there, sequestered in the common rooms with the other lunatics for the rest of her days—which will be short in number when you consider the filth, disease, and criminal activity in those places."

"An asylum!" he muttered, and he shivered.

"Should a child result from her fornication with you, it will be drowned at birth, the corpse tossed in the pauper's grave behind the building. I will see to it myself."

"Why?" was all he could ask.

"She will do as I say. She will not disobey me."

He was struggling to regroup and have the last word. He couldn't bear to acknowledge that she'd gotten the better of him—even though she had.

"You're quite good with your threats."

"I'm not a woman to be crossed."

"I've never supposed you were."

"Caroline has a fine life stretching ahead of her. It guarantees an excellent marriage to one of her own kind, and an ideal—if somewhat subdued—existence as the wife of an important gentleman."

"You don't make it sound like much of a blessing."

"For most females, it's more than enough."

"Not for her."

"Who are you to judge what she needs?"

"I'm the man who loves her," he boldly asserted, amazed that he'd finally declared himself, and to *her* of all people.

"If you actually love her—and I must admit I'm dubious—then you should do right by her. You should disappear without creating a fuss, and let her quietly and privately wed Mr. Shelton."

"But that's not what's best for her! You haven't a clue what would be best!"

"And you do? Why? Because you crawled between her thighs a few times?"

He was staggered by her crudity, by her cold, hard demeanor, and he thought of Caro and what it must have been like to be raised by such a brutal, heartless witch. He was astounded that the Countess hadn't drummed out every spark of compassion and decency.

"I know what Edward Shelton is like," he pressed, "and I suspect you do, too. If you would bind her to him—in spite of his proclivities—you're a monster."

"A monster?" She laughed in an unnatural way that sent chills down his spine. "I've been called much worse."

"I'll just bet you have," he agreed. "Why would you do this to her?"

"Mr. Clayton, you are a baseborn, poverty-stricken nobody. Why I decide to do anything is none of your business."

She started out, and he was so angry that he seriously contemplated rushing over and beating her to a bloody pulp. The urge was so intense that he could practically see her collapsed on the floor.

"I won't let you get away with this," he insisted. "I'll talk to the Earl."

"Will you? You seem to have forgotten our devil's bargain: You can be silent and she'll have a husband, children to mother, and the other niceties that all women crave. Or you can stir up trouble, and give her the asylum and the drowned, dead baby, instead. The choice is yours. Will you be responsible for killing your own child? I doubt it, so I suggest you think carefully about what it is you wish to do."

She left, and Ian went to the window and watched as her servants hefted her into her coach. He tarried, observing, till the team of horses pulled her away, and he lingered long after she'd vanished down the street.

His mind whirred with all the things he should have said, all the things he should have done, and he felt like a fool.

Why had he stood in his own parlor, in his own

home, and permitted the old shrew to hurl insult after insult? When had he turned into such a milksop?

He trudged to the sideboard and poured himself a whiskey, sipping it as he reviewed his options.

He refused to believe the Countess, and he had to confront Caro directly. If she told him to go away, that she hadn't been earnest, so be it. But he had to know for sure. If she was in danger, or if they'd locked her away, and she was hoping he'd come for her, he had to arrive. He couldn't abandon her to the fate her mother had engineered.

He had to see her, but how should he proceed? If he politely knocked on the Earl's door, he couldn't expect to be welcome, so there wasn't any reason to be courteous. So . . . he'd begin by knocking—like a civilized human being—but if courtesy didn't work, he'd be a bit *un*civilized. After all, he was half-Scot, his full name Ian *MacDonald* Clayton. The blood of centuries of warriors flowed in his veins.

Maybe it was time to remember the MacDonald clan's war cry.

He rose and hurried to the hall, shouting for his horse to be saddled.

Chapter SEVENTEEN

Father, wait!"

Bernard ignored Caroline's mournful summons and kept walking. He was heartsick and drained, fearful over what Britannia might have done, and fretting over what his next act should be.

Should he go to the authorities? Should he speak out regarding his suspicions and implicate his wife in murder? He was too distraught to think clearly or make rational decisions. His family was more detested than ever, their tiresome demands like a buzzing gnat he yearned to swat away.

He wasn't concerned about Caroline's petty troubles and wouldn't listen to her trivial complaints. The bloody girl had been given everything—everything!—but she constantly whined about her plight.

He reached his library, his sanctuary, and had almost shut the door, when she caught up to him.

"Father!"

He whipped around. "What is it, Caroline? Must you hound me in the halls like an annoying beggar?"

His virulent look brought her up short, and as they came face-to-face, he saw that she had a bruise under her eye, as if she'd been punched. Though he was disturbed by the prospect, he wasn't worried enough to inquire as to how she'd received it.

He was dying inside! Dying! He hadn't the energy for her silly chatter, and he wished he could utter a magic spell and make her vanish.

"I need your help," she tediously claimed.

"Well, I don't choose to give it."

"Please?"

She placed her hand on his arm, and he promptly removed it.

"You're trying my patience," he snapped.

"Why? Merely because I've asked for an audience with your eminent self?"

"Yes. Merely because of that."

"It's Mother," she persisted.

"Isn't it always?"

"She says I must marry Mr. Shelton, and she—"

"Of course you shall marry Mr. Shelton. I won't hear otherwise."

At his gruff treatment, she appeared so young, so hurt, and he suffered a small twinge of conscience, but it was a *small* twinge. Did she suppose she was the only person in the world who was unhappy? Did she suppose she was the only person in the world who had problems?

She was an ungrateful, spoiled child.

"Don't you care," she pressed, "that I'll be miserable for the rest of my days?"

"No, I don't. You're my daughter, and you will do as I bid you. Stop pestering me!"

"Mother is insane."

"Yes, she is. Have you only just now noticed?"

"She beat me!"

"Well, if you were behaving as you are currently, you deserved it. Someone should have pounded some sense into you years ago."

"But she actually contends that she kill—"

"How many times must I explain the situation?" he hissed, cutting her off. "I arranged the best match that was available. Why continue with your quibbling?"

"Is it *quibbling* when I inform you that I am terrified of the man and what he will do to me once I'm his wife?"

"It is Mr. Shelton, or no one," he tersely said. "Why can't you understand?"

"If those are my two options—Mr. Shelton or no one—then I would rather have no one."

"Would you? What about what I want? Which is to have you out of my hair at the earliest possible moment."

He'd finally been sufficiently brutal that her banter ceased. She gaped at him, stunned, incredibly sad, her big blue eyes filling with tears. She was such a beautiful, tragic figure, and for a fleeting instant, he was ashamed.

She was a daughter any father should have loved unconditionally, a daughter to make any father proud, but he'd never felt a connection to her. The fact that she had Britannia's blood flowing in her veins was repellent. They'd never been close, and to his surprise, he suddenly and vehemently regretted the distance that separated them.

Yet as quickly as the absurd sentiment occurred to him, he shook it away. She was nothing to him! Nothing!

She would wed Edward Shelton, because if she didn't, Bernard would have to fuss with her all over again. How many husbands was he required to find for her? How often should he have to wallow in the marriage market and drag out the last apple at the bottom of the barrel?

After the Wakefield debacle, she was lucky there was somebody willing to have her! She should be glad! She should be celebrating!

"Am I such a burden to you?" she asked. "Is it all I've ever been?"

"Yes," he said, not meaning it and wondering when he'd grown so cruel.

At being disavowed, she jerked back as if he'd slapped her.

I'm sorry, Caro, he yearned to say, but he couldn't form the apology.

"Go away!" he ordered instead. "Leave me be."

"I will, and you needn't worry. I won't bother you ever again."

Britannia saved them both by appearing at the end of the hall.

"Caroline!" she yapped. "What did I tell you about badgering your father?"

"You insisted that he wouldn't listen, and you were correct."

"Come away from there at once," Britannia commanded.

"Madam," Bernard barked at Britannia, "you must supervise your daughter's grievances without involving me. These household crises are none of my affair, yet she keeps carping about them. I'm weary of her protests."

At his stern rebuke, Britannia seemed to ripple with triumph. "How can I make matters clearer to you, Caroline? In the subject of your marriage, the Earl and

I are united in our resolve to have it transpire. It's futile to persist with your objections."

She continued screeching, her voice like cartwheels grating on rocks. "I warned you, Caroline, of what would happen if you whined to anyone. Must I now carry out my threat?"

"You wouldn't dare," Caroline retorted.

"Wouldn't I?"

Whatever intimidation Britannia had devised to force the nuptials, Caroline was chastened into silence, and he used the awkward interval to escape, slipping into the library and slamming the door, the action defying either of them to follow. To be on the safe side, he spun the key in the lock, sealing himself in.

He stumbled to his desk and sat, his head in his hands. He wanted to visit Georgie's home, to offer condolences and chat about the funeral, but he couldn't embroil himself in the sordid situation.

His life stretched before him, an empty void, and he couldn't imagine how he'd ever be happy again. He suffered all alone, lamenting, mourning, so it was a great irritation when a ruckus erupted in the hall and footsteps marched in his direction.

"You can't go in there!" a servant pronounced.

"The hell I can't," a very angry, very determined male replied.

Bernard frowned as the interloper tried the knob.

"Sir!" the indignant servant huffed.

Before Bernard knew what to think, the furious fellow began kicking down the door. Gad! Was it the law? Had they come to question him about Georgie and Britannia? What should he say? What should he do?

"Sir! Sir!"

The servant was shouting, but to no effect, as wood splintered and the man stormed in.

From the commotion, Bernard had been expecting a horde, so when he saw that it was only Ian Clayton he blinked and blinked, his mind struggling to make sense of the sight.

"Mr. Clayton?" he muttered as he rose.

There were two footmen on his heels, and they'd each clasped an arm, but Clayton was so irate that he shook them off as if they were a breeze of wind. They lunged to grab him again, but Bernard gestured for them to desist.

"We tried to stop him, milord," one of them said.

"It's all right," Bernard answered. "Mr. Clayton is an acquaintance. I'll meet with him. You're excused."

They departed, Clayton sullenly staring as their strides faded, and Bernard was irked by his presence. Bernard had no desire to talk to Clayton, but it was obvious that Clayton was in a state over some perceived slight. If he wasn't allowed to vent his wrath, he'd likely tear down the entire house.

"What is it, Mr. Clayton? And might I suggest you be brief?"

Looking noble and splendid, like some ancient Celtic warrior, bent on mayhem, Clayton approached. They faced each other across the desk, and Bernard didn't invite him to sit, nor did Clayton anticipate any courtesy.

Clayton braced his feet and announced, "I want to marry Lady Caroline."

"You want to what?"

"I want to marry Lady Caroline—as rapidly as the details can be finalized. I ask for your permission and your blessing."

"Don't be ridiculous. I'd never agree. Your appointment is concluded. Shall I have the butler show you out, or can you find your own way?"

"For the prior month, she and I have been having an affair."

"You have not, and I would caution you to be wary of your wagging tongue. I won't have my family slurred."

"Even as we speak, she could be increasing with my child."

Bernard studied him. He seemed very sincere, and though Bernard had heard many stories about his character, he'd never heard that Clayton had a penchant for fabrication or deceit. He was generally an honorable person, which—considering his blood relatives—was saying a lot.

Why would he lie about something so vital? What purpose would be served by telling tales and ruining Caroline's wedding? Clayton wasn't cruel in the manner his father or brother could be, so what was he hoping to accomplish?

A pathetic notion dawned. There'd been gossip that—having fought with Wakefield—Clayton was in dire financial straits. Caroline's husband would receive a substantial dowry.

Would he spread rumors just to get his hands on her fortune? Was he that desperate?

Money—or the lack of it—made people behave in strange ways, and if poverty was driving him, he'd be capable of any treachery. He was half-Scot and half-Clayton, so there wasn't a man in the kingdom who had a more contemptible lineage.

Bernard would put nothing past him.

"What are you really after, Mr. Clayton?"

"I told you: I wish to marry your daughter."

"Why?"

"Because I . . . I . . . love her."

Bernard was extremely surprised. He'd never expected such a strident declaration, especially one that had been so difficult for Clayton to utter. It seemed to have been wrenched from his very soul.

"You *love* her?"

"Yes."

There was no prevarication, no hesitation. Could it be? Had Caroline commenced an affair with him? How could she repeatedly sneak out undetected?

If Clayton's account was true, if the pair had instigated a catastrophe, heads would roll! Starting with theirs, then moving on to whoever should have halted the foolish flirtation but hadn't.

"Does she love you back, Mr. Clayton?"

"I couldn't say, Lord Derby."

"You couldn't? And why is that? Were there no promises made?"

"She is a woman. I couldn't begin to guess her opinion."

"If I accused you of sniffing after her dowry, I suppose you'd be offended."

"I suppose you'd be correct, and if you ever again voice such a dastardly insinuation about my integrity, I'll come around the desk and beat you to a pulp."

Bernard eased down in his chair, frowning at the younger man. He perceived genuine emotion, and he was humored that Clayton felt so strongly about Caroline. If Bernard had possessed any fondness for her, he might have been proud that someone could love her as much as Clayton seemed to.

Bernard couldn't remember ever being so passionate about anything. His life was all gray, smooth edges and always had been. There'd been no great swings from joy to despair, until Georgie, and even his grief was blunted. He simply didn't know how to feel powerful sentiment.

Clayton loved her, did he? So what?

"No," he murmured.

"No, what?" Clayton inquired.

"You may not have her. I'm amazed that you had the gall to ask. Please go home and don't return."

A weariness crept over him, and he wanted to drag himself upstairs, to crawl into bed and stay there forever.

"Summon her," Clayton annoyingly commanded. "I would speak to her at once."

"Get out!" Bernard motioned toward the door. "Go on your own, or I shall call for the footmen and have them cart you off like so much rubbish."

Looking lethal, Clayton leaned forward, braced on his palms. "Do you think they could?"

They engaged in a visual standoff that Bernard was in no condition to wage. He just wanted to be left alone, but Clayton was in an awful temper, and Bernard couldn't imagine the brawl that might ensue if he didn't relent. People might be injured or even maimed, which was demanding too much of any employee.

"What are you assuming she'll say, Mr. Clayton?"

Clayton dropped into a chair without its being offered, and the tense moment passed. "We were set to elope—"

"Elope!"

"She wrote to me that she was coming, but she never arrived."

"Show me the letter."

"I didn't bring it with me."

"Of course you didn't," Bernard smirked. "So what would you have me do?"

"I have to know if she was merely toying with me, or if your wife intimidated her into changing her mind. If Caroline didn't mean any of it, then I'll leave your family in peace, but I have to hear it directly from her. I have to know that she's all right."

"I must advise you, Mr. Clayton, that Caroline and I recently discussed her marriage. She's not too keen on Mr. Shelton, but her reasons had nothing to do with you. Your name never came up in the conversation."

"I want to hear it from Caroline," he stonily repeated.

Another staring match developed, as Bernard tried to figure out the best path. With Caroline's wedding only days away, Clayton was a loose cannon who could wreak havoc. Shouldn't Bernard agree to a confrontation? Clayton had to be placated, then silenced, or he'd career through London, spewing stories that couldn't be retracted.

Bernard knew Caroline. She would never shame herself by admitting to such a filthy liaison. It was wisest to let the pair meet, and Caroline would put an end to Clayton's drivel. Bernard wouldn't have to do anything.

He rang for the butler and instructed the man to locate Caroline and escort her to the library.

"If she contradicts you, Mr. Clayton, and tells me there was no affair, you will be good at your word and go away."

"I will be good at my word, sir."

"Don't get your hopes up."

"We'll see," Clayton said.

They watched the door, waiting for Caroline to step through and join them.

🙎

aroline walked down the stairs, feeling like a felon at the gallows.

As she approached the room, her mother emerged from the shadows. Caroline pulled up short and they glared, a thousand hateful messages flowing between them. They were fighting a private war, and her father—without knowing any of the facts—had sided with Britannia.

Caroline hadn't even had the chance to apprise him of Britannia's claims that she'd killed his mistress—a pesky detail that would definitely interest him—and Caroline wouldn't enlighten him now. He was no ally, and due to his odious conduct, he'd never receive the crucial information. He could go hang!

She was on her own, would have to chart her own course, and her primary goal was to ensure that Britannia hurt no one else.

"Remember what I told you," Britannia said.

"And what is that?"

"If you don't marry Edward, I will murder Mr. Clayton." She raised a brow, her confidence alarming and sickening. "It might not happen today, and it might not happen tomorrow. But it *will* happen and soon. I guarantee it."

Caroline ignored her and swept into the Earl's library. She'd only been allowed in it on a handful of occasions, so she should have felt honored. Instead, she was disgusted by the pomposity and fake grandeur it symbolized.

He was seated at his desk in the rear, and there was another man with him, when she couldn't fathom why he'd want anyone to overhear their conversation.

Head high, shoulders squared for combat, she marched toward him.

"Thank you for coming, Caroline."

"Father." She nodded.

"I believe you know Mr. Clayton?"

He gestured to his visitor, forcing her to look at him.

Ian was the last person on earth she'd been expecting, and his presence was so odd and so unanticipated that she was confused about what it indicated.

He was so beautiful, so angry and alone, and she'd just turned to throw herself into his arms, to beg him to save her, when he rose and furiously said, "Your eye has been blackened. Were you beaten?"

"I . . . I . . . ran into a pole."

She had no idea why she lied. The thrashing administered by the Countess had been too humiliating, and she couldn't admit to it. For some reason, she felt as if *she* was at fault for it having transpired.

"A pole?" he asked, incredulous.

"It was a stupid accident."

"It certainly must have been."

It was the moment when he might have reached for her to bridge the distance between them, but her coolly delivered falsehood restrained him. They seemed to be strangers, and the opportunity to stand united in front of her father evaporated in an instant.

The Earl interrupted her reverie.

"Mr. Clayton has made some wild accusations."

"About what?"

"He claims that the two of you have been having an affair. Is it true?"

She was mortified to have her father mention such private business, and she had no background that would enable her to confer over salacious details. She scarcely knew her father, and as the past few weeks had revealed, he cared nothing for her or her welfare. She was merely a burden he was tired of assuming. How could he suppose she'd blithely confess to licentious misdeeds?

Footsteps sounded behind her, and she glanced around, dismayed to see Britannia lurking. Her eyes glowed, the insanity wafting out, smothering Caroline with her evil intentions.

Caroline's heart began to race, her palms to sweat.

She thought about Ian, about how much she loved him, about how she couldn't cause him harm. If she disavowed him to her parents, he'd never forgive her, yet if she spoke up, she'd deliberately place him in peril. What was best?

"I have sneaked off with him a few times," she cautiously disclosed.

"So it was naught but a lark?"

She shrugged, which could have signified any number of responses. It mollified her mother, confounded her father, and exasperated Ian.

"He says it was more involved than that," the Earl charged. "In fact, he says that the two of you were planning to elope. Were you?"

"He had suggested it," she acknowledged. She felt as if she was negotiating a battlefield. One wrong move and she'd be blown to bits.

"He insists that you agreed to go, then didn't arrive." The Earl scoffed as if the story was ridiculous. "I've advised him that you didn't follow through because you weren't serious and that you're proceeding with your wedding to Mr. Shelton."

Ian butted in. "Tell me the truth, Caro. What has your mother done to you?"

"Stay out of this, Mr. Clayton," the Earl snapped; then he addressed Caroline again. "Mr. Clayton is laboring under the mistaken impression that you were coerced into changing your mind, when we all know that you would never shame me by running off and doing something so horrid. Isn't that right?"

He was so smugly confident of what her reply would be. He'd always terrorized her, had always cowed her, and he presumed that he could on this occasion, too. She peered at him, at her mother. When they hated her, and Ian loved her, was there really any doubt as to what her answer should be?

She had to pick a side, and Ian was the easy choice.

She opened her mouth to talk, when Britannia stepped into the circle of light cast by the lamp on the desk.

"I've counseled her on this topic," Britannia said. "She understands that her actions have consequences, and she will behave accordingly."

Ian hadn't realized Britannia was present, and he whipped around and snarled, "Shut up, you old bat. No one asked your opinion."

The Earl leapt to his feet. "That's enough, Mr. Clayton. I've been more than courteous. Good-bye."

"She bribed me," Ian alleged. "She barged into my home and offered me a huge sum of money to disappear."

"That's a bald-faced lie!" the Countess sneered. "As if I'd lower myself!"

The encounter disintegrated, with Ian hurling more accusations, Caroline's mother denying them, and the Earl bellowing for footmen to attend him. Several burly ones dashed into the room. They rushed for Ian, grabbed him, and started wrestling him out.

"Come with me, Caro," he roared over the din. "I know you want to! Don't stay here with them!"

Her mother leaned in and whispered, "If you go, I'll kill him. You'll be responsible for his death. Is that the conclusion you desire?"

Ian was shouting, her father was shouting, while her mother was murmuring a litany of the painful effects of poison. Caroline was dizzy, caught in a whirlwind. Ian's affection pulled her to him, but her parents' malice doused any display of bravado. She was paralyzed with indecision, yearning to flee with him, but desperate to protect him, too.

Ian was in the threshold of the library, struggling with the servants. He was so far away, as if at the other end of a long tunnel, and he was indistinct, his shape blurring, the edges fuzzy.

For a brief second, Time seemed to stop, and there was just the two of them.

"Caro!" he begged. "Come! Please! Don't do this for them. You don't have to!"

Britannia clasped her arm and brutally pinched it, her fingers digging deeply enough to bruise.

"I'll murder him," she hissed. "I mean it."

Caroline blinked, and Ian was gone.

"Ian!" she cried, but he couldn't have heard her over the commotion.

Britannia pushed her into a chair, then braced her hands on either side, blocking her in.

"Ian!" she attempted again, but Britannia clamped her palm over Caroline's mouth, stifling any further outburst.

She and her parents were frozen in place, waiting as

the noise in the foyer abated, as Ian was tossed bodily into the street. Silence descended, and Britannia glared over at the Earl.

"She's completely out of control," Britannia said. "What should I do with her?"

"Whip her, then lock her in her bedchamber," he ordered.

"I already tried that. Obviously, it didn't work."

"Whip her harder," the Earl urged. "If you have to, use a thicker belt. Now take her away and leave me be."

Britannia jerked Caroline to her feet and led her out.

Caroline stumbled along, like a puppet on a string, terrified over what would happen next.

Chapter EIGHTEEN

H ow dare you butt your nose into my private affairs."

"I didn't," Rebecca insisted.

"Liar," Ian hissed.

He was across the room, sitting in the dark, the light of a single candle illuminating him. He'd been drinking, and he was very, very angry. She kept her distance, nervous about approaching him when he was in such a state.

"Truly, Ian," she persisted, "you seem upset, and I'm confused as to why. What's wrong?"

"Jack tattled, Rebecca."

Jack again! The bastard! What was his problem? Why was he so determined to ride a moral high horse?

"What has he said?"

He narrowed his gaze, focusing in, peering to the center of her wicked soul, but she didn't flinch from his scrutiny. She wouldn't cower to any man.

On seeing that he couldn't rattle her, he shook his

head with derision. "My God, but you're a nasty piece of work."

"You call it *nasty;* I call it pragmatic."

She was weary of his superior attitude. By going to the Countess as she had, she'd acted out of self-preservation, and she wouldn't be sorry for thinking of her own needs first. She had no regrets.

Well, maybe a few, but they weren't worth noting.

"Have you any idea," he snarled, "what her parents are like? Can you begin to imagine what they'll do to her?"

"Her dilemma is none of my concern," she replied, giving up the pretense. "Why was she sniffing around anyway? She had to realize there'd be consequences if she was caught."

"How can you rationalize your conduct?"

"She was completely indiscreet, visiting you at all hours. If I hadn't told, someone else would have. It was only a matter of time."

"So that makes your perfidy all right?"

"What do you mean? I was doing you a favor."

"A favor! If this meddling is your concept of a *favor,* promise that you'll spare me from any more of your good deeds."

She was intrigued by the notion that she'd merely been trying to help—it sounded less terrible than the reality—and she pressed on.

"Honestly, Ian, you're behaving as if she was the love of your life. You're making too much of it."

"Am I?"

"Yes, you know what she was like," Rebecca said.

"What was she *like?* I can't wait to have you tell me."

"She was a flighty, pampered child. She always was."

"Your point being?"

"She was having a spot of fun before she entered into her stuffy marriage to Edward Shelton. But her fling is over, the wedding is almost here, and we'll all move on."

She took a step toward him, then a few more, coming closer, as if her remarks had smoothed the route. When she drew near enough to see his face clearly, she was stunned to discover that he was distraught in a fashion she'd never presumed he could be.

"You cared for her," she accused.

After a lengthy pause, he admitted, "Yes, I did."

He grabbed a whiskey bottle that was on the floor next to his chair, and he took an ample swig.

"But . . . why?"

"Can you really suppose my reasons are any of your business?"

"Can you really suppose they're not? Last I checked, we had an understanding, and nothing's happened to make me believe otherwise." Except her having had sex with Jack, but she disregarded that pesky detail. "You've sneaked about and developed an affection for another woman. How could you assume I wouldn't be irked?"

"Get out of my house."

"Don't be ridiculous."

"Get out! And don't come back."

"You're trying my patience. Stop being so surly."

She went to the sideboard and poured herself a brandy. She sipped it, desperate to appear casual, despite her racing pulse.

He couldn't toss her over! He absolutely couldn't! Yet his vexation was growing by leaps and bounds, and she wasn't positive how to calm him.

"I'm ordering you to leave!" he commanded. "Are you deaf?"

"No, I'm annoyed. You've positioned yourself to suffer a broken heart, and you're blaming me for it."

"This disaster is my fault?"

"Yes. You're aware of how fussy Lady Caroline is about status and class. If you truly thought for one second that she would disobey her father and choose you instead of Shelton, then you've turned into a blithering fool."

"Have I?"

"Yes. Now then, let's forget the past and look to the future."

"And what future would that be?"

"Why, *ours,* you thick oaf! It's time for us to marry."

"Marry? Is that why you accosted Lady Derby? Were you hoping she'd keep Caroline away from me?"

"Yes."

"At least there was a basis for your cruelty—twisted as it might be."

"I wasn't being *cruel.* I was being realistic. Caroline was all wrong for you, while you know we'd be perfect together."

"I know nothing of the sort."

"You are so full of it! You've been contemplating a proposal, as have I, but Lady Caroline was distracting you."

"She definitely was."

"So . . . as her wedding approaches, we'll proceed with our own. We should probably leave London after it, though."

"Really?"

"We'll journey to Italy, or some other exotic locale, and I'll cure you of your lovesickness. Lady C. will be but a distant memory."

He nodded, as if he was considering her suggestion; then he repeated, "Get out of my house."

"Didn't you hear a word I said? We'll sail to Italy so you can be away as she weds. You'll avoid the gossip. Why are you being such a beast?"

"I have no desire to travel to Italy with you—or anywhere else for that matter. Now go!"

Like a toddler having a tantrum, she stomped her foot, but her temper was wasted on him. He uncurled from his chair, like a cobra about to strike, and he advanced until he towered over her. He pinned her against the sideboard, a palm across her throat as if he might strangle her.

"If I killed you," he absurdly warned, "it would be no more than you deserved."

"*Kill* me! For pity's sake, cease with your dramatics." She shoved his hand away, exhibiting a bravado she didn't feel. "You're being an ass."

"You're lucky that's all I'm being. You're lucky I don't take a switch to you."

He grabbed her and dragged her out of the room, and though she struggled for all she was worth, she couldn't halt their forward progress.

"But Ian, I . . . I . . . love you," she spuriously claimed.

He scoffed. "Now who's being dramatic?"

"I do love you! I do!"

"You've never loved anyone but yourself. You're the most unbearable, selfish female I've ever met. Your antics used to humor me, but after this stunt, I merely find them tedious and degrading."

He threw her into the hall, just as Jack chanced to walk by so she was literally flung into his arms. She was trapped between the two irate, unsympathetic brothers. They glared down their Clayton noses at her, making her feel contrite and ashamed, both conditions which she hated.

"What's going on?" Jack inquired, as she squirmed to regain her balance.

"I don't want her here," Ian replied. "I asked her to depart, but she refused, so I'm tossing her out bodily."

"Why didn't I ever think of that?" Jack retorted.

"Speak to the butler, would you?" Ian queried. "I'd appreciate it if he could figure out a way to ensure that she never slithers back in."

"It will be my pleasure," Jack chirped. "I'll see to it immediately."

"Thank you."

Ian slammed the parlor door so hard that the windows rattled, and she was left alone with Jack.

"Hello, Mrs. Blake," Jack said, his tone frosty with dislike. "What brings you to our fine abode? Let me guess: You *love* Ian; you were hoping you could convince him to ignore your treachery toward Lady Caroline."

At realizing that he'd overheard her dismal declaration of amour, she blushed and peered at the floor, wishing she could snap her fingers and vanish.

She was like a child, caught doing what she oughtn't, and she was suffering from the most irritating urge to defend and explain, which was preposterous. Long ago, she'd learned that it was impossible to make a man understand anything.

Yet she couldn't tamp down her need to persuade him that her visit to Lady Derby had been the only logical choice. She hadn't planned to harm Lady Caroline. She'd simply wanted Caroline to desist with her futile pursuit of Ian. How could such an innocuous goal be deemed malicious?

Her conscience—that had lain dormant for years—had been rudely awakened, and it was needling her to be sorry, to make amends. To her horror, she felt as if she might start weeping and plead for his forgiveness. Her eyes actually welled with a bit of moisture.

"What's this? Tears?" He scrutinized her. "My God, it is! Well, you can turn off the spigot, Mrs. Blake. A display of waterworks will have no effect on me."

"I'm not crying." She slapped him away. "I have something in my eye."

"Oh, of course you do." He yanked her down the hall. "Let's go. Ian wants you out of here, and so do I."

Much before she was ready, he was marching her out, and she stumbled to keep up, which pitched her right back into his arms. For an embarrassing moment, their feet were entwined, her skirt tangled around his ankles. Her breasts were crushed to his chest, his thigh between her own. He felt strong and wonderful and perfect, and she was disgusted with herself all over again.

Like a pair of dancers frozen in the middle of an intricate move, they stared and stared; then Jack muttered, "Well, hell, Rebecca. What am I supposed to do now?"

"About what?"

"Quit looking at me like that."

"Like what?" She sounded breathless as a schoolgirl.

"Like you're as eager for a tumble as I am."

"You think I want to have sex with you?"

"You can't wait."

"Hah! I don't even like you!"

"Rebecca?"

"What?"

"Shut up."

He shoved her to the wall and fell on her like a wild beast. He kissed her as if they'd been separated for an eternity, as if they'd survived a catastrophe, as if he were the last man on earth and she the last woman. He kissed her as if he'd been dying to do just that—and nothing else—his entire life.

She joined in, furious that she couldn't restrain herself when she was with him.

He was the wrong damned brother! He was poor, and he was arrogant, and she refused to be attracted to him!

He lifted her, guiding her legs around his waist, and he carried her into the next room, kicking the door closed behind them. He dropped her on a small sofa, and he knelt on the rug, unbuttoning his trousers.

As quickly as that, he was prodding into her, just the slightest inch. He was smug and magnificent and so very aggravating, and she humiliated herself by wiggling her hips to pull him nearer. She was desperate to have him impale himself, but he wouldn't oblige her.

"Don't ever tell me," he said, "that you don't want this from me."

"I don't," she lied.

"Don't ever pretend that I don't mean anything to you."

"Finish it!" she commanded.

"Finish what?" He was all innocence, all mocking, exasperating male.

"I want you! Please!"

"I love it when you're reduced to begging."

With one smooth thrust, he was inside her, and he flexed several rough times, then came. There was no finesse, no wooing, and no attention paid to her own body's needs. He simply took her on the couch in the cold, empty salon as if he'd forced himself on an anonymous parlor maid.

The event over, he drew away, arranged his trousers, and stood. In a thrice, he was completely composed, not a hair out of place, not a wrinkle in his garments. The bastard wasn't even breathing hard, while she was in a pathetic state.

Her combs had fallen out, so her hair was drooping. Her dress was bunched up, the stitching torn at the waist, but her anatomy was in the worst condition. She was perched on the edge of some very sharp desire, but he couldn't be bothered to accommodate her.

His passion spent, he glared down at her, any tenderness having vanished.

Feeling chastened and sullied, she sat up and straightened her clothes.

"You know, Rebecca," he scolded, "if you could at least feign remorse for what you did to Lady Caroline, if you could show a smidgen of regret, there might be some chance of you turning into a human being."

"I'm sorry," she mumbled.

He chuckled, but miserably. "You don't know the definition of the word. You can barely pronounce it."

"I *am* sorry," she mulishly insisted. "I didn't intend to get her into trouble with her parents."

"Then why did you proceed?"

"I just . . . just . . ." She shrugged, unable to explain why—initially—it had seemed like such an excellent plan, but why it seemed so terrible all these hours later. She sighed. "It doesn't matter now."

"No, it doesn't."

She rose, too, and gazed up into his blue, blue eyes.

"I wish you were someone else," she said. "I wish you were a man I could love."

"I'm glad I'm not."

There was the oddest twinge in the center of her heart, and she was intolerably sad, as if she'd relinquished a precious gift.

"Is your carriage here?" he asked.

"Yes."

"Let's get you going."

He started out, looking so poised and in control, and the sight made her angry.

"Is that all you have to say?" she snapped.

"Yes, it is. Why? Were you hoping for something more?"

"No. I've never hoped for *more* from you."

"A wise assessment."

She pushed past him and hurried to the foyer, hating how he tagged after her. Their slothful butler had anticipated her departure, and he had her coat and hat ready. She jerked her belongings from him, and he scurried off. Jack tried to help her with her coat, but she shook him away. She was overwrought, her emotions careening so riotously that she considered throwing herself against his broad chest and blubbering like a babe.

He urged her over the threshold, which, of course, had her determined to resist. She dragged her feet, so he physically heaved her onto the stoop. With him inside the warm house, and her outside in the chilly night, she felt like a homeless waif.

"Don't come back," he said. "You're not welcome."

"Really?" She crudely focused on his crotch. "I'm pretty sure I was *welcome* a few minutes ago."

"It was another bout of temporary insanity. I'm over it. Good-bye."

As he moved to close the door in her face, she was overcome by the certainty that it wasn't merely *good-bye*, but farewell forever. The notion was distressing and even a tad frightening, and she shamefully implored, "Could we talk for a bit?"

"No, I'm busy packing."

"What?"

"Ian and I are leaving London."

"Leaving?" The news hurt her in ways she didn't understand. "Where are you going?"

"Ian is heading to Scotland."

"When will he return?"

"Maybe soon. Maybe never."

"How about you? Will you travel with him?"

"I haven't decided."

"But if you don't go to Scotland, where will you be?"

"I know it's difficult for you to believe, but before I arrived in London, I had a full and interesting life. I'll take it up again."

"You're serious."

"Yes. Ian has no stomach to stay and observe the disaster you've wrought, and I'm not too keen on continuing my acquaintance with any of the people I've met since I've been here." His harsh expression told her that he was referring to *her* and no one else.

"You don't have to leave London because of me."

"Don't flatter yourself. I'm not."

"Will I . . . will I . . ." She had to swallow three times before she could finish the sentence. "Will I ever see you again?"

"If I'm very, very lucky—which I haven't been so far—no."

He shut the door with a resounding click, and she stood, forlorn and forgotten on the front steps. The tears that had threatened earlier finally flowed down her cheeks, and she sniffled and swiped at them.

Ultimately, her carriage pulled up, and she climbed in and went away. As she peeked out the window, watching the gray buildings pass, she wondered how she could ever fix any of the mess she'd made.

Chapter NINETEEN

"Postponed!"

"It has to be, I'm afraid."

"I demand to speak with the Earl."

"That won't be possible."

Edward glared at Britannia. He'd been invited for supper, and he'd accepted, having assumed it would be one of Britannia's typically tedious soirees. With the wedding two days hence, he'd felt it important to pretend familial harmony, but with her announcing the delay, she'd blindsided him. His temper flared.

"Britannia, I don't know what's going on in that devious head of yours, but I insist on discussing this with Bernard."

"He's not receiving anyone at the moment."

"The man can't simply disappear. His daughter is about to be married."

"No, she's not! I've explained a dozen times. We have to reschedule."

"Have you any notion of the stories that will circulate? The gossip will crucify me."

"Circumstances can't be helped. Bernard has refused to participate, and I can't dissuade him. Lord knows I've tried, but he won't listen."

"I have a marital contract," Edward griped, "and I won't tolerate any mischief. If you two suppose you can renege on our agreement, I suggest you think again."

"We have no intention of *reneging*—as you so commonly put it. I'll see to it that Caroline marries you if it's the last thing I do!"

She vowed it with such fervor, her eyes aglow with the uncanny shimmer they'd recently adopted whenever she saw him, and he took a step away, embarrassed to find himself rattled by her zeal. She looked like a lunatic escaped from an asylum.

"I have no idea why Bernard has relegated such an imperative issue to a mere woman, and I must talk to him directly."

"He won't involve himself in the situation. You know how he is."

"No, I don't *know* how he is, and it seems to me that if he's changed his mind, he's quite involved."

"We have to reset the date," she claimed. "What else can you expect me to do? I can't very well hold the ceremony without a father to walk her down the aisle!"

"Where is your husband? Produce him at once!"

He pushed past her and marched toward the stairs, even as he speculated over his purpose. Was he prepared to search the mansion, room by room, until Bernard was located? Since he'd never behave in such an uncouth fashion, what was his goal?

Britannia saved him by pulling him to a halt. She leaned in and murmured, "He's having a personal crisis."

"A crisis? Oh for pity's sake! What sort of calamity

could make him postpone his daughter's wedding? Is he ill? Is he injured?"

"His dearest acquaintance has died."

"Who?"

"His latest trollop," she casually said. "Haven't you heard? She drank herself to death."

"She what?"

"She perished in a fit of inebriation. Apparently, he was fond of her, and he's distraught."

There had been rumors about the girl's demise, but he hadn't given the matter a second thought. Why would the passing of a nameless light skirt have any bearing on Bernard or his family?

"So he'd defer because of a . . . a deceased mistress?"

"Isn't it hilarious? He says we're welcome to have the wedding without him, but if we want him to attend, we have to wait until he's feeling better. He recommends that we utilize the original date."

"But . . . but . . . that's three weeks away."

"Yes."

"It would be my right to proceed as planned," he blustered. "I could insist on it."

"Yes, you could, but he won't do it. I don't see how we can make him."

"Let's continue without him."

"You're the one who was worried about gossip. Can you envision how the tongues will wag if he isn't there?"

He stared her down, trying to unravel her ploy. She'd always been anxious for him to marry Caroline, even when Caroline had been engaged to Wakefield. Now she was perfectly content to dawdle.

What was she really attempting? By delaying, what would she gain? What would *he* lose?

"I wish to speak with Lady Caroline," he finally said. "I assume she'll be down for supper?"

"No, she won't."

"Why?"

"She's indisposed."

He chewed on the response, working it over and over, struggling to delve to the inner meaning it contained.

"As I'm about to be her husband, I demand that she join me. Have a servant fetch her."

"Why would you bother with her?"

"I don't trust you, Britannia. I haven't seen Caroline in days, and I'm suddenly wondering why not."

"She's having cold feet."

"Is she?"

"Can you believe it? She doesn't care to be your wife! I can't imagine why. Can you?"

She cackled like a witch stirring her cauldron. Her enjoyment of Caroline's dilemma was out of proportion to reality, and Edward was beginning to question whether she wasn't completely crazed.

"Get her for me."

"You don't need to—"

"Get her!" he hissed. "I'll wait here."

"Very well," Britannia huffed. "You may see for yourself that she's fit and present. She's merely being disobedient, and I'm keeping her locked in a closet so that she doesn't run away. That's how desperate she is."

She stomped out, and a few minutes later, she returned with her daughter in tow. Caroline entered first, with Britannia behind her, and Britannia blocked the door, as if fearful that Caroline would bolt through it and escape.

Caroline approached until they were toe-to-toe, and

she appeared confident and stubborn, when in the past she'd been meek and submissive. From where had this adamant person sprung? How could she have metamorphosed into a totally different individual from the one he'd always known?

The alteration was unnerving and infuriating. He didn't want her changing! He wanted the timid, quiet girl she'd been previously. If she'd developed a backbone, it would be much more difficult to bend her to his will.

"Have you something to say to me?" he sneered.

Boldly, she replied, "I don't want to marry you."

He was so stunned by the insult that he was amazed he didn't slap her.

"Why would you consider your opinion to be relevant?"

"I've been told, over and over, that it's not. I simply thought you should know."

Her obstinacy spurred him to crave the nuptials more than ever, and he started calculating the ways he would punish her for her impudence, commencing on their wedding night.

"Here's what we will do," he said to Britannia. "The ceremony will be held in three weeks—but only three—so don't ask for another extension. It won't be granted."

"I won't go through with it!" Caroline contended, but he ignored her.

He continued to Britannia, "We shall disseminate whispers that Bernard is sick. To quell speculation, Caroline, you, and I will show ourselves at Westmoreland's ball on Saturday, which would have been our wedding day."

"She shouldn't be let out in public," Britannia mentioned.

"Why not? What could she possibly do? Is she so out of control that her own mother can't make her behave as she ought?"

The jibe had its intended effect. Britannia rippled with rage. "We will be more than happy to attend the Duke's ball with you."

"Fine," he said. "I will pick you up in my carriage at eight."

☙

I realize it's horridly presumptuous of me," Jack began, "but might I speak with Lady Wakefield?"

"And you are?"

At the butler's question, Jack was disconcerted about how he should answer. He was loitering like a supplicant on the stoop of the great and notorious Viscount Wakefield, so he wasn't about to proclaim that he was a Clayton bastard son. Nor would he brag that he and the Viscount were half-blood brothers.

"My name is Jack Romsey. I met her once prior. I was introduced to her by Mr. Ian Clayton."

The reference to Ian brought a smile to the butler's stony face. "Are you a friend to Master Ian?"

"Yes."

"How wonderful. We've missed him terribly these last few months. Please come in."

From remarks Ian had made, Jack had assumed that alluding to Ian would get him tossed out, so he was surprised by the warm reception.

He was led into a fancy parlor, but at viewing the grandeur, he was hit by a wave of nerves. The ornate decor emphasized the disparities between who he was and who his siblings were. Luckily, he was dressed appropriately in clothes Ian's tailor had sewn, but no matter the extravagance of the garments, they couldn't alter the ordinary man within.

"I am Rutherford," the butler said. "May I pour you a refreshment?"

A hearty shot of liquor would have stilled his trembling, but he didn't think he should greet the Viscountess while sipping on a brandy.

"No, thank you."

"Very good, sir. Make yourself comfortable"—Rutherford pointed to a sofa—"and I shall notify Lady Wakefield of your arrival."

Jack tried to sit, but he was too anxious, so he ambled around, looking at the paintings on the walls, the flowers in the vases, the figurines on the tables.

He wasn't sure why he'd come. He and Ian had reached a truce of sorts; then Ian had departed for Scotland. He'd invited Jack to tag along, but Jack had declined, not being eager to intrude on Ian's homecoming.

Ian had urged him to remain in the London house, insisting that it was Jack's home, but without Ian in residence, Jack didn't feel that it was. So after Ian had left, Jack had packed a bag and left, too. He was at loose ends, at liberty to go wherever he wished and do whatever he wanted, but he received no joy in his freedom.

From the time he was a very small boy, he'd been alone, so it was his usual condition, but since he'd had a brief taste of *family* with Ian, the sudden severance of their connection was frightening and humbling.

He was sad and forlorn in a way that was different from ever before, and as he'd walked down the street—ready to flip a coin and pick a destination—he'd found himself proceeding to Viscount Wakefield's door instead.

During his previous encounter with Lady Wakefield, she'd been kind and unpretentious, so Jack doubted she'd be offended by his improper visit. If she was, at least he'd have tried, so he wouldn't have to fret over what might have been.

Much sooner than he'd expected, footsteps sounded in the hall, and like a ray of sunshine, Lady Wakefield rushed in. She was petite and beautiful and very pregnant. She grinned, and instantly he wanted to know her better. He wanted her to consider him a friend.

"Jack Romsey! It really is you! When Rutherford announced you, I didn't believe him."

"Hello, Lady Wakefield."

She hurried over and held out her hands. He seized them in his own as she rose on tiptoe and kissed him on the cheek. He hadn't had many women fuss over him in his life, and the sweet gesture made him feel welcome as nothing else could have.

She studied him, assessing his features. "My Lord, but I can't get over how closely you resemble my husband. If you were a few years older, you could be his twin."

"I've often been told as much."

"I'm so glad you're here," she said.

"So am I."

"You're not as stubborn as your two brothers, are you?"

"I'm hoping I'm not."

"After I met you that night with Ian, I was going to call on you, but I let John convince me that I shouldn't. Can you imagine?" She chuckled in a merry way. "I actually listen to him occasionally—even when he's being foolish."

"Why was he being foolish?"

"We could see that Ian was still furious. John was afraid that if I went to his house, he might refuse me entrance, and then they'd have had another row, which would have been awful. There's already been such terrible talk."

"I thought Lord Wakefield was the one who was angry."

"Oh, he was. They both were. They said some dreadful things, but they're too proud to apologize, yet each is miserable without the other."

"Ian would never have snubbed you. He's very fond of you."

"I know. John was just being silly. It's a Clayton trait. I pray you were blessed with not inheriting it. Come!" She dragged him into the hall. "John is home today. He's been dying to meet you, but too pigheaded to do anything about it."

They halted at the end of the corridor and marched into the library without knocking, and Jack was amazed by the informal nature of the imposing residence and its occupants. They were like a normal couple, with a regular routine, and he didn't feel out of place. It seemed as if he'd always stopped by.

Lord Wakefield was across the room, seated at a massive desk and absorbed with reading through a voluminous stack of papers. He was aware of his wife's arrival and knew it was she without glancing up.

His nose buried in his work, he grumbled, "Emma, if you keep interrupting, how am I to get my chores done?"

"John! We have a guest."

"Will I be pleased?"

"I'm certain you will be."

"Does he want something from me?"

"Yes." Lady Wakefield winked at Jack and whispered, "I'm constantly bringing in people who need his assistance, when he hates doing good deeds. He assumes you're here for a charitable contribution. It makes him cranky."

"I can hear you, you know." Wakefield pushed his papers aside and sighed. "Very well. What is it this time?"

He stood, smiling at Lady Wakefield, as she beamed. "Look who's come!"

The Viscount stared at Jack, scowled in confusion, then recognition dawned, and he muttered, "I'll be damned."

"John!" Lady Wakefield scolded. "Don't curse! He'll think you're a barbarian."

"I *am* a barbarian."

"John!"

"Sorry. It slipped out." He didn't seem contrite.

"Haven't I cured you of your bad habits?"

"Not all of them. A man has to keep a few."

"I don't see why."

He gazed toward the door, then frowned at Jack. "Is Ian with you?"

"No." At the news, Wakefield visibly deflated, and Jack hastened to explain, "He's moved to Scotland."

"Scotland!" Wakefield said.

"It's a long story."

"I hope you'll tell it. I'm eager for every detail of how he's been."

Wakefield rounded the desk and approached. They

were the same height, the same build. The Clayton bloodline was strong, and Jack felt as if he were peering in a mirror and seeing how he would appear in another decade.

After a thorough evaluation, Wakefield murmured, "My goodness."

"Hello, Lord Wakefield."

"Your name is Jack?"

"Yes, Jack Clayton Romsey."

Wakefield reached out and laid a hand on Jack's shoulder, as if touching him to be sure he was real. His emotion was evident and genuine, and it was the strangest sensation, but Jack felt as if he'd always known the man, as if they'd merely been separated for a short while.

"Isn't it wonderful, John?" Lady Wakefield inquired.

"Yes, Emma, very wonderful indeed."

"It's like a gift," she said.

"I'm presuming"—Wakefield spoke to Jack—"that you have the most interesting tale to share as to where you've been and how you came to be living with Ian."

"Yes, I do."

"You must tell me all about your mother—and our father."

Lady Wakefield added, "We were just about to sit down to dinner. Will you join us?"

Jack's initial reaction was to decline, but they seemed to truly want him to stay, and his heart was aching with delight that he'd have the chance.

"I would love to stay," Jack replied.

To his surprise, his response caused Lady Wakefield to burst into tears and, as if her weeping was a common occurrence, Wakefield pulled out a kerchief and tenderly dabbed at her eyes.

"Why are you crying now?" he asked her.

"I'm so happy for you."

She fell into his arms, and he hugged her tight as he glanced over at Jack.

"Have you had much experience with pregnant women?" Wakefield queried.

"No, sir."

"I've learned that they cry like watering pots. She might not stop for hours, so let's go eat. We could starve before she's finished." He started out, his wife safely tucked at his side.

Jack followed them, and as they stepped into the hall, Wakefield gazed over his shoulder.

"I'd like it if you'd call me John," Jack's older brother urged.

"I will," Jack said, and they proceeded into the dining room together.

❧

I've had him kidnapped."

"You what?"

Caroline was stunned. Was there no crime Britannia wouldn't commit?

"You heard me: I've had Mr. Clayton kidnapped."

"But . . . why?"

"He's my insurance."

"Against what loss?"

"Due to your father's reduced mental state, the wedding is twenty days away instead of two."

Thank God! Caroline muttered to herself. "Why would the date of the ceremony have spurred you to abduct Mr. Clayton?"

"You now have an eternity in which to thwart me.

Should you refuse to marry Edward Shelton, I will have Ian Clayton killed."

"Yes, Mother, you've been very blunt about what you would do."

"He will be my collateral to prevent any bad behavior on your part."

"Can you expect me to believe that you have him hidden away in some hovel, awaiting the moment I say my vows?"

"I don't care what you believe."

Caroline scoffed. "What did you do? Sneak into his home and club him over the head?"

"Actually, he'd fled London. He was sick of you and your antics, and he was scurrying back to Scotland where he belongs. I had a pair of ruffians attack him on the road. It was very simple."

Caroline studied her, but she couldn't decide if Britannia was lying or not. She had grown so crazed that any nefarious conduct seemed likely. Then again, Ian might be just down the street, sitting in his own parlor and oblivious to the drama unfolding in the Derby household. How could she know for sure?

She had to contact him, had to find out if he was all right.

He'd been fond enough to fight for her, to force his way into her father's mansion and demand that she leave with him. His show of support was the sweetest, kindest deed that anyone had ever done for her. He really was her knight in shining armor.

"I have a gift for you," her mother said, and she handed over three letters.

"What are these?" Caroline asked even though she knew. Her spirits flagged.

"They are messages you managed to pen and have

delivered to Mr. Clayton. As you will see from the attached note, he has left the city, and his residence is shuttered indefinitely."

Caroline ran a thumb across the top letter, reading the words someone had jotted on the front. It was as her mother had claimed. He was gone, and Caroline felt his absence as heavily as if he'd died.

She clutched the small pile to her bosom. The letters were her last link to him, as cherished as if they'd been a strand of hair or miniature locket with his portrait tucked inside. On seeing her pathetic gesture, Britannia yanked them away and tossed them in the fire.

"I've been so cautious," Britannia mused, "so I'm perplexed as to how you were able to draft a plea for assistance, but you won't dare another such outrage. I have fired the maid and footman who abetted you. They've been turned out without a penny. If they apply for a new position, and a reference is sought, I shall say they were thieves. They'll never work again. Because of you, they'll probably starve in the gutter."

Tears welled into Caroline's eyes. Disaster struck whatever she touched. Was she tainted? Was she cursed?

"You are so wicked," Caroline charged, hating Britannia as she'd never hated anyone. "When did this happen to you? How is it that I didn't know?"

"Now that I'm aware of how sly you can be, I'll watch you even more closely. If you solicit aid from the other servants, I'll foil you, and the penalty to the involved employee will be worse than ever. Am I beginning to get your attention?"

"Yes, you are."

"You will marry as you've been commanded by your parents. You can't evade your fate."

"I realize that."

Her father was lost in his sorrow. Her brother detested her. She had spurned Ian. There was no one else who might have been worried about her, who might have intervened.

She was on her own, floating free of what had tethered her to her prior life. She felt invisible, unloved and unwanted. What would become of her?

"And don't forget," her mother taunted, "in the end, I have your precious Mr. Clayton. Nothing would please me more than to kill him for his audacity. I almost hope you give me an excuse to proceed."

She chuckled, sounding every bit like the deranged person she was, and she whipped around and walked out. The key spun in the lock.

Chapter TWENTY

"D on't turn around."

At the sound of a female voice coming from directly behind her, Caroline stiffened but didn't move. The Duke's grand ballroom was packed with people, and oddly enough, whoever had approached her seemed to be hiding in the drapes.

Edward had vanished in the throng, but Britannia was a few feet away and observing her every second, so Caroline was pretending to be very meek. She'd hoped to beg someone for help, but the crowd was an unfriendly mob.

Any person present would think her mother to be perfectly reasonable in forcing Caroline into a horrid marriage. They would deem a refusal as childish and reprehensible on Caroline's part.

"Who's there?" Caroline asked, keeping her expression carefully blank.

"It's me, Rebecca Blake."

Though astonished, Caroline showed no reaction. "What do you want?"

"I'm the one who told your mother about Ian."

"Why am I not surprised? How wicked of you."

"It was, and I'm . . . I'm . . . sorry." There was a pause, and she added, "And I don't apologize very often, so I'd appreciate it if you wouldn't gloat."

"I'll try not to."

"Are you in trouble because of me?"

"Of course I am. What would you suppose?"

"I've heard terrible rumors—that she beats you, that you're being locked in a closet."

Caroline thought about denying the stories and asserting that everything was fine, as was her tendency, but Mrs. Blake was the type of individual who'd be brave enough to assist. Caroline had to seize what might be her only chance.

"It's been awful," she admitted.

"I figured as much."

"Do you know where Ian is?"

"He's left town," Mrs. Blake confirmed.

Caroline nodded, calculating the response and what it meant for her future, what it meant for his. Did Britannia have him as she claimed?

"I need your help," Caroline said.

"I suspected you might. Is your mother watching you?"

"Like a hawk. I can't take a breath without her noticing."

"I just saw John Clayton go into the parlor down the hall. He's sitting alone, having a brandy."

"So?"

"I'll create a diversion and keep your mother occupied. As soon as I've distracted her, sneak off and talk to him. You'll have to hurry."

"To Wakefield? Why would I?"

"He's a man, as *I* obviously am not. Plus, he's powerful—as powerful as your father—and he loves Ian. He'll aid you as no one else would dare."

Caroline recognized the wisdom of Mrs. Blake's statement, but she was loathe to parley with Wakefield. He'd hurt her in too many ways to count, but Mrs. Blake was also correct in suggesting that Caroline solicit his support. Of all the people she knew, he was the most likely to stand up to her parents.

If his brother was in danger, he'd want to be notified, and if rescue was necessary, he would act on her behalf.

"All right," Caroline decided. "Go ahead."

She felt a rustling; then Mrs. Blake stepped into view. She walked between Caroline and Britannia, passing by until she was on Britannia's opposite side.

"Lady Derby," Mrs. Blake greeted much too loudly, "the death of your husband's mistress is so shocking. Everyone is whispering about it. Couldn't you just expire from mortification?"

As Britannia prepared to do battle with Mrs. Blake, her back was to Caroline, and Caroline slipped away and ran down the corridor. There was a room at the end, and she rushed in and slammed the door.

Wakefield was seated on a sofa, staring into the hearth. He glanced over at her, frowned, and rose.

"Caro?"

"Yes." Her heart was pounding.

"I'm having a brandy." He grinned his devil's grin that, for years, had had women swooning all over the city. "You won't tattle to my wife, will you? She doesn't approve of my bad habits."

His marriage to the vicar's daughter was still a sore subject. "Please don't mention her to me."

As she neared, he could sense her anxiety. "What is it? What's wrong?"

"You must help me."

"I'm happy to. Tell me what you need."

"My parents are foisting me off on Edward Shelton."

"So I've heard."

His smile wavered. Apparently, he felt guilty over his role in her current fate. Good! The bastard! If he'd wed her as he should have done, she wouldn't be in such dire straits.

"I don't wish to marry Mr. Shelton."

"It's what your father selected for you, and you should—"

"I love Ian," she declared, cutting him off.

"How grand for Ian," he murmured kindly, "but your parents would never give their consent."

"I don't care about their opinion."

"Yes, you do."

"You don't know me, John, and you never did. I love Ian, and I won't accept Mr. Shelton as my husband. I won't!"

"Would you like me to meet with them? In light of our past, I doubt they'd pay any attention to me."

"I don't need you to speak with them. I need you to find Ian. I need to be sure he's safe."

"Ian's in Scotland."

"I'm not certain that he is. My mother is mad and—"

"Well, I don't know if *mad* is the word I'd choose."

"No, she's crazed. She insists she had Ian kidnapped while he was on the road and that—if I don't go through with the ceremony—she'll have him killed."

"She said that?"

"Yes."

"You must have misunderstood."

"She was very clear."

"It can't be true."

"What if it is?"

They were both silent, and she could see the wheels spinning in his head. Since their botched engagement, they'd scarcely crossed paths, yet here she was, ranting like a lunatic. He was probably rejoicing that he'd had the foresight to break off with her.

"Now, Caro"—he used his most annoying, placating tone—"you're obviously distraught over recent events."

"You think I'm suffering from some sort of . . . of . . . delusion?"

"No. You've simply been under a lot of pressure."

He was lucky she didn't slap his imperious smirk off his perfect face. He'd always thought he knew best, always thought he knew more than she did. She grabbed the lapels of his coat and shook him.

"Listen to me, and listen well: I would do anything for Ian. I would walk through hell and back. I would drown myself in the deepest ocean. I would jump from the highest cliff. I would even marry Edward Shelton. But I absolutely must know if he's all right."

He studied her, then shrugged. "You're serious."

"Yes. Locate him, and if he's free and unharmed, bring him to me so he can take me away from here."

"If it's so terrible at home, don't wait. I'll assist you now. If you're afraid or if you're being mistreated, I'll intervene and place you under my protection."

"I can't jeopardize Ian. If she has him as she claims, and she learns I've met with you, she'll hurt him. I'm positive she will. She's increasingly deranged."

"I'll find out where he is."

"Thank you."

She raced to the door and opened it.

"Caro?"

"Yes?"

"I'm glad you came to me."

"I'm not!" she rudely replied. "I'd rather cut off my arm than ask you for help, but you care for Ian."

"I love him. I always have."

"Then don't fail me. Don't fail *him!*"

"I won't."

"Swear it!"

"I swear!"

He put his hand over his heart, and the other was stretched out as if he'd laid it on a Bible. Their gazes locked and held, and he seemed sincere. Maybe he'd changed; maybe he'd come through for her. For once.

The hall was empty, and she tiptoed out, then hurried to her mother before Britannia had noticed that she'd sneaked off.

Mrs. Blake had continued insulting Britannia, and a huge crowd had gathered to titter over the fireworks. Mrs. Blake saw Caroline approaching. She raised a brow in question, and as Caroline responded with a quick nod, Mrs. Blake stumbled forward pretending someone had pushed her. She had a full glass of wine, and she spilled the whole red mess down the front of Britannia's dress.

"Oh, Countess," she gushed, "I'm so sorry."

"You little fiend!" Britannia hissed. "My gown is ruined."

"I'd buy you another," Mrs. Blake offered, "but my brother-in-law has my money tied up in court. Would you speak to him for me? If you could convince him to relent, I'd compensate you."

Britannia was so furious that Caroline worried she might explode. Caroline leaned in and scolded, "Mother, you're making a scene. Why don't we go?"

"Yes, why don't we?"

Britannia flashed such a look of hatred at Mrs. Blake that the bystanders blanched and stepped away, presenting them with an easy path to the foyer.

Britannia hastened through the gauntlet, Caroline hot on her heels, departing so swiftly that they didn't even wait for their cloaks and hats to be retrieved.

Caroline passed by Mrs. Blake and mouthed, *Thank you.*

You're welcome, Mrs. Blake mouthed in reply, and suddenly Caroline didn't feel so alone.

For the first time in so very long, she was hopeful. She had Wakefield and Mrs. Blake as her allies. Perhaps she would survive her ordeal, after all. Perhaps everything would work out for the best.

❧

Explain yourself!" Bernard demanded.

"What do you expect me to say?" Britannia retorted.

Bernard skimmed the note he'd received from Wakefield. "He maintains that you've kidnapped his brother! Where would he come by such a ridiculous notion?"

"How would I know?" Britannia scoffed. "The man's a lunatic. He always has been. I have no idea why you'd interrogate me over something so preposterous."

"Am I to believe he pulled the insane nonsense out of thin air? That he's making bizarre accusations with no proof?"

Britannia didn't answer, and Bernard scrutinized her, wondering what the actual account was.

Wakefield was a pain in the ass, but he wasn't crazy.

Nor was he prone to hysterics. If he would allege such severe misconduct by Britannia, it likely had some basis in fact.

Bernard couldn't guess what scheme Britannia had concocted. She was a riddle he didn't care to solve.

"Caroline must have gotten word to him," Britannia said. "She's filled his head with twaddle."

"To what end?"

"She's determined to stop the wedding."

They were back to the wedding again? He gnashed his teeth.

"Madam, I told you to handle this situation. Must I assume—once more—that you can't manage your daughter? How many more discussions must we have on this topic? If you cannot deal with such a simple problem, what use are you to me?"

"I have her completely under my control."

"Do you?"

"No one sees her. No one confers with her. She's totally isolated."

"Then why is Wakefield pestering me? At this very moment, he's racing to Scotland on some wild-goose chase."

She chuckled in a way that frightened him. Anymore, she seemed a bit mad, which had him unnerved and terrified as to what would become of her.

"So . . . he's off to Scotland, is he?" she reflected.

"Yes."

"Marvelous. He'll be out of our hair."

"I didn't realize he was *in* our hair."

"The Claytons have always been a nuisance."

He couldn't disagree. Still, he was bewildered over the strange letter and fretting over what it might portend. If Britannia had done something despicable in her pursuit of Caroline's marriage, he ought to respond, but in what fashion?

When he was desperate to have Caroline wed and gone, why would he interfere? If Britannia was only furthering a difficult conclusion, who was he to complain as to her methods?

"I don't wish to be advised as to what folderol you've instigated," he stated, "but whatever it is, be sure nothing happens to Ian Clayton. Or if it does, be sure your hands are clean. I won't be dragged into a scandal, merely because you can't carry out your plan with any degree of circumspection.

"Don't worry, *dear* Bernard. I shan't get caught. Nor shall you."

She grinned and strolled out, while he mulled in the quiet.

Her comment had him more uneasy than ever. What was she implying? What had she done? What *would* she do?

He couldn't bear to know.

He poured himself a brandy, drank it down, then climbed into bed. Refusing to be disturbed, he closed the privacy curtains so he could ruminate—without interruption—over Georgie and the awful hole her death had made in his life.

♄

"May I speak with Jack?"

Rebecca tugged off her gloves and tossed them on the table in the foyer, acting as if she were welcome in Ian's home, acting as if she hadn't been bodily evicted during her previous visit. She feigned confidence, behaving as if she would saunter into the parlor and make herself comfortable as she always had in the past.

"He's not here, Mrs. Blake," the butler confirmed as he discreetly but competently blocked her entry.

"I'll wait—if it won't be too long. When are you expecting him?"

"I don't believe he intends to come back."

"What do you mean?"

"Master Ian has traveled to Scotland."

"Jack went with him? I thought he was staying in London."

She hadn't thought it, at all. She'd just *hoped* he wouldn't tot off and abandon her. Not that she wanted him to remain, precisely. Not that she'd given him any reason to remain.

"He's gone, too, but not to Scotland. He packed a bag that contained only the clothes with which he arrived, and he left."

"I see."

She peeked into the nearby salon. A footman was covering the furniture with sheets, as if the house was being shut down.

"Is the staff leaving?"

"Yes."

"Forever?"

"I haven't been notified of what Master Ian will do next."

Liar, she mused. "Were Jack and Ian fighting?"

"I'm certain they weren't, Mrs. Blake."

His stony reply indicated that, even if they had been, he would never gossip. It was an attitude she generally respected, but in this instance, when she was dying for information, she wanted to throttle him till he spilled all.

"Has Jack provided a forwarding address?"

"No."

"Have you any idea how I could reach him?"

"No," he said again. "Would you like to jot a message in case he contacts us?"

She considered what type of communication she might convey, when she wasn't even clear on why she'd stopped by.

She was simply feeling so morose. She was embarrassed that she'd caused so much trouble, and she hated that Jack was upset with her. To make amends, she'd involved Wakefield in Ian's little drama. If anyone could go against the Countess with impunity, he could. She'd done the right thing for once, and she'd rushed to apprise Jack, to see if he might be proud of her, but the ass had vanished.

Wasn't that just like a man! She'd finally conducted herself in a manner that would have pleased him, but he'd fled before she could boast.

She was frequently labeled a shrew, when she didn't mean to be. She knew how to be a faithful friend, but she'd had so few chances to display any loyalty.

She wanted to tell Jack that she was sorry, that she was inundated by guilt, that she wished she could retreat in time and start over.

But what she said to the butler was, "No, I don't have a message. Thank you anyway."

She grabbed her gloves and walked out, and she loitered on the stoop, remembering their last encounter, when they'd had wild sex, when they'd parted on such bad terms. How could he just go off and leave her?

She didn't understand him, and she was furious that she didn't. If she'd had a heart, he might have broken it.

"Bastard," she grumbled.

A tear tried to leak out, but she wouldn't let it surface. She'd already cried once over the unappreciative oaf, and she wouldn't give him the satisfaction of crying over him again.

※

A re you positive you don't want me to come with you?" Jack inquired of his brother John.
"Yes."

"I'd be happy to accompany you."

"It's not necessary. Stay here and escort Emma to the country. That's the best help you can offer me."

"I will," Jack said.

John had promised to take Emma home to Wakefield Manor for the birth of the babe, but Lady Caroline's cryptic warning about Ian had altered their plans. Their initial inclination had been to disregard it, but what if she was correct and something nefarious had happened?

John was anxious to discover Ian's true condition, just as he was eager to redeem himself to Lady Caroline by going to check. Jack was delighted to witness such honorable behavior from someone about whom there'd always been such dreadful rumors.

"When will you return?" Emma asked.

"Very soon. The wedding is scheduled for March fifteenth, so if I am to be of any assistance whatsoever, I must get back before then."

"It doesn't give you much time," Emma cautioned.

"A little more than two weeks," John agreed.

"So you mustn't dawdle."

Emma led him out to the drive where his horse was saddled for the fast trip north. She tugged at his coat, tightening it to ward off the chill, and she pulled out a scarf she'd knitted and wrapped it around his neck. John teased her for fussing, but she wouldn't be denied.

The sky was gray and angry looking, with snow or freezing rain seeming likely, and Jack pondered the wisdom of John riding off in inclement weather. A frisson of worry slithered down his spine, and he said, "Why don't you send a letter, instead, to see if he's there?"

"If the answer was slow in coming, and I learned that he hadn't arrived, what would I do? It would be too late to intervene in the wedding, and Caro would kill me."

"And she'd be married to Mr. Shelton," Emma added.

"Which would be a nightmare. I don't know what her father was thinking in proceeding with such a horrid engagement."

"Well, he had her betrothed to *you* for years," Emma wryly retorted, "but he didn't seem to notice how awful it was for her."

"Very funny."

"I'm glad she's so devoted to Ian," Emma mentioned. "He needed someone to love him."

"Yes, he did," John concurred. "Whether it's Caro remains to be seen."

Emma sighed. "It's so romantic."

"Only a female would find it so."

Emma elbowed him in the ribs, as John grinned over her head and winked at Jack.

The pair said their farewells with a lengthy kiss and much quiet whispering that Jack struggled to ignore. In the days he'd been with them, he was regularly disconcerted by their open affection. He'd never been with a married couple that was so besotted, and it reinforced how lucky he was that Rebecca had refused him. If he was ever to take a bride, he craved what John and Emma had together. He'd hold out for love, for friendship and abiding fondness.

Rebecca would have furnished him with none of those things.

If there was a tiny, idiotic voice deep inside that kept insisting they could have forged a different conclusion, he was an adult man, and he didn't have to listen.

John gave Emma a final hug, then leapt onto his horse. He leaned down and caressed her cheek, saying, "Don't you dare have that child without me."

"I won't," she pledged, "and don't you dare come back without Ian."

"I won't do that, either."

"Be careful. Stay warm. Stay dry."

"For you, my dearest Emma, I will."

He straightened in the saddle and vowed, "I'll meet up with you at Wakefield Manor."

"I'll be waiting. Don't disappoint me."

"I wouldn't dream of it." His gaze moved to Jack. "Watch over my wife while I'm away."

"It will be my pleasure," Jack responded, proud to have been entrusted with the important task.

John waved, yanked on the reins, and cantered off.

Long after he'd disappeared, Emma stared down the street, and Jack tarried a short distance off, loathe to interrupt such a private moment.

Ultimately, she drew away, her smile a tad strained, her eyes watery.

"It's the first time we've been separated since we were married," she explained. "I've gotten used to having him around."

"I can certainly understand why."

"He can be exasperating, but he grows on you."

Jack chuckled. "Yes, he does."

She hesitated, peered down the street again, then nervously asked, "He'll be all right, won't he?"

"Of course he will. He's just traveling to Scotland. It's not the end of the world."

"It seems like it to me." She walked over and linked her arm with his. "Let's go in and eat, and I shall spend the entire meal regaling you with stories of John as a boy."

"Are you sure he'd want you to?"

"He'd hate it, so we won't tell him. It will be our little secret."

They laughed and went inside.

Chapter TWENTY-ONE

Ian stood on a rocky outcropping and stared down at the small valley, studying the haphazard assortment of sagging huts owned by his relatives. With snow covering the hillsides, and smoke curling from the chimneys, it should have been picturesque, but the view was so depressing.

While scarcely more than a boy, he'd left at his father's behest. He'd journeyed to England to befriend his half brother, as well as to become a prosperous gentleman and betrayer. He'd shed his accent, his poverty, and rural mannerisms like a snake shedding its skin, as if heritage and tradition meant nothing.

Since then, he hadn't visited, so his recollections were those of a lad of twenty, who hadn't known how poor he was, who hadn't grasped the differences he'd encounter in the outside world.

His kin had once been powerful and wealthy, had owned huge tracts of Scotland, had fought and died for their legacy and customs. But history had worked its toll, and they had so little remaining. His uncles seemed content, but they were all so old!

Poverty and hardship had worn them down early, had them gray and stooped and weary from the struggle of keeping on.

They were all thrilled to see him, and they'd welcomed him like the prodigal son, but he felt so guilty. Over the years, his father had encouraged him to take so much money from John, and he gleefully had, but he'd never sent a single farthing to his family. His childish memory was that they'd been affluent from whiskey and wool, so they hadn't required any assistance, and he was shamed to be so painfully confronted by reality.

He wasn't like them, and he didn't belong, which shouldn't have hurt or surprised him, but it did. He'd never belonged anywhere. Growing up in Scotland as he had, he'd been an oddity, the bastard offspring of a rich nobleman. In England, he'd been an oddity, too, but snubbed and demonized because of it.

So what was he to do now?

He couldn't return to London. With Caro having married Edward Shelton, there was nothing for him in the city. Neither was there any reason to keep on in Scotland.

His uncles had begged him to stay, but he wasn't a farmer and couldn't see himself engaged in the toil it took just to get by. Should he move to Edinburgh? To do what? For how long? And if he didn't go there, where should he go?

He had no answers. Everything seemed futile, and his emotions were at their lowest ebb.

A brisk wind blew past, the cold making him shiver. He trudged down the trail to the hovel where his bed and bag were located. A hot fire burned in the grate, and he hung his coat and hat and went to sit in the chair by the hearth, his shoulders draped in a shawl an aunt had woven, when someone pounded on the door.

He frowned but didn't budge. He didn't want to chat, but his caller didn't realize that he was sulking and in no mood for company.

The intruder knocked again, and again, and finally, Ian cursed and stomped over and yanked on the knob. Though it was mid-afternoon, the sun gave off a pitiful bit of light. The sky was leaden, and with him standing in the dim cottage, he could barely focus.

There was a man on the stoop, and it seemed to be John, which was impossible. He was wrapped from head to toe against the bad weather, his face partially concealed by a scarf, but it had to be John. It couldn't be anyone else.

Was he hallucinating? Had the isolation driven him mad?

"There you are," the vision muttered, "and about bloody time, too."

"What?"

"Have you any idea how difficult it was to find you?"

"John?" he asked.

"Yes, it's me. What do I look like? A ghost?"

"Yes."

"Since I've just ridden from one end of this godfor-saken country to the other, might I suggest you invite me in?"

"John?" he said again, astonished and certain he'd lost his mind.

The apparition stamped snow from his boots and snarled, "And if you still have a stick up your ass about that fight last summer, and you decline to grant me some of your supposed Scottish hospitality, I can't predict how I'll react."

In a daze, Ian stumbled out of the way, and the man entered. Ian watched, stupefied, as he shucked off his heavy garments, regally tossing them in the middle of the floor, expecting a servant to magically appear and pick them up.

It really and truly was his brother. At least, Ian thought it was. Perhaps it was a Scottish fairy, playing some terrible prank.

"What in the hell are you doing in Scotland?" he demanded.

"Hello to you, too, Ian. I'm pleased to note that you haven't been kidnapped or murdered."

"Murdered!"

John glanced around the tiny space. "Where do you keep the liquor?"

"In the cupboard in the corner."

Ian gestured to it, wondering if he might blink and John would vanish. But no. John marched over, rummaged for a glass, and poured himself an ample quantity of Ian's uncles' finest brew. Then he proceeded to the fire and stood, letting his backside be warmed by the flames.

Ian stated the obvious. "It's the dead of winter."

"Yes, it is."

"Yet you're here."

"And I should receive a medal for a job well done, too." He gulped the whiskey and poured himself another. "It's a lucky thing this bottle is full, and I hope you have more than one. While I'm away from home, I like to catch up on my ration of vice."

"Why?"

"I can't drink a drop in front of Emma. It's the kind

of wicked behavior that sends a vicar's daughter into a righteous frenzy."

Good for you, Emma! Ian mused. John had spent most of his adult life inebriated. Any person who could convince him to get sober and stay sober was a miracle worker.

"You poor, poor man." Ian oozed sarcasm.

"I admit that being married has its disadvantages"— John wiggled his brows and laughed—"but it has its *advantages,* too. Especially when your bride is as humorous and entertaining as Emma. You should try it sometime."

"I'll keep that in mind."

The moment was so bizarre. He couldn't remember when he'd last heard John laugh. Maybe he never had. In all the years they'd lived together, his brother had always been so despondent.

Now he was smiling and making jokes. If he'd suddenly sprouted a second head, Ian couldn't have been any more stunned. John was carrying on as if they hadn't been separated a single day, as if Ian hadn't irreparably damaged their relationship.

"Aren't you still angry with me?" he had to inquire.

"Yes. I'd like to beat you to a pulp, but I think the icy trip has frozen my temper. And my hands. If I struck you just now, my fingers would crack into a dozen pieces."

Ian slumped into a chair. Was he dreaming? He'd pondered a reconciliation with John so often and with such intensity that it was entirely possible he was imagining the scenario all over again, with the difference being the precise amount of detail.

"Why are you here?" he queried.

"I've come to fetch you to London."

"But I don't wish to go."

"You have to. Caro needs you."

Once, he'd have been thrilled by the news, would have instantly raced to England to assist her, but he was wiser now. The summons was nonsense.

"No, she doesn't. She made her opinion very clear: She's married her Mr. Shelton, and I'm certain she's happy and settled."

"She hasn't married him yet," John maintained.

"Yes, she has. The wedding was held on the twenty-fourth. That's why I left. I couldn't bear to watch it happen."

"You know, you might have told me how much you cared for her. I could have helped the two of you. We could have avoided this whole mess."

"I tried to tell you—that one time. You didn't seem inclined to listen."

They both flushed, recollecting the night at Wakefield Manor when John had stumbled on Ian as he'd been kissing Caro. A brawl had ensued, and before it was concluded, they'd both been bruised and battered, their friendship ruined by harsh words and bitter revelations.

"We were pathetic, weren't we?" John mumbled.

"*Pathetic* doesn't begin to describe it."

"Afterward, I was so sorry."

"I knew you were. So was I." Ian went over so that they were face-to-face. "Our father was an ass."

"He definitely was," John enthusiastically concurred.

"I can't figure out why I agreed to work for him to your detriment."

"You were young and stupid and destitute."

"That pretty much covers it."

"Yes, it does."

"I hated taking your money—I hated it every day—but Father said I should, and I forged on, even though I knew it was wrong. It's been an albatross around my neck. I want to return it to you. I want to return every penny."

"I wasn't upset about the money." John waved away a decade of duplicity as if it had been of no consequence.

"You should have been upset. You're being too kind to me."

"You were the eldest," John stated. "I always thought you deserved a share. If you'd simply asked me for a portion, I'd have filled a bank account for you. I still would."

"If you persist with this casual attitude about your fortune, I can't see how you'll remain a rich man."

"Neither can I. Between you and my wife—with all the charities she makes me fund—I'm surprised I have a farthing to my name."

"You love her, don't you?" Ian murmured, amazed.

"More than my life."

"I'm glad for you."

"I think she saved me."

"I think she did, too."

As easy as that, they were friends again, the squabble of the previous summer swept away as if it had never been. Ian was so relieved he felt dizzy.

Why had they fought? He could scarcely recall. In hindsight, it all seemed so silly.

John was blushing, embarrassed at having confessed his fondness for his spouse, and he switched subjects.

"Now, about London . . ."

"What about it? What has brought you all this way?"

"Caro's wedding has been rescheduled for the original date."

Ian's pulse pounded with joy, but he tamped down any elation. What was it to him if she hadn't followed through? What was it to him if she'd altered her plans?

She was the most fickle female he'd ever met, and it was typical of her to change her mind. He'd have expected nothing else. Her future had no bearing on his. Whatever she elected to do—or not to do—she'd made it very plain that he would have no role in how events played out.

He was over it. He was over her! When push had come to shove, when she'd been forced to choose between himself and her parents, she'd cast him aside like a worn pair of slippers.

As he'd stood in her father's library, being dragged out by burly servants, as he'd bellowed her name and pleaded with her to pick him over them, she hadn't bothered to take a final glance in his direction.

"So she isn't married," Ian cautiously ventured. "How could the delay possibly matter to me?"

"Caro begged me to find you for her."

"She did?"

"Her mother claims she's had you kidnapped and that you'll be killed if Caro doesn't marry Mr. Shelton."

"The Countess said that?"

"Caro is extremely frightened. She insisted that—if she knew you were all right—she'd defy her mother and refuse the match, but if there was a chance the Countess might harm you, she'd have to proceed."

"She'd wed Shelton to keep me safe?"

"Yes, and you can't let her sacrifice herself like this."

Ian reflected, then blew out a heavy breath. "I don't want to be involved. This is none of my affair, and I can't believe she's requested my assistance."

"Why wouldn't she have? You're smack in the middle of it."

"The Countess is such a witch!" Ian seethed. "I'd love to see her get her comeuppance."

"So would I. You could make it happen by coming to England with me."

"I don't know. . . ."

"Won't you help me redeem myself in Caro's eyes? I hate that she has such a low opinion of me."

"If you cajole me into going with you, are you supposing she won't detest you quite so much?"

"Precisely."

"Her loathing is fairly intense. You're hoping for an awful lot."

John shrugged. "I promised her I'd bring you home, and if I have to, I'll bind you, gag you, and throw you over my saddle like a sack of flour."

"You wouldn't."

"I would, but I'd rather you agreed on your own and came without all the fuss."

"To do what?"

"To prove that Britannia is a lunatic and a liar, which will keep Caro from a hideous marriage."

"That's worth something, I guess."

"And I have to admit"—John grinned from ear to ear—"that it will be hilarious to see Britannia's expression when you foil her by showing up alive and unscathed."

Ian spun away and went to the window, staring out at the snow that was drifting down.

He'd gone to Caro like an adoring fool, and with hardly a thought, she'd tossed away what he was offering. If he rushed to London and she spurned him again, he didn't know how he'd survive her rejection.

Still, when John had braved such a distance, Ian couldn't imagine declining to accompany him, and in consenting to go back, Ian didn't have to do it for any emotional purpose. Obviously, Caro was a damsel in distress. He could steel himself against heartbreak, could aid her because she needed him to, then he could be on his way, with his sentiments in check and his detachment visible and firm.

He peered over his shoulder. "Why would she put herself through all this just for me?"

"She loves you, you dolt!"

"No, she doesn't," Ian scoffed. "I spoke to her father, before I left. I asked for her hand. Didn't she tell you?"

"No. She didn't exactly have time to share the details of your affair. Thank God."

"I begged her to stand up to them, to leave with me, but she wouldn't. She was content to stay, and I can't decide why I should go to so much trouble for a woman who's been very clear that she's not interested."

"She's interested, Ian. Believe me. She was so worried about you that she actually sought me out and talked to me."

"Considering how much she despises you, that's definitely a sign of her desperation."

"It is, so you must return with me. If you don't, I'll never hear the end of it from Emma. You wouldn't do that to your brother, would you?"

Ian chuckled. "No, I wouldn't."

"You'll come?"

"Yes." Ian sighed, wondering what kind of predicament he'd gotten himself into. "When must we arrive?"

"By the fifteenth."

"But . . . that's only five days away."

"You'll need a fast horse, and we'll be off at first light."

"What if it keeps snowing? We might not be able to ride out of the valley."

"I can control many factors," John replied, "but I can't do a thing about the weather. We'll just have to cross our fingers."

"What if we don't make it by the fifteenth?"

"We have to," John said. "There's no other choice."

Chapter TWENTY-TWO

D o you ever wonder about Caroline?"

"What about her?"

Britannia stepped in behind Edward, whispering so that no one could hear. Not that anyone was listening.

The church was closed, the door locked tight so their exalted family could have a private ceremony. No guests had been invited, so the rows and rows of pews were empty.

Bernard was over by the altar railing, awaiting the vicar, and he was so disconnected from the marital events that he might have been a stranger who'd wandered in by accident.

Her surly, unpleasant son, Adam, was off in the vestibule, sulking over her command that he attend despite his protestation that he didn't care to participate.

Caroline was seated in the front row. She'd chosen a silvery blue gown as her wedding dress, and with her blond hair and fair complexion the color washed out her skin so that she looked pallid and frozen. She might have been a carved statue, except that she kept glancing around, hoping for a last-minute rescue by Ian Clayton.

Britannia smirked.

Wakefield could find a magic horse with wings to fly him to Scotland and back, but he and Clayton would never return in time, not with the blizzard on the border. The distance was simply too far, the roads too hazardous.

In a few minutes, Caroline would be married to Edward. Britannia would finally have the revenge she'd sought for so long. She'd never been so happy!

"Weren't you ever curious," she inquired, "about the date of her birth?"

"No. Why would I have been?"

"Don't you recollect our affair, Edward?"

"Vaguely."

He always pretended that their liaison hadn't impacted him, while on her end she'd suffered daily.

"How typical of you to deny me," she fumed.

"Good God, Britannia! It's been twenty-five years. Let it go."

"I don't wish to. At the moment, there's nothing I'd like to talk about more."

He whirled on her, his fury clear. "We will not discuss it! Be silent!"

"No, I shan't be. In fact, I believe I shall chatter about you—and my prior relationship with you—all day."

"Are you completely insane?" He glared at Bernard, who appeared to be in a trance. "Madam, as your husband is in no condition to advise you as to your comportment, I shall speak in his stead: Get a grip on yourself!"

Britannia chuckled, assessing woebegone, pathetic

Bernard, who was so weak of character that he'd been felled by the death of a mere strumpet.

He only thought he was miserable. Before the festivities were concluded, he'd likely be comatose with shock.

She grinned at Edward. "The last sexual encounter occurred in early May. I've never forgotten."

"What encounter?"

"Why, yours and mine."

"Oh, for pity's sake, Britannia! Why dredge up ancient history? What is the matter with you? Your sense of decorum has utterly fled."

"Caroline was born in January."

"Thank you for letting me know. I'll be sure to buy her an appropriate bauble when next the day rolls around."

She walked off, amused that he couldn't unravel the true message she was trying to send.

He was so thick. He wouldn't figure it out till it was too late. She'd tell him in the morning, after the consummation, after he was beyond the point where he could fix what he'd done. She'd tell Bernard, too. She'd provide every sordid detail, and she'd watch and laugh as her words pushed him into an even deeper stupor. If she was very lucky, she'd drive him to an apoplexy.

He'd be at her mercy, bedridden and unable to escape, but she wouldn't kill him right away. She'd slowly torment him until he expired from rage and fear.

She stopped directly in front of him and mused, "Ah, Bernard, look at your daughter. Isn't she lovely?"

"What . . . ?" He struggled to focus on her. "What is it? Why can't we start? What's the delay?"

"Are you in a hurry?"

"Yes. I want the blasted thing finished, and I have no idea why I'm here when I'm feeling so poorly."

"You wretched soul! Imagine! Having to attend your own daughter's wedding! Such a chore! Such a burden!"

"I didn't mean it like that," he grumbled.

"Didn't you? You've never felt much of a connection to Caroline, have you?"

"I felt as much as any father would."

Which wasn't much at all, Britannia had learned. What good was a daughter? What benefit was there to having one? A daughter was like a fattened hog, auctioned off to the highest bidder.

"Have you ever noticed how she doesn't resemble you?" Britannia taunted.

"No, I haven't."

"Well, she doesn't. She hasn't any of your features. When she was younger, people gossiped about it constantly."

He peered over to where Caroline was morosely balanced on the edge of the pew. She was like a frightened rabbit, ready to bolt.

"I assume you're trying to tell me something," Bernard huffed, "but I'm in no mood for riddles. What is it, Britannia?"

"It's nothing. I'll explain tomorrow."

"You do that."

He turned away, signaling their discussion to be over, and she moved on to Caroline, who had just cast another longing glance at the door.

"He's not coming," Britannia said, sitting next to her. "There's no need to torture yourself."

"*Who* is not coming?" Caroline asked, playing dumb.

"Your Mr. Clayton, of course. I'm aware that you contacted Wakefield. You were hoping he'd locate his brother and that the despicable pair would ride to your rescue."

The news stunned Caroline, and she abandoned any pretense. "How did you know?"

"Wakefield wrote to the Earl. He complained that you'd approached him like a madwoman and were spewing wild tales."

"I begged him to travel to Scotland for me, to find out if Ian is safe."

"When will you accept reality, Caroline? Clayton is hidden away—by me—and he shall remain so until after the vows are spoken and the union consummated. You can't evade your fate."

"The ceremony hasn't commenced yet, Mother. John may still arrive."

"*John* has gone to the country. His wife wanted to have her baby at Wakefield Manor, and he's taken her. He's a busy man, and he couldn't be bothered with your petty request. He never went to Scotland."

"That's a lie! He swore he'd help me."

"He may have promised you, but his only follow-up was to compose a scathing letter to your father. He suggested that Bernard consult with medical professionals about your mental condition."

"He did not!"

"Bernard had considered locking you away in an asylum, but I convinced him the better punishment was to proceed with the nuptials."

Caroline stared at Bernard, studying his diminished capacity, his lack of interest in the present affair. Her mind was awhirl with calculating the odds of how truthful Britannia was being, and ultimately, she shook her head.

"John did nothing of the sort. He'll come through for me. Just you wait and see."

"Believe what you will"—Britannia shrugged as if she couldn't care less—"but why you would suppose you could rely on a scoundrel like Wakefield is beyond me. He's failed you your entire life. At this late date, why would you expect him to act any differently?"

The vicar emerged from behind the altar, his vestments on, a prayer book in hand. He motioned for them to assemble.

Caroline didn't budge, and Britannia snapped, "Come. It's time."

"I can't. I can't do it."

She was so pale and trembling so ferociously that Britannia wondered if she might faint.

"Think of Ian Clayton," Britannia goaded. "Think of what will happen to him if you don't behave as I've commanded."

The grim reminder had its desired effect. Caroline rose and stumbled over to join Edward.

❧

Dearly beloved," the vicar intoned, "we are gathered here in the sight of God . . ."

As he droned on, Caroline blocked out his words, gazing at a spot over his shoulder where a beautiful tapestry hung on the wall. She concentrated on the colors, trying to separate herself from what was transpiring.

She'd arrived at the church, certain that a miracle would occur, that John would walk in and halt the service, or that Ian would swoop in and carry her off.

Neither man had appeared, and she had to stop anticipating a happy ending.

Edward was clasping her arm very tightly, holding her in place, and her parents were positioned directly behind her to hinder any escape.

In a few seconds, she would have to speak her vows—or not. What was best? Should she save Ian? Should she save herself?

Caroline couldn't do both. If her mother had kidnapped Ian, Caroline couldn't cry off. If she refused Edward and rushed out of the church, she'd be leaving Ian to whatever hazard Britannia had devised.

If she disobeyed her parents and forsook Ian, she would be alone, without even the aid of an unreliable scapegrace like John Clayton. Who would take her in? Sadly, she couldn't conjure the name of a single person. She'd be on her own. How would she support herself?

She was nearly hysterical with despair, surrounded by people who hated her, and so lost in her rumination that she didn't notice the vicar had paused and was glaring at her.

Her father hissed, "Answer him!"

"What?" Caroline stammered.

"Answer the question with *I do*."

Britannia butted in. "Vicar, if you would read the line again, I'm sure she'll chime in as she ought."

"These promises are important, Lady Caroline," the vicar scolded. "Please pay attention."

"I'm sorry. What did you ask?"

The vicar repeated, "Do you, Caroline, take Edward to be your lawfully wedded husband?"

She gnawed on her lip, delaying a response, when suddenly noise erupted outside the church. Someone was shouting and pounding on the door.

"Keep going!" Britannia decreed.

The vicar began again, but the commotion grew, and he hesitated.

"Perhaps we should see what he wants."

"Don't be absurd," Britannia scoffed. "Do you recall how much money the Earl donates to this parish every year? You're trying his patience. Get on with it!"

The uproar became a frenzy, and Caroline struggled against Edward's firm grip.

"Caroline!" Edward reproached. "You're making a scene. Desist! At once!"

"I have to know who it is." She was prying at his fingers, but he wouldn't let go.

"Vicar!" the Earl barked. "Continue on, or explain to me why you can't, and I'll confer with the Archbishop tomorrow as to your lack of regard for my family's business."

The vicar was in a quandary, with the bride clearly wanting to run off and her rich, powerful parents and fiancé determined to proceed.

Caroline gave a vicious yank and pulled away from Edward, only to be grabbed by her mother.

"Ian!" Caroline wailed, but Britannia clapped her palm over Caroline's mouth.

Caroline fought and kicked at her mother's shins, as Britannia whispered, "I will not be thwarted. If it is he, and he thinks to intervene, he will pay in the end. So will you."

"Lady Derby," the vicar admonished, "this is a house of worship. I can't have a . . . a . . . brawl in the middle of the ceremony. It's obvious that Lady Caroline doesn't wish to keep on, and if she—"

"Shut up!" Britannia growled, sounding like a rabid dog.

Caroline's brother was tired of the tumult, and he pushed open the barred door to reprimand whoever had interrupted.

Looking aggrieved and travel weary, their clothing damp and muddy, Ian and John Clayton hurried in, the two brothers side by side. They were tall and handsome and filled with a fury that was thrilling to witness.

Caroline had never seen a more magnificent sight.

She bit Britannia's hand as hard as she could, and she sprinted down the aisle and fell into Ian's arms.

"Are you all right?" He kissed her cheek, her hair.

"Yes, yes," she panted. "Now that you're here, I'm fine."

"In case you were wondering, you're not marrying Mr. Shelton."

"I won't. I can't."

Ian linked their fingers and, with John bringing up the rear, they marched toward the altar.

"Who, sir, are you?" the vicar inquired of Ian.

"I'm the man Lady Derby claims to have kidnapped."

The vicar gasped. "Kidnapped?"

"Be gone, you bastard devil," Britannia seethed.

The Earl stepped forward and frowned at John. "Wakefield, take this half-blood nuisance, and get out of here."

"I'd rather not," John flippantly retorted.

Ian glared at the vicar. "I apologize for being late, but I'm afraid I missed a section of the vows. Could you repeat it?"

"To which one are you referring?" the vicar queried, trying to inject some sanity into the scandalous scene.

"Ask me if anyone objects to the union. Ask me if

there is anyone who would like to 'speak now or forever hold his peace.' "

"I take it you're opposed?"

"Damn straight I'm opposed!" Ian snarled. "You
can't have her, Shelton."

"How do you plan to stop me?" Edward replied.

"You're naught but a disgusting pervert, and I'm
prepared to accuse you to the entire world."

"Now see here!" Edward indignantly spouted. "You
will not cast aspersions on my character!"

"Why shouldn't I? You're aware that any story would
be true. And as for you . . ." Ian advanced on Britannia
until they were toe-to-toe. "I wish we were at Wakefield. I'd have John order you to the stocks in the village square and have you publicly whipped."

"You little weasel!" Britannia raged. "How dare you
barge in! How dare you insult me! Bernard, do something!"

"What would you have me say, Britannia?" Bernard
sighed. "Your scheme has been foiled. I warned you to
be cautious, yet you've made a total mess of it. Why
should I rescue you?"

Caroline scowled at the Earl. "You knew about Ian?
You knew she was threatening to kill him?"

"Well . . ." Derby blushed and tried to assert, "Not
really."

"You encouraged her!" Caroline charged. "What is
the matter with you? You've known John since he was
a baby. You were friends with his father, yet you could
let her murder Ian? You're as deranged as she is."

"I've had enough of this," Ian said.

He drew her away and started out, with John staying
behind to prevent any of them from coming after her.

"Where are you going?" the Earl demanded.

"Wherever Caroline would like," Ian answered.

Edward was finally rattled into action. He stomped toward John, as if he'd tromp over the slighter, younger man, but John delivered a hard punch to Edward's chest that cowed him into halting.

"This is my wedding," Edward bellowed at Ian, "and Caroline is my fiancée. You can't abscond with her. Who the hell do you think you are?"

Ian grinned. "I'm the fellow who ruined her."

"What?" Edward nearly swooned. "What are you saying?"

"She's damaged goods, Shelton," Ian confessed. "I've had her dozens of times. Didn't her parents tell you?"

Edward was about to commit mayhem. "You'd better be lying."

"I'm not. Just ask them. They both know all about it. The Countess even bribed me to be silent and go away, and I'd considered it, but it appears I've changed my mind."

"Clayton!" Bernard shouted. "Don't you leave this church with her. I'll hunt you down, I'll find you, I'll sue, I'll . . . I'll . . ."

Ian assessed Bernard, then Caroline, and shrugged.

"Let's go," he said.

"Let's do," she replied.

They started down the aisle again, when Britannia hurled herself at Edward. She grabbed his lapels and shook him.

"You have to stop them," Britannia insisted.

"I don't see how I can," Edward said, "or why I'd want to now. You treacherous witch! You were about to pawn her off on me when you knew she was a whore."

The insanity that had been simmering inside Britannia bubbled to the surface.

"She's your daughter!" Britannia screeched. "You can't let him take your own daughter! You can't!"

"Britannia!" Edward snapped. "Control yourself."

"She's your daughter!" Britannia claimed again. "You have to marry your own daughter. I must have my revenge! I can't be denied! Not after I've waited all these years to see you punished!"

The crazed pronouncement seemed to suck the air out of the room. Everyone froze in place.

John frowned at Ian. "Did she say what I think she said?"

"Yes, she did," Ian responded.

Caroline dropped Ian's hand and came back to her mother. She studied Britannia's unhinged expression, then she shifted her gaze to Edward, and the assembled group turned with her. They all observed the same thing: She and Edward looked exactly alike.

She peered at the Earl, studying him, too, and deeming it curious that she had no features in common with him. How was it that she'd never before noted the differences? No wonder the Earl had never felt any connection to her. There wasn't one.

"You had an affair with Edward, didn't you, Mother?" Caroline correctly deduced. "You hinted at it once, but I ignored you. That's what you were trying to disclose, wasn't it? You were planning to marry me to my own father."

"Oh, my God." Edward lurched away from Britannia as if she had the plague. "Woman, you are mad as a hatter! You always have been!"

Britannia's beady little eyes darted around the sanctuary, seeking an escape route, and she resembled a rat caught in a trap. For a moment, Caroline was certain Britannia would scoff at the accusation, but instead, she laughed an eerie laugh that raised the hackles on Caroline's neck.

"Yes, I had an affair with him," Britannia admitted. "I was young and foolish, and he made me love him, but he never arrived to take me away as he promised he would."

"I didn't come for you," Edward interjected, "because you were a lunatic, and as far as I can tell, nothing has changed in the intervening decades."

"You see?" Britannia fumed. "Even now, he insults me. Even now, he has no idea how to be sorry. He must pay!"

Her arms outstretched, she stumbled toward Edward, lumbering like an automaton and intent on inflicting bodily harm.

"Britannia!" the Earl commanded, and he marched down from the altar and stepped between Edward and her mother.

John positioned himself between them, too, but Britannia was such a large person, and in such a muddled state, that Caroline wasn't positive they could restrain her. Not that Caroline cared if they could or not.

For once, she was unconcerned about the Earl and his countess and how their predicament was resolved.

She scrutinized the Earl, who'd always detested her, then Edward, who was unveiled as her true sire, and she shuddered with distaste. She'd been mere seconds away from an incestuous union, orchestrated by a maniac. She felt tainted and revolted, but at the same juncture, strangely freed.

The Earl was struggling to contain Britannia, as Edward scurried out, led to safety by the vicar. For a brief instant, Caroline's gaze locked with the Earl's, and he appeared stricken and apologetic, but it was probably a trick of the light.

"Lord Derby," she said, her mode of address severing her ties to him, "your countess previously informed me that she murdered your mistress. With poison."

"She what?" he wheezed with shock.

"She confessed her homicidal crime a few weeks ago. Directly after, I tried to notify you, but you wouldn't listen. I thought you should know." She turned to Ian. "Please, take me out of here. I don't want to see either of them ever again."

"You won't ever have to," he vowed. He glanced over at John. "Will you be all right?"

"Yes," John said. "I'll stay and clean up the disaster. You get going."

Together, she and Ian walked out of the church.

Behind her, she could hear her mother shrieking, "Let me at him, Wakefield. Let me at him!"

Her brother was by the door, having watched all with his typical disdain. As she passed, his sole participation in the event was to mutter, "Good luck. You'll need it."

Caroline swept by him without a word, judging it peculiar that he was now only a half brother and scarcely related, at all, but not being especially saddened by the realization. He'd always been awful to her, his dislike as blatant as her parents' had been.

She followed Ian outside. His horse was tied in front, and he escorted her to it, tossed her up, and jumped on after her. The animal was winded from the journey that had brought Ian to London, but it was hale and spirited, and as Ian pulled on the reins, it eagerly leapt to action.

They raced off, cantering down the road, the church quickly vanishing from view. She didn't even have on a coat, and the cold bit into her skin. She wrapped her arms around Ian's waist, held on tight, and never looked back.

Chapter TWENTY-THREE

I demand that you have me released!"

"I could, but I won't."

Bernard stared at Britannia, wondering how he was to deal with the reality that his countess was a raging lunatic. He'd never liked her, had definitely never loved her, but honestly!

She was pacing incessantly across the small cell. Her dress was ragged and dirty, her hair sticking out as if the gray strands had been altered into snakes. She looked inhuman, demonic even, like a wicked creature from an ancient Greek legend.

The hospital where he and Wakefield had delivered her was the best of its kind, but the accolade was a sorry statement on the level of modern convalescent care. She'd been housed in the private wing, with the other members of affluent families who had to be permanently locked away, but the conditions were sparse and disturbing.

"You can't mean to keep me here," she said.

"Oh, but I do. You're completely insane. And you're

dangerous. You can't be out among normal people. There's no telling what mischief you might instigate."

"I've done nothing wrong!"

"Nothing!"

"I was entirely justified in seeking revenge against Edward."

"Madam, I suggest you be silent. The very fact that you would mention your affair to me only underscores how crazed you are."

"You are a philandering roué. You always have been. Don't try to seize the moral high ground."

He'd been an awful husband; he couldn't deny it. He'd chased after every trollop who'd strolled by, but with all that had recently occurred, his liaisons seemed to have been so pointless.

He wished he could go back and do so many things differently. He wished Georgie were alive and being courted by some fine fellow her own age who would have cherished her as she'd deserved. He wished he'd been a better father to Adam and Caroline.

After the fiasco at the church, Adam had packed his bags and left, claiming he'd never return, and Bernard hoped that time and distance would calm him, but he wouldn't count on it.

Mostly, he wished he knew how Caroline was weathering her mother's revelations, but he had no idea where she was and no one he could ask who might inform him. She wasn't an earl's daughter, after all, so everything she'd understood about herself was false.

She'd been born during his marriage to Britannia, so in the eyes of God and the law she was considered to be his child and always would be. He wouldn't repudiate her. It was so strange, but when he'd believed himself to be her actual father he'd constantly snubbed her. Now that he'd found out he *wasn't* her father, he was desperate to make amends, to take the faltering steps toward a continuing relationship.

Instead, he would head to his empty mansion. The family he'd loathed was in tatters. His spouse was deranged, his son had fled, and his daughter was missing and would likely never talk to him again. It was a pitiful situation, indeed.

"If you aren't here to fetch me home," Britannia nagged, "why have you come?"

"I've brought some of the items you requested."

"Pen and ink?"

"No."

"But I need to write letters. I have to notify my friends of how heinously I'm being treated!"

"You have no *friends*, Britannia. Not any who'd like to hear from you anyway, and I won't allow you to share your venom with the outside world. You've done enough harm."

"You can't refuse to let me correspond!"

"I already have." He placed the satchel of her belongings on the narrow, rickety cot where she slept. He didn't know how it held her enormous weight and girth.

"Now then, I'm off."

"When is your next visit scheduled?"

"It's not. In the future, if you must contact me, you'll have to send a message through my solicitor. I don't intend to confer with you in person ever again."

"Don't be ridiculous. You shall come whenever I summon you."

"No, Britannia, I won't. I'm leaving you to stew in your own juice."

"Stop being melodramatic."

"I could have had you tried and hanged."

"For what crime?"

"For murder."

She laughed. "There's not a jury in the land that would have convicted me for killing your mistress. You were going to divorce me. The girl had you bewitched."

He could have made a thousand replies. He could have admitted all the ways he'd erred; he could have reminded her that his failings weren't Georgie's fault, or that he was genuinely sorry for everything that had transpired.

But she was crazy, and he was so very weary.

"You must listen to me," he told her, unsure of how to get her to focus. "Should you need anything, tell your nurse, and a note will be dispatched to my lawyer."

"I won't speak with your lawyer. I will speak with you directly, or I will speak to no one, at all."

"So be it."

He sighed, gazing at the gloomy cell, at his mad wife who hadn't yet paused in her pacing. She was like a spinning top that couldn't be stilled.

"I doubt you'll ever thank me," he murmured, "but by keeping you here, I'm doing you a favor."

"A favor! How?"

"At least you're alive. That's better than swinging from a gibbet, I'd warrant. Good-bye."

He knocked for the guard to let him out, and to his dismay, she hurried over and stood as if she'd walk out with him.

"What are you thinking, Britannia?"

"I'm coming with you."

He sighed again. "You're not. You can't. You must remain here."

"With all these lunatics?"

"Well, since you put it that way, yes."

"I'm coming with you!" she repeated, growing agitated.

He rapped more forcefully, and the guard arrived. Bernard stepped out, and Britannia tried to step out, too, but the guard held up a hand, signaling her to halt. Without warning, she grabbed his wrist and twisted it so hard that he howled in pain, and he began struggling with her.

It was a hideous scene—his demented, obese wife grappling with her jailor—and Bernard was too stunned to assist or intervene.

On whose side would he have fought? Britannia had to stay, but he couldn't bear to be the one to physically restrain her. He was paying the staff, and paying them well, to do that exact sort of thing.

The guard's yowling brought several others running, and it took five burly men to wrestle her to the floor. One of them produced a type of jacket, and they shoved her arms into it. The sleeves had long strings attached at the cuffs, and they were wrapped around her waist so that she was trussed like a Christmas goose.

The sweating, bruised men eased her to a sitting position, but she was too large for them to move her farther until she was ready to go. She glared up at him, and her hatred was so evident that Bernard blanched.

"I waited thirty years," she hissed. "I planned how I would wound you in the worst possible way. I finally told you the truth about Caroline, but you don't care!"

"I *care* that you hurt her, when she didn't deserve it. But I'm unconcerned about you. Your misery is all your own doing."

"When I get out, I'll kill Edward, then I'll kill you. You'd best keep looking over your shoulder."

"You'll never get out," Bernard vowed. "I intend to see to it."

He left, and she started screaming, "Bernard! Bernard! Bernard!"

He shuddered and hastened down the lengthy labyrinth of corridors, and even after he was in his carriage and proceeding home, he was certain he could hear her bellowing his name.

&

E dward entered his club, and he tarried in the foyer, impatient for the butler to take his coat and hat, but no one appeared, and his temper flared.

How dare the servants fail to attend him! His exclusive membership cost a pretty penny, and their sloth would be reported.

He marched up the stairs to the library, positive he would bump into some person of authority to whom he could vent his wrath, but to his surprise, he encountered no one. The place was busy—male laughter drifted by as he approached the stately chamber—but as he strolled into the room, the closest gentleman coughed discreetly, alerting the other patrons. The noise was a warning that wafted through the crowd.

Heads turned; brows raised; whispers swept by. The words *Shelton* and *his own daughter!* were bandied by all. Every man stared him down, their indignation and censure clear. He stared back, angry, defiant, and refusing to be cowed.

From out of nowhere, the butler emerged, his fake smile firmly fixed.

"Is there a problem?" Edward asked. As if he didn't know!

"No, Mr. Shelton. If I might speak with you downstairs?"

He was much smaller than Edward, but he had a nimble and diplomatic knack for steering out an undesirable guest. On a dozen previous occasions, Edward had chuckled when it had been some other poor fellow who was cast out.

To realize that it was now himself! To understand that he was being shunned!

For the briefest instant, he dragged his feet, thinking that he might defend himself, that he might hurl the facts at their pathetic faces.

I had no idea that she was my daughter, he imagined himself saying. *It was all Britannia's doing. The woman is mad, I tell you! Mad!*

But as he frowned at their stony expressions, absorbing the collective resolve to eject him from their eminent company, he recognized they couldn't be dissuaded, and he wasn't about to grovel.

Without comment, he whipped away and stomped out. He was mortified and fully aware that his years of residing in London—perhaps in England—were at an end. He'd never be invited to another social event. He'd be ignored by everyone who mattered.

Who had tattled? Derby? Wakefield? Why would they? Or had it been that weasel of a vicar? Who could be trusted anymore?

He stormed to his carriage and climbed in, advising his driver to take him to his favorite brothel. There was no situation that a bit of illicit fornication couldn't cure, and within minutes he'd sneaked through the shrubbery to the secret entrance.

He knocked the special knock, expecting to be greeted immediately, but he waited and waited, and no one came.

Finally, the madam peeked out, a brawny houseman lurking behind her.

Edward straightened and flashed his most imperious glare. "I seek an afternoon of entertainment. I demand to be admitted."

"We don't serve your kind," she sneered. "Be gone, you disgusting pervert!"

She slammed and barred the door.

Gad! Even the whores were revolted by him! Considering some of the foul deeds he'd attempted in the woman's establishment, that was saying a lot.

He was so shocked he couldn't move. He loitered on the stoop, his cold cheeks red with humiliation, the icy rain wetting his shoulders. He wanted to raise his fist, to pound and howl until his furious summons was heeded.

He'd inform the old harlot of how he was an innocent victim, how he'd done nothing wrong. It wasn't as if he'd married the accursed child. Yes, he'd privately lusted after her, but with no overt action being undertaken, how could he be judged guilty? Was it his fault that Britannia was deranged? Why should he be punished?

He trudged to his carriage and gave the directions to hurry home. He'd pack his bags and flee the city in the dark of night where he wouldn't be seen scurrying away like a rat in the sewer. But where the hell was he to go? And when would he ever be able to return?

※

Rebecca was snuggled under the covers and staring at the ceiling when she first noted that someone was banging on her front door. It wasn't that late, only midnight or so, and she was plagued by her usual insomnia.

Her butler and housekeeper were away for the week-end, so neither was available to respond. The other servants were asleep in their rooms in the attic, and even if they could hear the commotion, they wouldn't answer.

Well, *she* wasn't about to, either. Whoever it was could come back in the morning when sane, rational people were up and dressed and receiving callers.

The thumping grew more determined, and she'd tugged a pillow over her head when a man bellowed, "Rebecca Blake! I know you're in there!"

Scowling, she sat up.

"Rebecca!" he continued. "Get your shapely ass out of bed and open the door!"

"What the devil . . . ?" she muttered.

Shivering against the chill, she grabbed a woolen shawl and marched down the stairs.

"Rebecca!" he yelled again. "Don't make me come in and get you!"

"Would you be silent?" she griped as she fumbled with the lock, yanked on the knob, and peered out. "You'll wake the dead."

There was no moon, so it was difficult to see, but from his tall height and halo of golden hair she was sure her visitor was Jack Romsey.

Her heart did a funny little flip-flop.

Wondering if she wasn't dreaming, she blinked and blinked.

"Jack?"

"Bloody right!" he growled, and he stormed over the threshold.

There was a gleam in his eye that made her nervous, and for each step he took forward she took one back until she was at the wall and could go no farther.

"It's the middle of the night," she pointed out.

"Yes, it is."

She could smell alcohol on his breath. "You've been drinking."

"Not nearly enough to keep me from coming over here."

"What are you doing? What do you want?"

"I have to talk to you."

"I believe you are."

She waited for more, but he seemed incapable of speech, which was hilarious. He'd always had too much to say, much more than she'd ever cared to hear.

"Well?" she pressed.

"I'm told that you did a good deed."

He hurled the remark like an indictment, and she scoffed.

"Me? Don't be ridiculous."

"When I was initially apprised of the story, that's what I said. I said, 'Rebecca Blake, hah! She hasn't a kind bone in her body.' "

"No, I don't."

"I swore it couldn't be true."

"I'm certain it wasn't."

"But the teller of the tale insists that not only were you very considerate—you were also very brave."

"How absurd."

She couldn't have false gossip spreading. She had a low image to maintain, and she wouldn't have others suspecting that she was a sentimental fool.

"Thank you," he murmured.

"For what?"

"For helping Lady Caroline—when she was in trouble. For trying to make amends."

"I did nothing of the sort."

"You did. Don't stand there and deny it."

"I lent minor assistance when she was in a jam. So what?"

"So . . . maybe you're not the shrew I've accused you of being."

"Aren't you a flatterer?"

"I'm leaving London," he said, abruptly switching the subject.

"I thought you already had."

"I'm here to say farewell."

"You've already done that, too."

"But this time, I'm asking you to come with me."

"To do what? Will I roam the rural highways like a player in a traveling troupe? Will I carry my belongings in a satchel and sleep in a tent in a ditch?"

She'd exasperated him, and he huffed out a heavy breath.

"Would you shut up and listen for once?"

"I'd *listen* if you had anything pertinent to say."

"My brother, John, has made me an offer I can't refuse."

"Knowing Wakefield as I do, that sounds either illicit or dangerous."

"He owns a small property in the country, and I'm to live there. It's not charity," he hastily added. "I told him I wouldn't accept charity. I want to earn my own way."

"You're a veritable saint."

He ignored the taunt and kept on. "I'm to work for him as his land agent, and the job comes with a fine house and an excellent salary."

"You're going to be a gentleman farmer?"

"I guess I am."

"What do you know about farming?"

"You'd be surprised."

"You'd have to factor the accounts, too. Can you read and write?"

She had no idea why she was so terrible to him. He simply brought out every bad trait she possessed, and she ended up lashing out when she didn't mean to.

A muscle ticked in his cheek. "I take it back."

"Take what *back*?"

"Perhaps you are a shrew, but do you know what?"

"What?"

"I like you anyway."

He leaned in and nibbled her nape.

"You smell good," he mumbled.

"You're drunk."

"Yes, I am, but it's given me the most keen insight."

"About what?"

"I never spend enough time convincing you to do what I want."

"There aren't sufficient words in the universe to persuade me to go off and be the wife of a country farmer."

"Then I'll have to utilize other methods."

"Such as?"

He picked her up and tossed her over his shoulder. Her bottom was next to his ear, her head dangling. She pounded on his back with her fists.

"Put me down!"

"No." He swatted her on the rear.

"Jack! You'll wake the servants. They'll see."

"Why would I care? Besides, I'm about to be their master, so they need to get used to me." He started climbing the stairs. "Where's your bedchamber?"

"My bedchamber! I'm not having sex with you!"

"Did I ask your opinion?"

He arrived at the landing and walked down the hall,

entering the first room he saw that had a bed. He dropped her onto it and crawled on top of her, pinning her to the mattress before she could scurry away. Not that she tried very hard. His tongue was in her mouth, his fingers in her hair, and as he kissed her she moaned with delight.

As always happened when she was with him, their ardor rapidly increased, and he clutched the neckline of her nightgown and ripped it down the center. The fabric fell away so that she was nude and stretched out beneath him.

He fumbled with his pants, and in a thrice, he was inside her and thrusting away. She wrapped her legs around his waist, taking him deeper, and as he reached between their bodies to touch her, she came in an instant.

With a hearty shout, he joined her, and as quickly as that, they were finished. Together, they soared to the peak, but as they floated down, he was chuckling and smug, reminding her of what a conceited oaf he could be.

She punched him in the chest. "Get off me."

"No." He kissed her again, his cock leaping to life and not the least bit sated. "Say yes. Say you'll marry me."

"We've been through this before."

"Yes, we have, and you keep giving me the wrong answer. Tell me that you'll have me. Tell me that you love me."

"I don't love you," she declared. "I don't love anyone."

"Except yourself. But isn't it lonely on that tiny island where you hide yourself away?"

"I'm not lonely," she insisted.

"Which brings me to point out how you'll behave as my wife."

"I haven't agreed, and you're already imposing conditions? You're really pushing your luck."

"I'm positive I'll convince you, so here are the terms by which we'll carry on: You can't ever own a pistol, and you can't ever lie to me."

He could have made any stipulations in the world, and he'd chosen those?

She giggled. "You are mad."

"Mad for you."

"I understand why you'd be nervous about pistols, but why would you worry about prevarication? I've always been candid with you."

"Have you? You just told me that you're not lonely, and that you don't love me. That's two gigantic fibs in a row."

"Will you get it through your thick head? I don't love you!"

"You do, too. Stop denying it, and marry me. Let me be the strong one. Let me fight your battles for a change. You don't have to be so damned tough."

She gazed at him. He was so handsome and sexy, so stalwart and dependable, and he seemed to be genuinely fond of her. It was such a novel and frightening prospect, having a man who actually wanted her. If she consented, she'd have someone on her side, would have a best friend.

"Marry me," he urged.

She sighed. "I suppose it wouldn't kill me."

At her tepid reply, he laughed and laughed. "I can see that I'm wearing you down, so I can't quit now. By morning, I intend to have a full-on *yes*."

He rolled them so that she was on top and he was on the bottom, and as he clasped her breasts and started to flex, she decided he wouldn't have to try nearly as hard or as long as he assumed.

❧

"Where is your brother?"

Caroline glared at John. As if he had any control over mulish, stubborn Ian Clayton!

"Gone to Scotland."

"Scotland!"

"I'm sorry, Caro."

When she'd run out of the church with Ian, she'd thought they were riding off into the proverbial sunset. Instead, he'd escorted her to John's town house and deposited her in the care of the butler. Then he'd cantered off without a good-bye.

Initially, she'd presumed that he'd returned to the church to help John with the aftermath of the wedding, but he hadn't come back. She'd tarried, expecting him, but as hours had become days, then weeks, she'd been flabbergasted and furious.

Eventually, she'd begged John to hunt for him, and he'd been searching high and low, while she'd been trapped in his home, hiding from scandal, and fretting over what to do next. Now, to learn that Ian would rather trot off to another country than be with her!

Would it have killed him to take her along? Would it have killed him to inquire as to what *she* wanted? Didn't the obtuse lout comprehend that she'd have followed him to the ends of the earth? Would she be forever plagued by Clayton men?

The bastard!

She was so angry that she could have bit nails in half!

"What is he doing in Scotland?" she asked. Her jaws were clenched so tightly she could barely force out the question.

"He's rented a house in Edinburgh, but I don't know how he's keeping himself busy."

"Why would he leave me here like this?"

John shrugged. "Ian has always been a mystery to me. I couldn't begin to guess."

"You must have some idea."

"He's contrary. You know that."

"But he came all the way from Scotland—just for me! Why would he simply turn around and go back?"

"Like I said, Caro, he can be perverse."

"Have you his address?"

"Yes."

She went to the window and stared out at the gray sky. It was late April, but it still seemed like winter. The temperature was frigid, the rain continuing to fall, the roads an impassible mire.

Her entire life, she'd lived under her father's thumb, and for the first time ever, she was free and alone. She could go wherever she wanted and do whatever she wanted, but there was only one thing that appealed.

She could have her pick of options, and what she picked was Ian Clayton. But the ass was in Scotland! In light of how much she loved him, was there any choice as to what she had to do?

"I need a favor."

"I'm completely at your disposal."

"Actually, it's two favors."

"I'm happy to give you whatever is within my power to bestow," he gallantly said.

"I have a large dowry, and considering what I've been through, I think I deserve to have it. I recognize this is a huge request, but would you speak to the Earl about it? If he plans to renege, I'll hire a solicitor."

"Caro!" His brows shot up.

"What?"

"That's so . . . so . . ."

"Unlike me?"

"Yes."

"You never did know me very well, John."

"I realize that now."

"Will you meet with him?"

"I'll try my best, but you're aware that—even if I can persuade him to release it—it has to be transferred to your husband, not to you, so you have to marry in order to receive it."

"Oh, I fully intend to wed," she asserted, "which leads me to the other favor."

"What is it?"

"May I borrow a carriage?"

"Certainly. Where is it you need to go?"

"I've suddenly decided I must make a fast trip to Scotland, and when I arrive, your brother had better watch out!"

Chapter TWENTY-FOUR

There's a woman in your bed, sir."

"A woman?"

Ian glared at his valet. The man had worked for him exactly two days, and Edinburgh—for all its metropolitan airs—was a very provincial place. He had to be shocked. Would he resign in a huff?

"Is she pretty?" Ian asked.

"She's English."

The answer provided no valuable information. As he tried to rebuild his life of vice and gambling, he'd met several intriguing females who hailed from London, but he hadn't acted on any of their blatant invitations.

Would one of them have dared breach the sanctity of his new home? Did he want one of them to?

Since he'd left Caro, his lust had fled, and he was so lacking in arousal that he wondered if he shouldn't just proceed to Arabia and become a eunuch. Obviously, he'd outgrown the need for his manly appendage, so why keep it attached?

"I don't suppose she gave you her name?"

"No, but she claimed to have traveled a great distance specifically to find you. She said she was hungry and tired and cold, and she demanded that I see to her. I advised her that she couldn't stay, but she wouldn't listen. She was extremely bossy."

Rebecca Blake? Rebecca had come from London?

It couldn't be anyone else. What was he to do with her? How would he get her out of his bedchamber? There wasn't a crowbar big enough to pry her out of it.

"Did you provide for her as she requested?"

"I couldn't very well refuse a lady."

"No, you couldn't."

"After she ate and washed, she nodded right off."

Ian sighed. "That will be all. You may call it a night."

"Are you sure?"

"Yes, thank you."

The man hesitated. "About the morning . . ."

"What about it?"

"I didn't realize you were a . . . a . . ."

"A what? A blatant fornicator?"

The poor fellow blushed bright red. "Well, yes, and I'm not positive of the protocol. Should I assist the two of you upon your waking? Or should I keep out till summoned? I should mention that I'm a bachelor. I don't imagine I ought to . . . to . . ."

He looked as if he might ignite with embarrassment, and Ian took pity on him, figuring he'd probably race to his room and pack his bags as soon as their conversation was finished.

"Go to bed. Don't worry about me. I'll be fine."

"Very good, sir."

His relief palpable, he scurried away, and Ian stood

in the foyer, watching him climb the stairs. After he'd disappeared, Ian trudged after him.

He was in no mood to tangle with Rebecca, and if he'd had another bed, he'd have picked her up and dumped her in it, but he hadn't had occasion to purchase much furniture. The sole bed was his own, and he wasn't about to sleep on the floor merely because she was deranged.

What was she thinking? Though the calendar indicated it was spring, the weather hadn't improved. The roads were treacherous, yet she'd ventured off on a fool's mission.

How many times should he have to tell her to go away? She'd be lucky if he didn't take a stick to her, and he wouldn't use it to paddle her bottom, either. In the hope of pounding some sense into her, he'd knock it over her hard head!

He marched into his bedchamber, tossed his coat over a chair, and rolled back his sleeves—as if preparing for a fight. A candle burned on the dresser, and as he approached her, his eyes plainly observed what his mind couldn't comprehend.

"Caro?" he murmured.

Caroline Foster was in Scotland? Why? It was painfully clear that madness afflicted her family. Had she inherited some of the dreadful traits?

He eased away, the sight of her disturbing in a fashion he didn't understand.

With her blond hair spread across the pillows, her creamy skin so pale against the dark quilts, she was so beautiful, like an enchanted fairy princess or an angel. He was so happy to see her, so joyous that she'd arrived. His absent lust returned with a vengeance. He was frantic to rip off his clothes, to crawl under the blankets and make love to her all night long, which had him wondering if *he* was the crazy one rather than she.

Her eyelids fluttered open, and she stared at the ceiling, scowling as she tried to recollect her location. When recognition dawned, she grinned a smile that alarmed him. He was certain Eve had flashed the very same smile at that imbecile, Adam, who'd been hooked like a fish on a line.

As it was, he was already ensnared, and he could barely keep from stumbling toward her as if she was reeling him in.

She looked rumpled and adorable, and his male parts were screaming at him to run like hell.

He was in trouble!

She rolled to the side, the covers falling away, to reveal a perfect breast. He honed in on it, immediately inundated with delectable memories he didn't want to have. He couldn't quit gaping.

"Hello, Ian," she said, her voice sultry with sleep. "I didn't hear you come in."

"Caro, you're in Scotland," he stupidly retorted.

"Yes, I am."

"Why?"

"I'm delivering some important messages."

"You couldn't write me a letter?"

"No. They're urgent."

"In what manner?"

"Your brother, Jack, needs you to come home for his wedding."

"He's getting married?"

"To your Mrs. Blake—which is definitely peculiar, and I don't wish to be apprised of the circumstances of how their amour flourished."

"Is that it?"

"No, as a matter of fact, it's not. John's wife is about to have her baby—she's convinced it's a boy, by the way—so you're about to be an uncle. John wants you home, too, to help him celebrate."

Ian was still raw over the recent twists in his relationships with his brothers, and he couldn't talk about them coherently. He switched to the only subject that signified.

"You're in my bed again."

"I am."

"Why does this keep happening?"

"Don't you know?"

"I haven't a clue."

"Come here." She rose up on her elbow and patted the mattress, coaxing him closer.

"Why?"

"I have a secret to tell you."

"I don't care to hear it."

"I'm going to tell it to you anyway."

She reached for the covers as if she would climb out, stroll over, and ravage him. The prospect was both electrifying and terrifying, and he was frozen in place, unable to flee as he ought. The blankets were down around her lap. As if teasing him, she stretched her arms over her head, which emphasized her fabulous bosom, her slender waist.

He ignored her and gazed at a spot over her shoulder.

"What possessed you to travel so far?" he snapped.

"You left me at John's."

"Of course I did."

"It was weeks ago."

"Yes, it was."

"You never came back for me."

"Why would I have?"

"You know, Ian, that is the oddest question."

"Why?"

"You saw no reason to return, while I was in London, impatiently waiting for you to arrive. Don't you find it a tad strange that we have such divergent views on the same point?"

He shifted nervously. He couldn't bear to discuss the jeopardy into which their affair had thrust her. Nor could he bear to remember the frenzied trip to England, through snow and icy rain, to stop her wedding. He and John walked in with only seconds to spare, and if they'd been delayed by even a few minutes, she'd have been Shelton's bride, and her mother's bizarre scheme would have been realized.

Every time he thought of the near result his negligence had caused, he felt ill. He'd always cared too much about her, and the notion that his folly had driven her to such a hideous situation was shameful and mortifying.

"I hastened to England as John requested," he said. "I interrupted the wedding as was proper and fitting. What more was it you wanted from me?"

"Are you really that thick?"

"I guess I am."

She stood, her nude body on full display, and she advanced until they were toe-to-toe. She snuggled herself to him so that her torso was pressed to his all the way down.

It took every ounce of strength he had not to hug her back. She felt so beloved and so familiar, and idiot that he was, he still physically desired her with every fiber of his being. Previously, he'd have done anything for her, but that moment had passed when he'd dawdled in the Earl's library and she had disavowed him to her parents.

Though he was over it now, when it was occurring he'd been crushed. He'd endured a life of insults because of his lineage, and he'd assumed he could handle any rejection, but hers had been more than he could abide.

He'd been happy to assist her in evading her mother, had been happy to see her safely under John's protection, but what more did she expect? They were never meant to be together. Their fates were never in accord.

She kissed him on the mouth, but he declined to participate. He was immobile as a statue.

"Kiss me back, Ian."

"No."

"I can sense how much you want to."

"I don't."

His phallus was hard as stone, and she stroked across the placard of his trousers. The feel of her hand, positioned precisely where he craved it to be, was like a jolt of lightning.

He whipped away from her, his eyes shut, his breathing labored, as he tried to calm himself and determine how best to deal with her.

"What is it, Ian? What's wrong."

"You can't stay here."

"But I journeyed all this way. Don't pretend that you're not glad to see me."

"Why wouldn't I be *glad*?" he lied. "We're old friends. I'm always charmed by your company. I'm merely thinking that perhaps I'll . . . I'll . . . proceed to a hotel or rent bachelor's quarters till we can get you home."

"Home?"

"Yes."

She chuckled, but in a forlorn fashion. "I have no *home*, so I have nowhere to go. Your carnal antics saw to that. You ruined me, and I demand that you give me shelter."

"For how long?"

"Forever. How long would you suppose?"

Forever? Was she insane? This was stuffy, conservative Edinburgh, not some squalid London neighborhood where sordid characters abounded and any low behavior was allowed. He couldn't house an unwed female. He'd be tarred and feathered and run out of town by an angry mob.

He spun to face her, ready to talk logically, but he'd forgotten she was naked, and he couldn't remember what it was he was going to say. It had been something about sending her away, about shielding her from ridicule and scorn, but she was unbuttoning his trousers, and he was too confounded to stop her. Shortly, her fingers had slipped under the waistband of his pants, and she was caressing him in every way he enjoyed.

She dropped to her knees and pushed the fabric aside, and he was paralyzed with indecision, unable to desist or progress. She pulled his cock free, and she licked him over and over, then sucked him into her mouth. He stared down at her, prostrate before him and pleasuring him as the most experienced harlot might have.

The sight was decadent and mind-boggling. He loved her; he hated her, and he rippled with every emotion between the two extremes.

His temper flared. Why had she come to Scotland? Why was she bent on tormenting him? Didn't she understand that her very presence was torture?

He fisted his hand in her hair, guiding her to take him deeper, and he considered spilling himself in her throat. If she wanted to act like a whore, why not let her? It would be so easy to use her badly.

As fast as the despicable notion spiraled through his head, he tamped it down and drew away. She frowned at him, hurt, confused, and so incredibly lovely.

"What's the matter?" she inquired.

"I don't want this from you."

"Liar."

"Go back to bed, Caro." He straightened his clothes and adjusted his rampaging male anatomy. "We'll figure it out in the morning."

"We'll figure it out now." She glared at him, suddenly ablaze with her own burst of temper.

He grabbed a blanket and wrapped it around her, covering her as he sighed with dismay. He refused to fight with her. He simply wanted her to leave, but apparently, she wouldn't be satisfied till they'd hashed out every contemptible detail of whatever absurd idea had spurred her to race north.

"Fine. Tell me whatever it is that's brought you here. Blame me for the whole bloody mess, then give me some peace."

"Give *you* some peace?"

"Yes."

"Have you the slightest clue as to what the past few months have been like for me?"

"I realize that they've been horrid." He sounded condescending and smug.

"*Horrid* doesn't begin to describe it! My mother is a deranged murderess who tried to force me into an incestuous marriage. My philandering, aloof father who I've known all my life isn't my father, at all. I have no parents. My family is destroyed." She punctuated each syllable with a jab of her finger at the middle of his chest. "I'm dying from the desolation for all that is lost me, and I've reached out to you for solace and friendship."

"I can't fathom why you would," he cruelly said.

"You are the only person who ever cared about me," she replied in a shout. "You are the only one who was ever genuinely kind to me, yet I come here, brokenhearted and needing you, and you can't so much as pretend to be glad that I've arrived."

"That's because I'm not *glad*."

"And why is that?"

"What do you want me to say, Caro?"

"I want you to declare that you love me. I want you to ask me to marry you so I can always be with you."

It would be so easy to spew a proposal, for she was correct: He loved her and always had. But so what? His heightened sentiment had no relevance to their situation. Throughout all the years of their acquaintance, she'd been very clear that ancestry was the most important factor. She'd endured a dreadful month or two, but a brief tribulation could never alter who she was deep down.

She'd had a crisis in her relationship with her parents, but it would pass. The Fosters would regroup and continue on as they had been. It was British tradition, the stiff upper lip for which they were all so renowned.

"I love you," he admitted, hurling the words like an accusation.

"Yes, you do," she agreed, not appearing any happier about the pronouncement than he was, himself.

"But you're forgetting something."

"What is that?"

"You're the child of an earl, and I am not," he tersely reminded her. "You are the prized daughter of one of England's premier families, while I am merely the illegitimate bastard of a dead Scottish commoner. Since the day we met, it's all I've ever heard from you. Don't prance about now as if it doesn't matter. I know you better than that."

Stunned by his remarks, she paused, then went over and flopped down on the bed, burrowing under the quilts. She studied the ceiling, fuming, ruminating, but not looking at him.

He wanted to rush over, to take her in his arms and offer comfort, but he didn't dare. He desired her so much, and the least bit of physical contact would make him behave like a moron, so they tarried, unable to move or speak, a void as wide as an ocean separating them.

"Ian Clayton," she finally grumbled, "you are an idiot."

"I won't argue the point."

"You said I'm forgetting something, but aren't *you* forgetting something, too?"

"What?"

"I'm not an earl's daughter. I'm not anyone, at all."

"You're Lady Caroline Foster, only daughter of the Earl of Derby. You'll never be anyone else."

"Weren't you listening at the church?"

"Well . . . yes."

"My father is not the Earl of Derby."

"It was a small group at the wedding. There was no one present who would repeat the truth."

She scoffed. "Someone told, and the gossip has spread. It's all over London."

"I didn't know. How awful for you."

"All these years, I've strutted around with my nose up in the air, certain I was better than you, being so horrid to you because of it. But the joke was on me. It was all a lie."

What a dolt he was! In the weeks he'd been sequestered in Scotland, he'd rarely thought of her. He hadn't wanted to feel sorry for her, so he hadn't let himself recognize that the pedestal upon which she'd been balanced had been shattered into a thousand pieces.

What did the change portend? Where did it leave them?

A spark of hope flared in his chest.

She turned toward him, her blue eyes poignant. "Can you ever find it in your heart to forgive me?"

"I already have."

"Thank you. It is more than I deserve."

He was inching to the bed, his feet carrying him directly where he should not go. He kept on until his thighs were pressed against the edge of the mattress, and he gazed down at her, so filled with affection that he worried he might burst.

She reached out her hand, and it hovered there, a lifeline, a tether, to the only thing he'd ever truly wanted. Dare he grab it? Dare he hold on?

He reached out, too, and he linked their fingers, the gentle touch connecting them, locking them together, sealing their fate.

"I have nowhere to go," she murmured. "Please don't send me away."

"I won't. I can't."

"I want to marry you," she proclaimed again. "I want to be your wife and have your children. Won't you let me?"

Two visions flashed—of the lonely, detached man he'd always been, and of the complete and contented man he *could* be with her by his side. He sank down next to her.

She was offering him a family to cherish, a home where he would always belong. He would be part of the whole, one of many. He'd have children to care for and a wife to love. In the past, he'd maintained that he didn't want any of it, that he didn't need any of it, but he'd been fooling himself.

He bent down and kissed her.

"I love you," he said, meaning it.

"I love you, too."

"I don't know how to be a husband."

"Nor do I know how to be a wife, but I suspect we'll figure it out."

"I suspect we will, too. Will you have me, Caro? I'm not much of a catch—"

"You're right about that!"

"—but I will protect you and watch over you, and I swear that I will love you till my dying day and beyond."

"Yes, I'll have you, Ian. Till my dying day and beyond."

The vow reverberated around the room, joining them more fully than any wedding ceremony ever could.

"So it's settled?" she asked.

"Yes, it's settled."

She blew out a heavy breath. "For a minute there, I was nervous."

"I can't deny it: I'm the thickheaded oaf you always accuse me of being."

"Yes, you are, but I'll make it my lifelong goal to save you from yourself."

"I can't wait."

How lucky he was! He smiled, and she smiled, too, and she tugged on his hand, drawing him closer.

"Now that the formalities are over," she said, "I was wondering. . . ."

"About what?"

"It's frightfully cold in here."

"Yes, it is."

"I would pay a fortune to anyone who agreed to climb under the covers and help to warm me."

"I know just the man you need."

He chuckled and started unbuttoning his shirt.

Look for these other sizzling reads
from *USA Today* bestselling author

CHERYL HOLT
Named One of the Top 25 Erotic Writers of All Time★

Forbidden Fantasy
ISBN: 0-312-94255-9

Secret Fantasy
ISBN: 0-312-94254-0

Available from St. Martin's Paperbacks

❧

. . . and don't miss the next novel in the series

Double Fantasy
ISBN: 0-312-94256-7

Coming in March 2008
from St. Martin's Paperbacks

"Holt delivers a delicious erotic romance
with heart and soul."
—*Romantic Times BOOKreviews*★